Praise for The Alford Saga

"For adventure seekers... a journey full of promise and danger."
— *The Globe and Mail*

"Can you talk about thrill-a-minute Canadian history? You can now. Paul Almond has worked for many years as a TV and film director, and his skill shows in the drama and pacing of this first-rate read." — Carole's BookTalk

"I believe this series should be placed into the hands of every young student learning the history of Canada... "
— Mrs. Q Book Addict

"The Saga has garnered much international and national acclaim, and for good reason — it provides an in-depth look into Canadian life in the late nineteenth century."
— Barbara Burgess bookpleasures.com

"These are important books in an essential series: essential reading for all Gaspesians, Quebecers and Canadians. Thrilling... enthralling... interesting and compelling."
— *The Gaspé Spec*

THE CHAPLAIN

BOOK FIVE of THE ALFORD SAGA

PAUL ALMOND

**SULBY HALL
PUBLISHERS**

Toronto

First published in Canada in 2013 by
SULBY HALL PUBLISHERS
28 Duncannon Drive
Toronto, ON M5P 2M1

Almond, Paul, 1931-
The chaplain / Paul Almond.
(The Alford saga ; bk. 5)
ISBN-13: 978-0-9919746-0-3
ISBN-10: 1483943577
I. Title. II. Series: Almond, Paul, 1931- . Alford saga ; bk. 5.

Cover photograph by Joan Almond
Map by David Stansfield
Interior design by Tania Craan

For my companion and wife

Joan

who walks beside me always

COLONEL THE REV. CANON ALMOND. C.MG.
PRIEST IN CHARGE OF THIS PARISH 1901-1904.

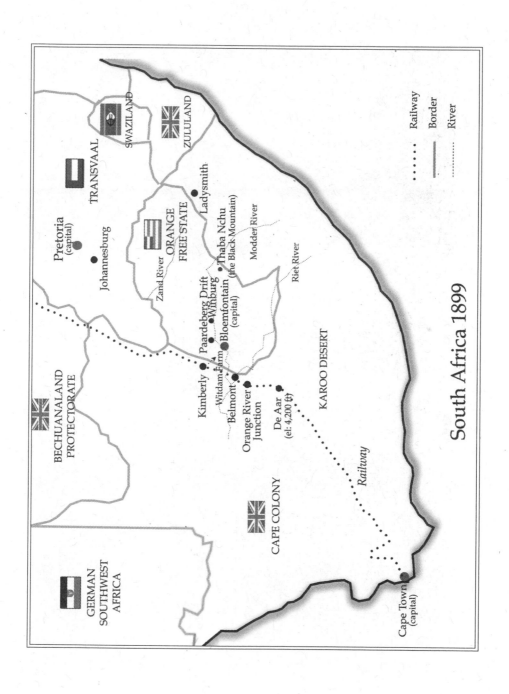

South Africa 1899

Preface

The Boer War is remembered nowadays for its famous, or perhaps infamous, inventions: Boer warriors roaming in *kommando* groups using guerilla tactics; the British policy of "scorched earth" so hatefully practised in later wars; and putting prisoners in concentration camps, where some fifteen thousand blacks and thirty thousand whites, including half of all Boer children, died.

The Canadians entered the war before any of these inventions were put into play. The first year was marked by fierce fighting, heroic acts, devastating disease, and especially — in contrast to today's battles — a gentlemanly attitude that above all bore witness to good manners in warfare.

The Royal Canadian Regiment, perhaps through a series of mistakes but also by great courage and fortitude, managed to turn the tide of the war in the historic battle of Paardeberg Drift in February 1900. Until then, a raggle-taggle bunch of farmers ("Boer"' means farmer) had roundly beaten a far larger army of Imperial troops. The Canadian victory in February 1900 gave a great lift to the British, although it ushered in a new and dirtier form of warfare. Boer leadership and tactics changed to focus on hit-and-run raids and sabotage; this later provoked a British scorched earth policy, with farm burnings and concentration camps, until victory was simply a matter of time, arriving with the Treaty of Vereeniging in May 1902.

This victorious first contingent, which left Canada on Oct 31st 1899, finally departed Capetown for England a year later to be cheered by the British public and congratulated by Queen Victoria. They arrived home before Christmas, 1900, before the war itself ended.

Paul Almond, Shigawake, Quebec

HISTORICAL NOTE

The South African (known as the Boer) War was Canada's first trial by fire. Great Britain, the preeminent superpower of the day, had decided to wage one of its little wars against the Transvaal and the Orange Free State: two white, Protestant, Dutch-speaking Republics in southern Africa, who had declared their independence from all European empires. The British government had become alarmed by the shift of economic and strategic power in this unpredictable Afrikaaner-controlled interior towards closer relations with Britain's European competitors, especially Germany. So they responded by sending more troops; then Paul Kruger, President of the two Boer Republics, issued an ultimatum demanding the British government withdraw these reinforcements from his Transvaal borders within forty-eight hours. At stake was the control of rich resources — gold and diamonds — and strategic advantage.

The Boer War's distant and bloody conflict occupied Canadians' discourse, engaged their imaginations, and claimed much of their time and resources. Popular literature fired young men's imaginations with the desire for adventure and travel — especially to defend their British Empire, which covered a fifth of the world's surface and on which the sun never set. Increasingly, the curricula of public schools inculcated patriotism and loyalty, discipline and leadership, which were reinforced by school drills, demonstrations, exercises and patriotic anniversaries. In this era of missions and missionaries, the Bible and the English language and flag seemed as indivisible as the Trinity.

Public support for the Canadian contingent was never in question. The public mobilized immediately to fête, honour, and support our soldier heroes. Once the government had announced its decision, public enthusiasm was infectious. Young men were urged to join this missionary crusade to win the world for Christ in their generation. Newspapers hailed the men as patriots; clergy, politicians, and public persons praised their courage and sense of Christian duty; poets sang their praises; no language seemed too exaggerated. Elaborate demonstrations were organized: parades, bands, banquets and interminable speeches by politicians, clergy and local notables. Cheering crowds lined streets decorated with flags, bunting, and patriotic slogans, and civic leaders granted their employees holidays to swell the noisy crowds cheering the Royal Canadian Regiment.

Verbatim from Carman Miller's *Painting the Map Red*, and *Canada's Little War*

NOTE: I have chosen throughout to use the language then in vogue: such as Kaffir (now a slur, from the Arabic *Kaffar* meaning infidel), Soudan for Sudan, kharki for khaki (the correct transliteration of the Urdu and Arabic), and the practise in wide use in 1900 of telling stories through the eyes of another narrator, as will be seen with Paardeberg. And Jack, or any English Gaspesian, never spoke with, or used, the accent on Gaspé. It was Gaspe, pure and simple.

Chapter One

Reverend John Alford awoke from frantic dreams of war, brutal soldiers, pure women sabered against pews, babies torn from tender wombs. He sat bolt upright. Where was he?

In his boarding house in Quebec City in October, 1899. Then what was this all about? Oh yes, those troops crowding the narrow streets. And rumours that the Boers in their devilry had attacked the good Queen's soldiers serving in South Africa. Jack, the nickname he preferred, pushed the images from his mind and dressed quickly.

After a good breakfast in his lodging, he hurried along the flat land below the great ramparts of Quebec, the oldest city in Canada. Three- four-story houses lined this narrow rue du Petit Champlain, just as in mediaeval Bordeaux. He turned up Côte de la Montagne, its steep curves crowded with young soldiers. A calèche rattled past loaded with rowdy recruits singing, shouting, celebrating their one last leave. Beside him an overloaded horse dug its shoes into cobblestones as it hauled more revellers up to the plateau above with its finer houses, important churches and government buildings. The soldiers wore Glengarry caps and kilts, or forage caps, some clad in the regulation rifle-green serge uniforms. All with loyal hearts, Jack could see, having assembled here from all over Canada for their great embarkation — volunteers, he reflected, who had been activated by the purest patriotism, responding to the call of religion, blood, glory and progress, to fight and bleed for the Empire's greatest need.

These past weeks ministering to his parishes in Northern Quebec, Jack had heard little of the rapidly approaching war in South Africa nor the frantic enlistments across Canada; far from newspapers on their remote but hard-worked acres, his farmers had little means of acquiring news. Only yesterday morning, as he checked in at the cathedral office, had Jack received his first earful. That alarming report, and the city busy with excited recruits, had overcharged his imagination and nourished his nightmares.

He heard from behind: "Beg pardon, Father..." He paused and turned. "Would you know where a fella might eat a good meal without all that Frenchie sauce?" The obligatory military moustache had begun to grace the young man's lips, but no uniform indicated that he'd just enlisted as he gleamed with enthusiasm. "It took us a long train journey to get here, fer shore. Now I'm rarin' to go, but I gotta eat something."

"Go? You're off to South Africa with the troops?"

"Monday, they told us. The sooner the better. No time to lose — them Boers went and invaded the British Colony of Natal. They up and attacked Her Majesty's forces on their own ground."

"Really? I knew the Boers sent an ultimatum three weeks ago. They demanded a reply from the British within forty-eight hours — got everyone in an uproar, so I'm told."

"Me too! Those hateful scum went and encircled Colonel Baden-Powell at Mafeking. And they're advancing on Ladysmith! That's why I volunteered. Hard to get in, you know, lotsa fellas got turned down: too short, too young, size of chest or fitness — though some got in because o' who they knew." He went on proudly. "They say about a thousand of us is gonna get on that there Sardinian Monday."

"Quite a force," Jack exclaimed.

"Bringin' two or three doctors, some nurses, even a YMCA man — all to look after us."

"And who is the chaplain, by the way? Someone from Ontario?" Jack wondered if the clergyman in question had volunteered or been selected by his bishop.

"Chaplain? No chaplain, Father."

Jack frowned. "You sure?"

"Yes, Father. My cousin, he's Captain of "A" Company, we're from Manitoba, regular churchgoer, so he got complaining last night on the train. The Frenchies, they got one, but we don't."

Jack absorbed that. How dare they send off this young laddie with others his age to face death and suffering without a spiritual counsellor?

He pulled himself together, and gestured. "Now if you just go on up straight ahead, turn left and go down rue St. Louis, you'll be sure to find lots of restaurants with whatever you like to eat."

The soldier thanked him and set off. Jack turned right before Place d'Armes and strode up Sainte Anne Street, now even more worried and still haunted by his dreams. These young Canadians going into battle... How would he have felt if, even before attending university, he'd had to face a murderous foe? Not many hardened veterans hereabouts — just happy-go-lucky fellows with little hint of malice. Here they all were, for the first time in their lives traipsing up and down the quaint, old narrow streets that might have belonged to some crumbling city in Europe. How would they survive against those beastly and bloodthirsty Boers?

He entered the close of Holy Trinity Cathedral, centre of the vast Quebec diocese, an area that included much of Labrador and most of Quebec, five times the size of England. As the seat of the Bishop, it drew Jack back every month or so from his little parishes around Lake St. John. The cathedral's day-to-day goings-on fell, as was usual, to the Dean, Lennox Williams, who'd been born in Lennoxville where Jack attended Bishop's University. Jack had even coached a bit of rugby across the St. Francis river at Bishop's College School which Lennox had attended, so they might have something in common. But no, on the whole the Dean paid Jack scant attention. And this weekend, the bishop, Andrew Hunter Dunn, would have far too much on his hands, so the Dean was his only conduit to resolving the question of a chaplain.

Opening the door to the church office, Jack saw his stiff figure bent over the desk of their prim secretary, Margaret. "May I have a word with you, Dean?"

"Not just now, Alford. We're expecting a packed cathedral tomorrow. Canon Scott is preaching." His high forehead over well-marked dark eyebrows, his dark, heavy moustache and short, neat beard, all signalled a fearsome presence to Jack.

"Oh? I look forward to that. So all the troops are Church of England then?"

"Mostly, I'd say," mumbled Williams. "Some Presbyterians, I'm told, and of course, Romans, mostly French from this province. Father O'Leary is leading a Low Mass for them tomorrow in the Basilica. He's embarking with them, we've heard."

As the Dean turned to go, Jack asked, "Have you heard who is representing us?"

"No idea. Whoever he is, he's not preaching tomorrow at any rate."

"I've heard they've not chosen a clergyman as chaplain yet."

"Impossible, Alford. Of course they have. They must've."

"No sir, I've heard not."

The Dean, preoccupied with tomorrow's service, was paying little attention.

But still, the horror of these young innocents heading off to fight and die for the Empire distressed Jack. Did they not deserve succour? Could it be true that not one of the clergy had volunteered? He had no intention of going off himself... But then again, as he reflected, ever since getting his B.A. degree recently he had wanted to visit that dark mysterious African continent.

He blurted out, "Sir, I'll take the challenge if no one else will."

The Dean stopped and turned.

Now where did that come from? Jack asked himself. A ghastly mistake? But Jack was not one to shirk a challenge. After spending two years in the most inhospitable environment on earth, the Labrador Coast, he made up his mind: let their tramp steamer be shipwrecked, let his regiment be devastated by cannonball or bayonet, let the chaplains be slaughtered by those Devil's henchmen, no matter — if he were chosen, yes, he would go.

"You, Alford?" Lennox Williams snapped. "Out of the question! What about your parishioners? How would they get along if you went off adventuring?" The Dean shook his head. "Can't have one shirking one's duties now, can we?" He strode off down the hall and closed his door.

So much for that. Jack's shoulders sagged, but he saw Margaret, tight-lipped, watching. A few months ago, he'd even gone so far as to ask her out. His heavy-set athletic frame was shorter than hers, but his large and piercing eyes, although almost black, carried some warmth as they looked into parishioners' souls. Well, with the ecclesiastic taboos on relations with parishioners, and his travelling, he'd not benefited from any female friendship since the Labrador, where the lovely Lorna had been a warm confidante, before she left. Margaret, though cold as those winter floes along the St. Lawrence, was at least a female. Still unmarried, she was skinny as a hoe, but ever since she had aborted his attempt at friendship, in his presence she kept extolling neat, handsome and well-dressed men, which of course quite excluded Jack, with his round moon-like face and his slightly rumpled appearance. But then, Lennox Willliams, of a wealthy family, could pay more attention to his wardrobe.

For this reason she seemed partial to the Dean, by no means a romantic figure. Perhaps, thought Jack, like him I should start being unpleasant to her. But in truth, she was about as inviting as an icicle.

Jack went to find a more sheltering environment: up the four cathedral steps he leaped and let himself in through the great oaken doors. For all its plain, block-like exterior and bold steeple, the interior was impressive. But Jack didn't notice. He paused at a pew, then slipped through its door, and sidled in to kneel. The small doors reminded him that only last year, the practice of pew-renting had been abolished. He glanced at the bold, brass eagle on the lectern from which he had occasionally read the lesson.

In the peace of the cathedral, a certain calm descended. After a few moments, Jack bowed his head. The dream images still haunted him. "Please Lord," he whispered, "in this great enterprise, make sure our lads have someone worthy to guide them spiritually." He felt strongly that in their righteous battle against such inhuman devils, the soldiers needed a wise and courageous padre.

After a time, Jack sat back on his pew, deep in thought. Should he press his point? No, of course not, he was much too inexperienced. He glanced up at the balcony to his left, which boasted the country's only imperial box, fronted by a brass balustrade and decorated in royal blue. The Monarch's coat of arms reminded him in no uncertain terms of the British Empire. As did the gift given by the King himself over a century ago: solid silver plate, chalice, pattens and candlesticks, all lying in a glass case along the right-hand wall. Jack's country parishes bore no such splendour. One day, he thought, I might be Curate here.

The doors broke open and the present curate, Ingall Smith, some ten years his senior, called out, "Ah, there you are, Jack!" He came up wearing a worried frown, frizzy hair falling about his ears but thinning on top, his large and piercing nose supporting thick steel glasses. "Jack, I'm frightfully sorry to ask, but would you mind doing me a tremendous favour, in fact doing us all one."

"Of course."

"The Bishop has asked me to get these orders of service to Canon Scott over at St. Matthews. But for some odd reason, I haven't been as diligent as I might and I'm afraid we don't have enough wine for all those troops' Eucharist tomorrow. Our delivery's not till Thursday. Would you mind awfully running down and picking up some? You do know our supplier?"

Jack nodded. "I'd be delighted, Ingall." Although the supplier was a good mile away, Jack saw he had no alternative. And indeed, a good brisk walk might do his spirit some good.

"Ripping of you, old man. You see, then I must run home and change, because the bishop has invited me, along with the Dean, to the banquet for the officers of the contingent. It's being given by members of the Garrison Club in the Citadel itself. I've never been. Have you?"

Jack shook his head. The Citadel, quite a landmark, had been designed in 1820 in the shape of a four-pointed polygon as a defence system; it covered thirty-seven acres and took thirty years to build. Jack would love to have gone, for it now served as the transit billet for the Royal Canadian Regiment's officers heading to Africa.

He watched Ingall whirl and hurry out. He had managed to throw not one but several barbs in Jack's direction. Barbs? How uncharitable! But nonetheless, it did bother Jack that he had not been invited to the Citadel.

Back at the office, he faced Margaret. "Any chance now of seeing the Bishop?"

None, the Secretary confirmed, and pressed her lips together.

Time's awasting, thought Jack. Repressing his annoyance, he grabbed the money in an envelope she held out for the wine and headed across the cathedral close, passing a railway clerk who came hurrying in, telegram in hand. On impulse, Jack followed him back into the office where the clerk handed his telegram to the church secretary. Savagely, she tore it open. In her floral cotton frock and prim hairdo, she stared at the telegram and then looked up abruptly. "You should see this, Mr. Alford, before I hand it to the Bishop."

Jack looked down at it — one of his favourite students in his parish of Blue Point, Eino Virtanen, a Finnish lad, had been drowned along with his father, Heikki, in Lac St. Jean. Their funeral was Tuesday. Would Jack please return Monday to perform the last rites?

He folded it and gave it back to the Secretary. What a shame. Such a fine student, and a good family too. Return for the funeral? Oh yes, he certainly would.

* * *

Jack walked into the store that already had a goodly share of visitors. Most of them were young men buying supplies to take on the troopship moored in the harbour. He threaded through the lads to the owner behind the counter, himself a rather portly English member of the Holy Trinity congregation. "I see business is good," Jack offered, "with all the troops arriving."

"Business may be good, but not the soldiers' mission, for sure."

"Oh?"

The storekeeper shook his head. "We've got no business, no business at all messing with people like those Boers — after all, they're colonists just like us. My wife says it's a crime — put on us by politicians and businessmen — they're just trying to make a dollar out of armaments and uniforms, and such. And you know what? They're after the gold and diamonds there. They want to grab all that through the blood of our offspring."

A voice from behind Jack spoke up: "What's that I hear?" A young lad with red hair and freckles had his dander up. "Say that again."

The plump, grey-haired storekeeper wiped his hands on his apron, looked at him, but did not speak.

"We heard what you said," the soldier went on. "No right to go over there? No right to go fight savages who've had the audacity to attack her Majesty the Queen?"

The storekeeper raised his eyes. "They didn't attack our Queen; they defended their land. Pushed into doing that by British politicians: Cecil Rhodes and businessmen like him. They be bigger savages than the Boers, if you ask me." The red-haired lad tried to interrupt but the storekeeper kept right on. "Gold, that's what they want. And diamonds! Once that got discovered in the Transvaal, those businessmen, they sure set their sights on that fortune. Why else go way down there and fight? That greedy bunch, it's their problem, not ours."

"Do you hear that boys?" the redhead said. "I'm putting back my supplies right now. I'm not buying from anyone who won't support Her Majesty and our fight for freedom!" With that, he dropped his supplies on the floor and stomped out.

Jack stared as one after another the soldiers, some reluctantly, placed their provisions on counters and barrels and walked out, too. Jack was left standing, with the storekeeper angrily returning the goods to the shelves.

Jack turned. "Are there many who feel as you do?"

"All my wife's family. She's French Canadian. They're against our fighting Britain's battles for them. Read the *Quebec Telegraph*, or the *Vérité* — even our own *Canadian Clergyman*. They're all against it, too. Not one single French Canadian in Quebec wants this war."

Jack frowned. "I've heard a good few French Canadians are leaving with the contingent."

"That's as may be. Always fools in any bunch. If you ask me, those politicians in London, Chamberlain and — "

"He's the Colonial Secretary?"

"Yes sir, and that Lord Minto, our own Governor-General, he's British too, just as bad as the rest — they all want us to go get shot or killed so's Rhodes and his bunch can get their hands on all the gold and diamonds. That's what my family says. And that's what I say too." He glanced up. "You've come for wine?"

Jack nodded and handed over the envelope from the church office. The man gave him two sizable bottles of port, and Jack went off, head spinning with new thoughts.

Chapter Two

By the time Jack reached the cathedral office with the wine, everyone had gone home to prepare for the evening's festivities — and festivities there were sure to be, packed with fun: the officers and their clergy being feasted just outside the gate at the magnificent Garrison Club.

At his desk, Jack found a message from the Rev. Lennox Williams saying that for the enlisted men, a grand smoking concert or party had been planned, and asking him if he would be kind enough to "show the flag" and attend that dinner beforehand, and say an appropriate Grace.

Jack walked down from the cathedral to the Lower Town, passing old draw-bridges and piers with barrels of oysters for sale; idle fishing smacks bobbing beside the last of the great sailing ships, moored incongruously next to docked steam-driven freighters loading freight from swaybacked horses' carts. As dusk settled, he turned onto one of the southeast piers that reached out into the icy St. Lawrence, and headed for the low barrack-like immigration sheds, the Quebec home of the enlisted men of the Royal Canadian Regiment.

He tramped through the gates of the high picket fence and joined a group gathering for supper. He lost no time in checking to see if anyone had heard of any Church of England chaplain being assigned. Not a one. When the doors opened, Jack went in with them and found himself at a folding table to the right of a grizzled old corporal at its head. "God Save the Queen" began the proceedings, concluding with huzzas and cheers, and then Jack rose and proclaimed a suitable Grace.

The Corporal proved quick to introduce himself as Joseph Ferguson, from Glace Bay. He asked, "You the new Chaplain?" Ferguson had a short mop of greying hair, trim frame, and grizzled brows under which knowing black eyes had clearly seen it all. But Jack saw that beneath the tough exterior and well-worn uniform beat a good heart.

Jack shook his head. "I'm staying at the cathedral this week, and my dean, he asked me to come down and say the Grace."

The ladies of the lower town had volunteered to help out, and now they dished up hearty knuckles of meat, mushy potatoes and coarse bread. Ferguson lost no time in tucking in. "We'll not be seeing a lot of this on the battlefield, I can tell you."

"You been though a few battles, have you?"

"Enough to know we should avoid them. Specially this bunch."

"You mean the enlistees who've come here?" Jack asked.

Ferguson nodded, glanced at Jack, and lifted a heavy knuckle to gnaw at it.

"They're inexperienced, I know," persisted Jack, "but they all seem healthy and hearty, and raring to go."

Ferguson nodded again. "Ask any o' them what a Mauser is. Ask any o' them what to do when you hear a shell whistling." He shook his head.

"A bit untrained?" Jack began eating, and oddly enough, found it tasty. Ferguson shot him a look, and put down his knuckle. "Half the boys here never fired a rifle, Padre. They think that me and us other NCOs are gonna whip 'em all into shape on that there cattle boat." He snorted in disgust, and went on eating.

"Cattle boat?"

"The *Sardinian*. Converted it into a troopship. Fit for five hundred, maybe, maximum, and they're gonna cram a thousand on it. You know how long it takes to get to South Africa?"

Jack shrugged. "No idea. Probably a couple of weeks."

"More." Ferguson shook his head, still chewing hungrily. "I'm not looking forward to it. You watch, they're doing this in such a rush, I'll take a bet there'll not be enough food, or maybe it's water, or maybe it's ammunition, there's always something missing, just when you need it."

His companion across the table, a corporal, nodded vigorously. "Corp's right. He's always right. Trust him."

"Lucky you're not coming, Father," Ferguson went on. "Stick to your nice safe cathedral up there on the hill. And just pray they don't pick you."

"So it is true they have no chaplain yet."

"Not on your life. You think we've had a chaplain with us these last fifteen years? No sir. Not since they stuck a couple of theology students on us in them Indian battles. I was a private then, saw no use fer 'em m'self."

Jack was shocked. "Not even when you had to fight?"

"Well... we haven't done that much fighting, I will say that. Few knockabouts with some Indians, but nothing to write home about." He coughed, and then shovelled in some mashed potatoes. "You just wait till we get to them dry deserts over there, crawling with blood-thirsty Boers. That'll give the lads something to worry about —" he swallowed a mouthful — "even if they do hand us enough rifles and ammo, which I still frankly doubt." He looked up as another corporal at an adjacent table rose, clearly primed with the demon alcohol, and proposed a rambling toast to the Queen and their own speedy victory — which should come in just a few months, long before the one year term they had signed for, and more than enough time to vanquish that raggle-taggle Boer army.

This was soon followed by other toasts, uproariously proclaimed and thoroughly enjoyed, for most men had already partaken of good amounts of intoxicants.

As they continued eating and drinking, Jack found his need to be a part of this Militia mounting, in spite of the Corporal's predictions. He admired the camaraderie amongst these men who had made the cut. In later conversations during the evening, he discovered that in Vancouver they had taken only seventeen of some sixty applications, in Nelson BC only eight out of seventy, and so on. These men clearly felt that they were "the chosen" and their spirit of patriotism was running high.

As Jack moved around after they had risen from the tables, he found himself gravitating towards the companies from Nova Scotia and New Brunswick. One group of young men were being entertained by a tall, craggy youth whose accent showed him to be a Maritimer, and Jack wandered over. His face seemed as beaten up by the elements as one much older, and carried a few pocks and pimples.

The merriment ceased due to Jack's clerical collar. He wished on occasions such as this he could be seen as one of the boys; after all, was he not a Maritimer himself? Brought up on a farm, and with the same life, at least until he'd gone into the church.

The lads formed a respectful circle, and after Jack introduced himself and where he was from, their leader took over. "Aye, a Gaspesian! Well sir, I'm from Dingwall, Eamon McAndrews at your service." A couple of the others, still intimidated by Jack's garb, bashfully gave their names.

"And what induced you to leave that beautiful Cape Breton and set off for South Africa, Eamon? A sense of adventure?" Jack didn't want to seem too patriotic at the start.

"I know what you expect us to say, Father, that we're off to defend her Majesty Queen Victoria. But none of us had that idea in our heads, did we boys?"

One shrugged, but the others agreed with him. He went on, "Six younger in my family, four o' them girls, so how d'ye expect mammy to feed us without me goin' to work? And no work out there on the Cape, I'll tell you. Pappy lost our boat last year when he drowned out in Aspy Bay. Lucky I had the grippe then or I would'a gone with 'im. So last summer we joined up — out of greed! Yeah, we need to eat!" The other gawky lads chuckled, but their skinny frames bore out his words.

Then they joined in recounting their own backgrounds, laughing and talking; they did seem a happy bunch.

"Yep, now we got three square meals and a roof over our heads that don't leak." The others chorused agreement. "And a set of new clothes. And I hear they're going to be handing out another set on the boat."

"Well, good for you!" Jack smiled at their infectious jollity. As Cape Bretoners, they were no strangers to bottles of beer.

"We send back what pay we can, and now looks like we get extra money fer goin' over there to beat the bejesus out o' that lot o' Boers. Not a bad deal, I'd say."

Jack winced at his swear word, and Eamon looked guilty. "Begging your pardon, Father. So you looking to come with us then?"

Jack glanced down, not knowing quite what to say. The Corporal had given him a quite other take on the whole proceedings, and yet... these lads here, they did need a chaplain, oh yes.

"You'll have a hard time with that Eamon there, Father. Only time he seen the inside of a church was when they buried his pa."

"Well," Jack offered, "they're saying it's not going to last too long. And perhaps it won't be too difficult."

Jack and his new friends left and joined the men surging up the hill and then along towards the imposing grey stone building of Quebec's Armoury, just outside the walls of the city. Jack pointed out to the Nova Scotians this local and ancient architecture, the steep, high roofs, tall, thin windows with green frames piercing the roof in dormer style, and slits imitating the gun ports of old.

Once inside the drill hall, the stone walls and hardwood floor magnified the raucous celebrations. In fact, the whole evening turned out to be rather more boisterous than Jack would have preferred. He found the entertainments a bit too "down home": some half-learned recitations, skits, songs, even a boy's choir from one of the churches, and a number of soloists.

That night Jack found it hard to sleep. His Queen had been assaulted by mindless hordes, as some of the more conservative papers would have it. The boys he'd met represented an ideal cross-section of Canadian manhood, the pick of the nation's sinew and brain. All they lacked was a chaplain. All well and good, but what about his duties northward in Lake St. John, with the Virtanen family facing their grief on Tuesday? How could he resolve this?

For two years he had been working over a broad swatch of the Quebec countryside, trying hard to build his little settlements into proper parishes: Lake Edward, Blue Point, Moose Park, Forrestdale, Arthabaska. He'd been travelling mostly on horseback, sometimes by sleigh, and recently the new train line to Lake St. John. And of course shank's mare. He had grown to admire his parishioners for their moral courage and hardiness, though their lives in no way approximated the harsh conditions of the parish in which he'd served the two years previously on the Canadian Labrador. But the similarity of the two postings was undeniable. And so was he not, he reasoned, ready for change?

This new experience of a foreign country, the dark, mysterious continent of Africa which he'd often thought about visiting — would it not help mature him, bring him new insights, and build his spiritual stamina for the days to come?

If only he knew someone to ask for guidance. The Bishop, from the Old Country, was altogether too haughty and the Dean usually overwhelmed with schedules. How he wished there was some way to speak to his father back on the Gaspe Coast. Old Poppa would surely know how to handle this with always good instincts and ideas, even though he was not really educated nor wise in the ways of city doings, nor indeed did he know anything of the ecclesiastical goings-on in the diocese.

In fact, Jack found himself caught by a wave of homesickness. It didn't happen very often: much as he loved the Old Homestead, he was always so involved with his parishioners and his busy life that he had little time to think back on those glorious days he'd spent growing up in Shigawake, on the Gaspe, that peninsula jutting into the Gulf of St. Lawrence. But now he visualised his three sisters again: Winnie, Jean and Lillian. The latter had spent a year with him on the Labrador shore, and was now teaching in Shigawake. Winnie would soon be off to the big city to become a nurse, but Jeanie, too young to leave, still helped her mother as best she could. He would have loved to discuss all this with his brother Mac. Clare, still a teenager, worked on the farm, and little Earle kept getting in everybody's way — but wanted very much to be a farmer like his brothers. Their dear mother, Mary Ann, so hard working — she would wear herself out. He hoped that Eric, her youngest, would be her last.

The restless night did nothing to improve his disposition. Sunday morning he arrived at church in the pouring rain. He stripped off his sopping coat, brushed his trousers free of the worst splashing, and set about helping the other clergy gathered from around the city. He stowed their umbrellas and arranged for each to receive the printed orders of service. Then he got himself into his cassock and surplice.

He just had to speak to the Bishop. But how? Right now the Bishop, tall and stately with an enormous white beard and moustache, was surrounded by clergy to whom he was giving last minute instructions and exchanging pleasantries. Should Jack discuss a matter of such importance, and at the same time so personal, here and now? Well, it did deal with the welfare of a thousand gallant soldiers going off to fight and possibly die, some of whom were already crowding into the cathedral. But did he feel secure enough in front of these others to make his proposal known? Unsure, he hovered nearby.

The Bishop spotted him through the small group. "Good to see you, Alford. How are we this morning?"

"Very well, thank you sir."

The Bishop went on without a pause, "I was wondering if you'd mind taking the evening prayer for the Dean and Curate tonight? We're all going to the Citadel again at the invitation of Lord Minto, to dine with the officers of the regiment."

"It will be a delight, sir." Blast it, he thought, not invited again.

"Very good then. Oh, and, er, would you mind holding the Bible for me when I read the Gospel? Ingall will carry the mitre."

"Of course."

The Bishop turned, but stopped himself, apparently feeling that he'd been a bit peremptory. "Well, how was your last time out in the province?"

"It went well, sir." And then Jack drew himself up and spoke out. "M' Lord, may I impart an item of some importance?"

The Bishop's frown cut him off. Clearly not a time to be interrupted.

But Jack pressed on regardless. "These young men coming to our wonderful service —"

The Bishop turned away, mumbling, "Indeed they are."

"But sir!" Jack blurted loudly, "they are going off to fight without any guidance. No Church of England chaplain!"

The Bishop turned back. "No Alford, that's quite impossible."

"Sir, it's true."

The Bishop stood stock-still.

"They do have Father O'Leary for the French Catholics," Jack pressed. "But, no one to care for our own."

The Bishop paused, looking hard at him. "Dear me! After this service, my day is full. All these ongoing celebrations." He stood, perplexed. The room had fallen silent. "How on earth does one find a chaplain now?" Then he added, "Alford, I'm sure the Primate has selected someone and the man is just a bit late arriving."

"You would think so, my Lord, but with the speed of the mobilization and the hectic enlistments, perhaps no one thought of it."

The cathedral bells began to peel. The gathering grew restless.

Jack had never seen the great man so stunned; he appeared to be grasping for an idea, but none came.

"Sir..."

"Yes?" The Bishop quickened. "You have an idea?"

"Yes sir." Jack paused. "Me!"

"You?"

"Yes sir. I am not only ready, but very willing." The words sounded extra loud among the assembled clergy. Jack blushed.

The Bishop seemed taken aback. "But you already have such an onerous and time-consuming position here."

"Yes, but one thousand young men," Jack pressed, "they are going forth to do battle, and perhaps to die..."

The Bishop looked at him for a long moment. Then he

turned, and as the organ blared out the opening bars of the processional hymn, he left the sacristy and with his retinue proceeded down a side aisle. Jack hurried to catch up, for his place was near the front.

Jack marvelled at the assemblage as he moved down beside the troops, all singing lustily. Nine clergy followed the full choir in their sparkling white surplices and black cassocks, ending up with Canon Scott, then Lennox Williams, and finally the Bishop carrying his golden mitre. "Onward Christian Soldiers" echoed round the vast interior as the thunderous voices of five or six hundred men, Christian soldiers all, gave voice to this coming battle against a dreadful foe.

Chapter Three

During the hymn before the sermon, Jack went with the other clergy down into the pews where they could look up at the commanding figure of Canon Frederick George Scott, speaking with fierce eloquence. He faced out over the congregation with his prominent nose making him look like the prow of a proud windjammer. His words made a strong impression on Jack's patriotic soul as he watched and listened.

"We stand today as an Empire," thundered Scott, "comprising one-fifth of the human race, in the van of civilization. The charter of the world's freedom, once grasped by the warrior hands of ancient Israel, surely rests now in the keeping of England and her great daughter empire of the West, Canada."

No doubt about it, thought Jack, if the Bishop finds a way for me to go, then go I shall, for no more uplifting words were ever said in defence of an approaching engagement.

Scott went on: "England and England's flag must remain the symbol of our common patriotism: liberty, brotherhood and the welfare of man. We conquer and advance. Wild lands come under our sway. Savage races are subjugated, or turn to us for protection. With the result that the waste lands are cultivated, the hidden mines of the earth yield up their treasures, continents are spanned by vast railways and the bed of ocean by electric cables, so that the savage may be brought under the yoke of civilization;

and religion, education and commerce raise him almost to the level of a European."

Jack felt a swelling of pride that perhaps he too might find a place alongside the gallant few. Even if, as more likely, he were to stay back here among his northern parishioners, at least he would have made the attempt. He turned his mind once again to the oratory.

"Cruel and terrible as war is, there could not surely be a cause worthier than the giving of light, liberty and religious toleration, not only to those oppressed in the Transvaal, but, in the end, to the oppressors themselves. No ordinary departure of troops to the front is yours. You are the pioneers of a new era in our history."

Indeed. But Jack could not help remembering the voice of his storekeeper: the businessmen were just after gold and diamonds...

"In the pause before the battle charge, in the silence of lonely picket duty, or during sleepless nights on the hospital pallet — the memory of this parting service in these hallowed walls will come back to you with the comfort that even the bravest need. And you will feel that in life and death *the Eternal God is your refuge and underneath are the everlasting arms.*"

Well said, Canon Scott! Jack thought. Well said...

"Then like the knights of old, consecrate today your hearts and swords to God's service. Go forth, then, in the consciousness of right, in the pride of patriotism, in the certainty of victory. The eyes of the Empire and the world are upon you."

And perhaps if I'm lucky, Jack concluded, I'll be with them. He could hardly wait to see what his bishop had decided.

* * *

After the service, Jack had lunch on rue St. Jean at a modest little eating-house crowded with young soldiers. He could not avoid hearing their excited chatter. This afternoon, Major

General Hutton, Officer Commanding the Canadian Militia would address the entire regiment in the Frontenac Hotel. Event piled upon event to augment the lads' thrill at being in this new and very foreign city: their anticipation built ever more towards the great endeavour they were about to undertake. But would Bishop Dunn command Jack to undertake it too?

What about the Virtanen family and their loss? They had become good friends, had taken him fishing on occasion, and often fed him a Finnish meal. He taught school sporadically and young Eino was one of his favourites. The needs both of parishioners and regiment were equally clear; but which way should he turn? Leave it in God's hands? But the Lord helped those who helped themselves...

When the recruits left the café for the Chateau Frontenac, Jack followed. This vast castle-like hotel towered over Quebec City. He smiled at the rumour, then prevalent, that it had been designed after an insane asylum in Buffalo, New York. Built and decorated just seven years earlier, the furnishings and open spaces were so sumptuous that it had every right to be considered the premier hotel in all the Province, if not all Canada. During the morning, onlookers and troops had crowded in to hear the coming speech. Jack was able to make his way through into the grand ballroom, above whose rows of brocaded chairs hung ten large crystal chandeliers.

Not being tall, he could hardly see past the onlookers. But this time his clerical collar stood him in good stead, for the troops let him through so that he could stand right behind the chairs. Then he heard a voice behind him: "Didn't we see you this morning in the cathedral, Father?"

Jack turned to find a tall junior officer looking down at him. From his accent, he sounded as if he too were from the Maritimes.

"Oh. Yes, you did. How did you like Canon Scott's sermon?"

"Inspiring, no other word. Seems we're off to do the right thing. Though sometimes, a man can have his doubts."

"Aye, but there can be no doubt about the rightness of this expedition," Jack said. "I only wish I were going on it."

"Oh, you're not, Father? Then why are you here?"

"Hard not to get caught up in all these proceedings, Lieutenant," Jack admitted. "And where do you hail from?"

"Down Fredericton way. Lieutenant George Dorsey, at your service." The young Lieutenant had a warm face under the close-cropped brown hair.

"And I'm John Alford, though my friends call me Jack. I'm from the Gaspe."

"And now you're regularly at the cathedral?"

"No, I minister in a few wee villages a good way north of Quebec City: Arthabasca, Moose Park, Lake St. John, places like that. I travel there three or four weeks at a time, trying to meld them into parishes, then I come back here to report and catch up. Then off I go again."

With fifteen minutes before the proceedings were due to start, Jack and the brawny fellow fell to talking. In no time, Jack found out that he had joined the Militia to pay his way through college, which he was now attending, and then had volunteered for this. An unlikely candidate for a degree, thought Jack, being chunky and muscular, with country hands and a stout neck, every inch a farmer's son. He surprised Jack with his hobby, the Romantic Revival: Byron, Shelley, and Keats.

"So what do you think you'll do when you return?" asked Jack, careful not to use "if".

"Not sure, Padre. Maybe I'll go in for teaching. Maybe I'll take up a trade, though I'm not much for engineering or lawyering."

"Ever thought of the church?"

"Oh no, Padre, catch me in a collar like yours? Looking after 'the lame, the halt, and the blind?' No sir. I'll only do this fight, help lick those dirty bastards, restore Queen Victoria to her rightful place down at the Cape, and then I'll get back to my studying again. And it looks like we're leaving tomorrow, now."

Tomorrow! Jack's heart sank. No matter what the Bishop did, he'd never resolve this before the morrow. The big farmer patted him on the shoulder. "There's lots like you who want to come, and cannot." He shrugged. "It may not be all that exciting."

"You know you don't believe that."

"No. You're right — lots of excitement for sure. But just for a short time. Nowheres near long enough to get any of us killed. We'll only stay until we can give them Boers a bloody nose."

Seeing Dorsey stiffen and crane his neck, Jack turned. Major General Hutton was making his way along the side aisle with his captains and majors. George pointed out the officer in charge of the actual regiment, Lt.-Col. William Dillon Otter, a regular army officer in his late fifties, wavy hair parted in the middle and sporting a bushy moustache — every inch the British officer. He had been born in Ontario, but his parents were British and his affinity for the Old Country well known.

The General mounted the three steps onto the plush stage draped in velvet and a hush settled. This British general officer commanding all the Canadian Militia recalled the great battles of the past that the British had fought on their behalf, mentioning brave General Wolfe, but careful not to rub this victory into the noses of his French Canadian troops, who made up parts of F Company. This war in Africa, he told them, was the greatest military movement that Canada had ever undertaken.

He had fought a campaign against the Boers and spoke of their tenacity. He'd taken pleasure in writing to General Buller, British commander of the Natal field force, that we were sending from the shores of Canada the best battalion that Canada could offer, headed by the best Canadian soldier he knew, Colonel Otter. Also he spoke highly of the second-in-command, Major Lawrence Buchan, who commanded four companies, and the third, Major Oscar Pelletier from Quebec, another four.

Jack felt his excitement grow as phrase after phrase built his enthusiasm. Captured by eloquence, his rational side could no longer subdue his inflamed thoughts. But then he lectured himself: just when I can see there's no chance of going, I'm getting all worked up. Better get out of here before I burst. He began to edge his way toward the entrance, and then the speeches ended.

Among the cheers and scattered cries of victory and encouragement, Hutton began heading towards the entrance, too. So Jack found himself right in front of the speaker. Spying Jack's clerical collar, Hutton paused for a second.

From nowhere, Jack heard his own voice blurt: "Wonderful speech, General — it made me want to go with you."

"Yes, my boy, my biggest disappointment is that I am not going myself."

"But General, you do know that the troops have no chaplain?"

He frowned. "Well, I believe we have a Catholic fellow."

"Yes sir, but none from the Church of England."

"No C. of E. chaplain? Are you sure?"

"Yes sir, I myself spoke to the Bishop of Quebec this morning. I'm sure he would welcome the opportunity of sending someone." And then he blurted out, "such as myself!"

The Major General raised an eyebrow. "And what is your name, Father?"

"John Alford, sir," Jack replied.

"Well, the Bishop is sure to be at the dinner tonight. I shall speak to him. And good luck!" The General moved off with his officers, who looked askance at this young upstart cleric taking precious time with their commanding officer.

Oh-oh, thought Jack, you're in for it now, breaking every rule of decorum, moving in where you shouldn't, stepping on the Bishop's toes, too. Dear me, in the doghouse for sure. And from the looks of the officers passing, he was heading into no small conflict with his own supposed comrades.

The peaceful pastoral life among his pleasant parishes did not seem so bad after all.

* * *

During a light supper, Jack decided that, to calm his manifest dilemmas, he'd order a carafe of his favourite red wine. And then a second. In all, rather too many glasses for someone preparing to give Evensong. At the cathedral he hurriedly boiled up a pot of black coffee to sober up, consoling himself with the knowledge that the service was simple: two lessons to read, clearly and loudly and his sermon, roughed out during dinner, a eulogy for the valiant troops going off to face the barbarous foe.

And so, while Ingall Smith, the Dean and Bishop were being entertained at the Citadel by the Governor-General Lord Minto, Jack led a peaceful evening prayer service. He spoke a few words, very few — for which the tiny congregation were appreciative — but foremost in his mind was which direction his future might take.

* * *

On Sunday night, Jack tossed and turned in his bed. What about his sorrowing Finnish family? Horrid visions blasted his sleep again: a rotting, blue-lipped Eino calling from the lake's murky depths, beseeching him with outstretched arms to lay them both to rest. Then his friend George reading a Keats poem in a trench — only to be smashed between the eyes by a Boer bullet, brains splattering all over as he fell backwards, crying Jack's name. What a night!

Finally, Jack gave up any attempt at sleep and opened his *Pilgrim's Progress*, always such a comfort when he'd been on the Canadian Labrador. But even this could not quell the daggers of dreams that pierced his brain.

What about Rudyard Kipling? He picked up the recently published *Captains Courageous*. He was at Chapter Eight, the description of young Harvey going with the Newfoundland cod-fishermen, an environment Jack knew and understood. It had a calming effect and, thus engrossed, Jack rid himself of these lingering nightmares. But he longed for the breakfast hour when his motherly landlady might place before him the morning porridge and maple syrup.

Finally day broke. Descending the narrow staircase, Jack heard a knocking at the door and paused. The landlady opened the door.

Young William, the Dean's son, burst in, out of breath. "I ran all the way," the youth blurted out. "I got this here message for ya, Mr. Alford sir."

Jack took the message and his eyes widened. "Be at the cathedral at quarter to nine sharp."

Chapter Four

Early Monday morning, October 30, two carriages pulled up at the gates of Spencerwood, the residence of the Lieutenant Governor of Quebec, Sir Louis-Amable Jetté, KCMG. The low, white building, over a hundred and fifty feet long with its servants' wing and winter garden, sat in the Bois-de-Coulonge, a park jutting out onto the river, commanding a view of the Isle d'Orleans and in the distance the Laurentian mountains. To accompany Jack and himself, the Lord Bishop had assembled a committee of Canon Scott and a couple of other senior clergyman to meet the recently knighted Sir Wilfred Laurier, Prime Minister of all Canada. The entourage got out of their carriages and surveyed the privileged enclosure, which many had not seen before.

"What are we waiting for?" asked Canon Scott.

"General Hutton said he'd join us, and mentioned that de Lotbinière might indeed come." About twenty years ago, he'd been the fourth Premier of Quebec for a short time; now he was Minister of Internal Revenue in the Cabinet.

"Goodness, two prime ministers in one day!" Scott commented. "Good for you, Bishop."

Promptly at nine, Hutton turned up with Sir Henri Joly de Lotbinière, now in his seventies and sporting enormous white sideburns. They were admitted to the elegant residence and shown into a living room.

After a short wait, the lieutenant-governor came out from

breakfast with his guest, Sir Wilfred Laurier. This first French-speaking Canadian Prime Minister was highly respected, though he had been in office only four years. Jack felt distinctly sheepish and stood well to the rear, listening casually at first, and then taken aback as he realized the Bishop was actually praising him.

General Hutton outlined the problem, and then the Bishop took over. "We have a young clergyman here who has done sterling work on that boldest of environments, the Canadian Labrador. He has undergone life-threatening blizzards, crossed icy waters, and done a thoroughly fine job of ministering to those lonely parishioners who inhabit such a bleak and wild coastline. Afterwards, I sent him northward to turn some small settlements scattered across the interior of Quebec into parishes that might soon be worthy of a church or two, a mighty challenge, I must say.

"He has filled both jobs with courage, honesty, and loyalty to the church. I beg leave, as General Hutton suggested, to have him accompany our troops, even at this late date."

Sir Wilfrid looked around. "Is that the young man at the back?"

The Bishop turned. "It is, sir."

He motioned and a stunned Jack came forward. Sir Wilfred shook hands and then spoke. "I see it as absolutely imperative that the Church of England be represented among our troops. And from what they tell me, you are the ideal man to do it. Godspeed, go in peace, and do your best to uphold the faith in what will doubtless be very trying times."

Hutton added, "Sir, I should like to gazette our fine Chaplains as Honorary Captains, if no one has any objections?"

Jack could hardly believe his ears — this simple Shigawake laddie was now finding himself a Canadian Army Captain.

Now that the deed was done, Jack did not know what to think. He sat in the calèche with none other than Canon Scott, who seemed to have taken a liking to him. In fact, Scott had not only complimented him on undertaking this great endeavour but hinted that he'd heard somehow that it had been Jack's own doing.

They trotted briskly along St. Louis Boulevard and then onto the Grande Allée with its large homes, and the Canon asked him about his previous ministries. Jack, delighted at the diversion, filled him in with some exuberance on the two years he had spent along the Canadian Labrador Coast.

"No finer people, and none hardier," Jack concluded, after describing some of his adventures to the older clergyman. "I was indeed sorry to leave."

"And then I gather you served as our travelling Missionary further afield in the northern reaches of the province, even as far as Lake St. John?"

At the mention of the lake, Jack found himself overwhelmed again at his dilemma with his drowned friend, Eino. Whatever should he do? He shifted in his seat and looked out the side of the carriage at the plains of Abraham now rolling past. Clearing his throat, he made himself respond, "Again, another fine group of parishioners, though perhaps these missions occasion rather too much travelling, though a good deal safer than the Labrador."

Thankfully, a plan sprang into his mind; he turned this conversation towards another vexing question. Perhaps the good Canon had an answer. "Sir, travelling in those far-flung villages, I returned with little news of the coming conflict. But once back here, I've been given to understand that not every Quebecer is behind our enterprise."

"Indeed no! During the last month Sir Wilfrid has been hard put to reconcile opposing factions. He's been under pressure from Lord Minto, Governor-General of Canada, appointed just two years ago, and also from the more conservative newspapers in Ontario, and one even in Montreal, all of whom want to send an even larger force.

"Last night, there was quite a fracas, or so the Bishop told me on our way to the residence. Hutton didn't take kindly to all the political interference in Ottawa associated with this whole event. He blamed the Minister of Militia, F.W. Borden, who, being drunk, took his remarks rather badly. Fine soldier, Hutton, though British born. Too bad he's not going with all of you."

With us... That's right, Jack was now part of the contingent, going off to fight. Taking his chances in skirmishes and battles right along beside his men, sharing their pain, ministering to their afflictions. He had hardly absorbed this enormity.

* * *

The calèche drew up outside the cathedral and Jack descended, thanking the Canon for his kind words and for the lift. He saw the Dean talking to a couple at the gate, and quickly went up to him as he excused himself from his parishioners.

"I hope you won't mind my bringing up the subject, sir," Jack began, "but as you may know, two of my parishioners in Lake St. John were drowned on the weekend. The funeral is to be tomorrow. Of course, I am pleased that the Bishop did end up putting the welfare of a thousand young fighting men ahead of this one funeral. But the family were my special friends, and I feel we must address the problem."

The Dean seemed somewhat taken aback. He scratched his chin. "We'll just have to let it go, I suppose," he said at last. "Perhaps some lay person could pronounce the funeral rites?"

Jack frowned, and shook his head. "May I propose a solution, sir?"

The Dean looked up.

"Ingall Smith does have duties here, but surely none too onerous that he could not make that long and possibly arduous journey. He'd make do so splendidly at the funeral." Jack watched the Dean. "You see, I hope you'll agree that my far off parishioners deserve a proper burial rather than some awkwardly managed business."

The Dean paused, thinking. Then he exclaimed, "Splendid idea!"

Jack was tickled pink.

"Only if you think he's up to it, sir," he added mischievously

"Course he is! And in fact, while he's there, he might as well stay for a bit. I know a young deacon who could fill his spot beautifully here at the cathedral."

Thanking the Dean, Jack rushed off to his lodgings, smothering his delight at Smith's comeuppance.

* * *

With his large and hastily packed bag, Jack had to hire a calèche, its top folded back behind, its large wheels clattering over the cobblestones as they set off. The city seemed deserted; most of the inhabitants were attending ceremonies up on the Esplanade where Sir Wilfrid, Lord Minto, and General Hutton were addressing the troops. When the calèche drew up at the Allan wharf where the *Sardinian* lay docked, Jack beheld a scene of apparently some turbulence.

Jack stepped down, paid the driver, and took in his future home. Just over four hundred feet long and forty-six feet wide and recently converted for this crossing, it sat ominously low in the water, with no fo'c'sle quarters nor any real superstructure for the bridge. Seaworthy? Hardly, Jack thought, but then, he had no good idea of what made a large vessel sail or sink. All night long, officers and various details of men had been busily loading stores from the wharf to the ship, and these operations were still under way: piles of blankets to be baled up, boxes of boots and uniforms loaded, men's kit bags checked over, and provisions for a thousand hungry men brought up gangplanks.

He lifted his bag out of the calèche and struggled with it toward the troopship.

A strapping private came over. "*Excusez moi, mon Père, est-ce que je peux vous aider?*"

"*Ah oui, merci,*" replied Jack. In his clerical collar, he knew he'd been mistaken for a Catholic priest, whose parishioners paid even greater respect to their clerics. The young man took his bag, and they walked along together toward the gangplank, while Jack asked if he were one of the contingent.

"*Certainement, un militaire de carrière,*" the young soldier replied proudly. Several regulars among the men had been posted to help sort out the departure.

At the gangplank, an NCO stopped them. "Good day, Father. Your name, please. *Votre nom, s'il vous plaît.*"

"Reverend John Alford." Jack knew this would be a futile exercise, and so it proved to be, after the NCO had scanned his lists. "*Vous avez dit* Reverend Fullerton? You have said — "

"No, Alford, and I'm English, but no need for translation — I'm just not on the list. I was only just seconded to the contingent this very morning."

"Very sorry, Father," said the NCO in broken English, "but no permission for go on ship. You must to wait for Adjutant. *J'ai reçu les ordres.*"

The private beside Jack frowned. Jack went on amiably, "There was a special meeting at the lieutenant-governor's this morning with General Hutton. I am definitely licensed to go on board."

"*Mais vous voyez,* many peoples, they say many things to

come wit' us. We must be extremely careful. Many men, they want come for fighting. *Déjà quatre*, four, I must reject."

"But surely, Corporal you can see that a priest would not stow away. We priests tend to be quite honest."

The NCO thought for a moment. Jack waited, wondering what his next step should be. Then the NCO shook his head, and sighed. "*Bon*, but please to report at the orderly room. I will make the note you have no permission."

Jack and his soldier went up the gangplank and onto the afterdeck where the officers were quartered. Before going down the companionway to the staterooms, the soldier showed him the orderly room. "The office, *mon Père*. When officers on ship, you must to see them 'ere."

"Thank you, soldier. Of course."

They paused to read the posted lists to find out Jack's stateroom; already some officers had arrived and stowed their bags before going back up to the Esplanade. Because of his last-minute posting, Jack found his name nowhere. "Oh, well," he said, "not the first time I've slept on deck."

His young friend persisted. "*Regarde. Ici, mon Père. Ici, il y a une cabine avec seulement un officier. C'est le seul avec un lit qui est libre. Je pense qu'on peut vous y installer.*"

"A double cabin with only one occupant? Yes, good idea."

Without further ado, Jack followed his guide down a passageway and into a cabin with two bunks: on one lay an officer's greatcoat and dunnage bag; Jack threw his gear on the other and thanked the private who saluted and left.

He stood for a moment, taking in his situation. In fact, he realized he had little idea of what was required of a chaplain. But then, who else would: this was the first incursion on foreign soil by any Canadian force. Jack had read something of the Indian wars: Otter at the battle of Cut Knife Creek, the capture of Batoche, Louis Riel's headquarters, and other battles where troops had seen action, but all on Canadian soil. So what actually did a chaplain do, apart from taking Sunday services? Well, he'd soon find out. Perhaps Father O'Leary would guide him. It couldn't be worse than being thrust into the Labrador with no training whatsoever. He had already seen at first hand poverty, starvation and death, and tried to reassure himself that whatever lay ahead would not prove beyond his powers of adaptation.

He had not long to wait. Through the open door burst Captain Forbes, officer commanding H battalion. He seemed slight, with white hair, pale skin, and the very lightest cold blue eyes, like an albino animal in winter, dead white and somehow cruel.

He stopped short when he saw Jack. "I'm sorry, Father, you seem to have wandered into the wrong cabin!" He stowed another small bag and turned to go. "Some enlisted men have been detailed to help — one of them should put you right." With that, he left. Jack saw that his future room-mate was not at all pleased with his intrusion. Well, no matter what, this was now his new home, and stay he would, consequences be damned.

Chapter Five

The noise in the distance grew louder. Jack hurried to the rail to watch the regiment in their new uniforms of dark green serge and white helmets, led by the bands of Montreal's Fifth Royal Scots, and Quebec's garrison of Royal Canadian Artillery, an impressive sight amidst the cheering spectators as they formed up in companies and then marched in double file towards the gangplank, row after row, dozens after dozens, hundreds upon hundreds. He wondered how on earth this converted cattle boat would ever contain them all. Glancing up, he saw three or four braided officers on the stern deck watching with what seemed equal concern.

After the last man boarded, a sudden, deafening whistle sounded their departure. The ropes were lifted from their bollards and the great ship's engines began to throb. Jack knew he had to report to the orderly room, but he wanted to watch them pull out into the black currents of the mighty Saint Lawrence. A wildly enthusiastic multitude cheered farewell as the vessel slipped past the sullen rocks of the Citadel. Guns from the Citadel, whistles from harbour ships, and cheers from the crowds and from soldiers in the rigging drowned out the sound of God Save the Queen from the little artillery band on the dock. Then steam yachts and tugs, pleasure boats and barges, all followed the transport as it steamed down river. Those on the escort boats rushed to the railings of their crafts, cheering and catching whatever souvenirs the departing soldiers threw them.

Finally, Jack made himself leave the rail and push his way aft. The ship was so cluttered and disorganized, the deck so blocked by baggage, crates and bodies, that he took a good while getting to the queue for the Regimental Adjutant, Major J.C. Brown. Upon noticing his clerical garb, those in the queue motioned him forward, placing him next in line.

The frazzled Captain at the Adjutant's door was fretting over the chaos of rapid comings and goings, orders being shouted, and the general tumult prevailing as men tried to locate their accommodations, sort out gear, and find their way around. This officer also had a list, which he surveyed skeptically on hearing Jack's name.

"I'm sorry, Padre, we have two chaplains marked, but no one else. You'll have to disembark on the next skiff with those two stowaways we've caught."

Army bureaucracy again. However, Jack persevered. "I'm sorry Captain, but I've been assigned to the regiment by the orders of General Hutton. Please let me see the Adjutant at once."

"The Adjutant," he snapped, "is busy, as you might imagine. I have orders that none but the most urgent cases be admitted."

"Mine is not urgent? If the commanding officer of all our forces and our Prime Minister both find out that some Captain has put their chaplain ashore, there might be trouble."

Jack watched the man's eyes narrow: he knew he was making another enemy. Careful — use more tact, he told himself.

The Captain turned angrily and went in, leaving Jack to ponder his indiscretion. After a spell, the Captain returned and jabbed his thumb, motioning Jack in with him.

The Captain announced with a grimace, "Major Brown, sir, this fellow claims to be attached, but we have absolutely no record of his name." With that he turned and stationed himself behind Jack at the door.

The Adjutant, a hearty man with a bulbous drinker's nose and florid face, appeared to be dealing with three or four crises at once. Jack waited patiently until he saw the officer glance up at him. "Name?"

"Captain, The Rev. John M. Alford, Church of England chaplain assigned to the 1st Battalion of the Royal Canadian Regiment of Infantry." And then he added as an afterthought, "Reporting for duty, sir."

That should achieve something, thought Jack, smiling to himself.

And achieve something it did. "Sorry, my good man, but every type of scoundrel has been trying all sorts of trickery to get on board. Not hard to lay your hands on a clerical collar and suit! I've sent three ragamuffins off already. So I couldn't help, even if you were a real chaplain. Captain Smith," he ordered, "take the imposter off and put him on the first skiff ashore."

Now what?

The tug at his arm compelled Jack to turn to the door, which the Captain opened with a complacent grin.

Once ashore, how would Jack get back on the boat? And if he did, could he manage that before the ship left Canadian waters? Something must be done at once.

At the door, he stopped and turned. "Major, I demand to see the Colonel!"

"What?"

"And I shall not move until I do."

The group around the Adjutant tensed as he straightened and looked at Jack. Silence fell in the room. No one ever challenged an officer like that. Major Brown paused, then controlled himself. "The colonel is busy. Captain Smith, please take this man away."

The Captain took Jack's arm firmly, but he shook it off.

"No! Major Brown, the Prime Minister himself, Sir Wilfred Laurier, at Spencerwood this morning, decreed that I am to join your regiment. If you would let me speak to Colonel Otter, I'm sure he could enlighten you."

Silence greeted this firm pronouncement.

Jack waited.

Brown got up.

Jack flinched, but tried to show nothing.

"For heaven's sake, man," the Adjutant said, "why didn't you tell us that right away?" But Jack saw his heart was not in it. "Come this way."

With that, the Major knocked at a door behind him. He opened it and motioned Jack forward.

Jack nervously entered the large stateroom with its portholes and heavy desk anchored to the floor. The door closed behind him. He faced the fearsome Lieutenant Colonel William Otter, every inch a commander.

"Captain the Reverend John Alford reporting for duty, sir."

Otter rose. "Ah yes, the new Church of England chaplain? I suppose we should be pleased —" He certainly didn't seem to be, Jack thought. " — that the Bishop of Quebec has seen fit to assign us one."

Jack relaxed somewhat.

"But would I be right," Otter went on, "in stating that you have absolutely no experience of military life? Battles? Deprivations? Of the hazards of the South African terrain? Of forced marches and nights under canvas, or out in the open?"

Jack frowned. How should he respond? Well, better try. He gathered himself. "Colonel, I have spent two years on the Labrador. I travelled six hundred miles in every sort of weather — by sail and by komatik pulled by a team of savage dogs. I have slept snowbound under trees, faced white-outs and blizzards at minus fifty, and nearly drowned on two occasions during that spring storms for which the Gulf is famous. I have also acted as policeman, magistrate, nurse, and doctor under the most trying and arduous circumstances. I would never have volunteered for this demanding position had I not the confidence that I could fulfill whatever duties you placed upon me. Sir," he added as an afterthought.

Oh dear. Although he might be reassuring Otter, Jack now saw he'd thrown down a challenge that would likely, as the voyage progressed, have unfortunate repercussions.

* * *

Two sittings of the officers' mess were scheduled in the regular saloon of the ship to accommodate the numbers; the second only for senior men so they could relax around the table afterwards; the first for junior officers, surgeons, nurses, and the clergymen — Jack's first chance to meet his brethren. Nurses possessed the rank, privileges and pay of a lieutenant.

When Jack came in, he spotted opposite him a small, slightly older man wearing a uniform with a clerical collar and talking in French to a Lieutenant from a Quebec regiment — the Roman Catholic Chaplain, Jack supposed.

He sat down at one of the empty places on the bench and noticed at the other end another clerical collar on a clergyman whose captain's uniform had a slightly worn look. Broad shouldered, balding though obviously in his thirties, this cleric had the usual military moustache gracing his rather handsome features. He noticed Jack's collar and nodded, but went on talking to the officer next to him.

The main conversation in the mess seemed to be between non-military guests, the four journalists who were accompanying the regiment: Fred Hamilton of the Toronto Globe, Stan

Brown of Toronto's *Mail and Empire*, Smith of the *Montreal Star*, and Kandinsky of the Montreal *Herald*. But Jack had little experience of the gentlemen of the press, and he wanted to avoid them at all costs. Some indeed ended up going to his services, but happily, they soon moved their meals to the second sitting, where they could speak to the senior officers, so his contacts with them were thus limited.

Sipping his soup, Jack waited for a lull in the dinner conversation opposite, and then remarked in his best French, "*Vous êtes du Québec, mon Père?*"

"That I am, Father," said Fr. O'Leary with an Irish accent. "And who might you be? I thought they let only two of us on board, me and Father Fullerton over there, though he doesn't like 'Father'. Them Presbyterians," he said in a loud voice, with a wink at Jack, "they like to ruin our standings by being called Mister — though I'm supposin' we'll all be callin' each other Captain, or Padre, now that we're under arms."

"Father O'Leary, we want none o' your papist nomenclature," said Fullerton in an attempt at humour.

Jack introduced himself to both of them. "My coming was all rather last-minute. In fact, only this morning did I get leave to come from the higher-ups."

"You volunteered?" frowned the little man opposite, who then introduced himself as Peter O'Leary.

"A crazy man, like all the Church of England," said Fullerton, attempting more humour. "You don't have a family back there, for sure, young Alford."

"No, I'm free as a bird." Jack noticed across the table one of the nurses turning to stare at him. She caught his look and dropped her eyes. "I most certainly did volunteer. I can't let our fine young Canadians be looked after by reckless Protestants (by which of course he meant Presbyterians) — or even worse, bigoted fellows from a great basilica." He winked at the good Father O'Leary, who grinned in response.

"Well, now that we all have our territories well staked out, I hope there'll be some areas in which we can all cooperate." O'Leary glanced back and forth between Fullerton and Jack, amused.

"Oh," said Jack, "I'm all for that, *mon Père.*"

"And you can stop this 'mon Père' stuff," cracked O'Leary. "I'm Peter, Irish, straight from County Killarney, though I spent thirty years in Quebec, starved out of Ireland by those very British for whose Empire we're going to fight. No idea why I'm here, actually. Except my bishop sent me."

"So you didn't volunteer?" asked Jack.

"Not bloody likely," said O'Leary, approaching blasphemy. "I was the only fella who spoke English well enough. They knew damn well only a real English speaker could hold his ground with this lot. Otherwise we French would get ourselves all walked over again, as Quebecers have for two hundred years."

"Ever since General Wolfe gave you that beating up on the ramparts of Quebec, I suppose," cracked Fullerton.

O'Leary glanced at him but didn't smile. Not a very good joke either, thought Jack. Was he the kind of clergyman who opened his mouth and inserted his foot?

To change the subject, Jack spoke to Fr. O'Leary. "Well, I've been serving up in Lake St. John, and Arthabaska, and all over your beautiful province," he remarked. "I myself was born in Quebec, on the Gaspe Coast, *la Gaspésie* as you fellows like to call it. Little English community, Shigawake, no fairer place in all the world!"

"I don't doubt it," replied O'Leary. "I've been dying to get there myself. But no, they put me in Montreal, they put me in Quebec city, last year they sent me to Cape Breton, they put me anywhere there's an English congregation of Catholics. Not a lot of English Catholics where you come from, are there, Jack, if I may call you that?"

"Please do," Jack answered. "Not a lot. Some from the Jersey Isles in Bonaventure, but in New Carlisle the English are mainly United Empire Loyalists from south of the border. Up New Richmond way, all Loyalist and C of E, too; otherwise, the whole Coast is French."

"We have a few French down in Prince Edward Island," Fullerton said, "but none of them have joined up. The French speakers from New Brunswick have been placed in F Company from Quebec. So our G Company is all English."

Jack glanced up and saw the little nurse looking at him again. He made a mental note to go and sit beside her at a future meal. The four nurses had formed their own cohesive group, talking quietly among themselves. Not a good time to open any new conversation. They appeared rather straight-laced, but the shy one who glanced at him had a fragile look. He wondered what she was doing, going off to fight a war.

"And you, Father," Jack asked O'Leary, "any experience with the troops?"

"I've taken a few services at the Citadel, but never party to an armed conflict, no siree."

"I hear you preached a fine sermon in the Basilica yesterday, so one of the lads said."

O'Leary shrugged, and Jack turned to the other cleric. "And you, Mr Fullerton?"

"I was, for my sins, already an honorary chaplain with the artillery in PEI, so there was nothing for it but to come. But Canadians have never fielded a Militia on foreign soil, I gather?"

There was general agreement from the other junior officers, who had begun to listen in.

Fullerton went on, "If only those cowardly and savage Boers had withheld their attack on the Cape Colony, we'd be back home now in our manse, slippers on, reading our Bibles by the fire." He finished with a chuckle.

"Serves you right," O'Leary kidded, "for accepting that honorary Captainship. Did you think it'd look nice on your stationery?" He winked, and smiled.

Fullerton did not take offense but rather grinned. "Actually it was my wife who pushed me into that. Now she's got herself into a right old pickle: alone at home, looking after all the children by herself, and fearing she'll lose her only support when a sharpshooter gets me... Not that I'm a great one at keeping her in a state she'd desire." He nodded at O'Leary. "They pay me poorly."

"Ah, you can say that again, Father," O'Leary chimed in. "You wouldn't believe the pittance I live on. Not an easy life." He looked over at Jack. "You Church of England chappies get more, perhaps?"

Jack shook his head. "Probably less. The two years I served up on the Canadian Labrador, they had to scrounge funds from the Society for the Propagation of the Gospel in England."

Both Fullerton and O'Leary reacted. "Pretty harsh environment up there, for sure," O'Leary offered.

Jack nodded. "But I rather liked that life. Born on a farm, and all that. Not that life is so tough on the Gaspe."

"So if life was good, why go into the church?" asked Fullerton. "When I grew up in Charlottetown, a steady job working for the Lord had its appeal, I can tell you, with us seven children going hungry most nights."

"In any case," Jack saw the Presbyterian was not quite so gung-ho, "I feel lucky being a part of all this now. I thank the Lord I got chosen."

Just then, the Orderly Corporal announced the end of the dinner.

Jack got up, taking good look at the young nurse who, he noticed happily, was even shorter than he was. But now that he'd met the other clerics, he foresaw that his job might be more difficult than he had envisaged — not much real support coming from that sector.

He made his way back to his cabin, thankful at least that his roommate, Forbes, would be out at the second sitting so that he could prepare for bed by himself, if only for tonight. But as he sat down on his narrow bunk and began to take off his shoes, he reflected that his life this one weekend had taken a complete turn: one full of surprises. In fact, just what he wanted.

Chapter Six

Steaming down the St. Lawrence River that first night out offered little hint as to what turbulence awaited them in the Gulf beyond, so Jack slept soundly. In fact, most of the men lucky enough to find beds did so as well, after all the festivities, excitement and inevitable inebriation — even among officers this first night on board. When the regiment was summoned by bugle and bell to breakfast, very few words were uttered.

When Jack emerged from his quarters, he found the troopship in absolute chaos. Some fifty men had slept on deck, unable to find accommodation; all manner of stores lay about; bales of uniforms and foodstuffs awaited stowing along with cases of arms and armaments. The few officers and NCOs, none of whom had any experience of shipboard life, seemed at a complete loss as to how to cope. Quite a change from the orderly parades Jack had seen on shore, with the trilling of bagpipes and rattle of drums. He hoped that this did not presage the South African battlefield.

On those calm waters with land still in sight, first on one side of the St. Lawrence and then on the other, the ship seemed seaworthy enough. But Jack's fears about crossing the great Atlantic were not allayed; it was rumoured that the voyage might even last a month. Would the regiment be restored to some semblance of order before they faced the enemy — if indeed they were not all drowned? His worries were somewhat mollified by the issue of a new green serge uniform, which he began to wear on board. Being of average size, somewhat heavy set but by no means tall, he was easy to fit.

A dense fog surrounded the vessel the next night and fog-horns blared in monotonous regularity from ship and distant shore. Had the large vessel hove to? This occasioned some grumbling from the men, but on the third night when a storm descended all its fury, they had every reason to wish for the previous becalming.

Jack had brought oilskins, being well aware of the vagaries of the Gulf of Saint Laurence and its currents. He put them on and lurched his way into the bow to stand clinging onto the railing — the best way to face a storm, for sure. The ship under him rolled and bucked, diving into wave troughs in spite of its four hundred and twenty-five foot length and then rising up high, only to splash down again with a mighty shaking. The blinding rain and freezing wind tore into him, but if he retired to his warm bunk and the ship sank, he'd have little chance of escaping. Of course, up here he'd have even less. He had always hated the sea and its torments, a fear he had retained since childhood.

Out on deck facing into the weather, his sou'wester pulled down, the heavy collar buckled about his chin, he avoided the claustrophobia of a cabin and his room-mate Forbes vomiting with dreadful stench into a bucket. He and the officer had shared few words after that initial antagonism.

He felt a tug at his elbow, and turned. "Captain sent me down to tell you to get off the deck," the sailor yelled. "Too dangerous. Go back to your cabin!"

"My compliments to the Captain, sailor, but this is my preferred post. If we're going to be sent to a watery grave, I want to watch and be fully prepared." They were shouting in each other's face: the wind and crashing seas made it difficult to hear.

"Sorry sir, but Captain's orders." With that the man turned and fled, a wave almost drenching them both.

Jack turned and faced the sea again. Oh yes, getting rougher! Just in front, a mountain of water rose seemingly overhead, and then at the last minute the boat climbed it safely — only to crash down again, sending spray everywhere.

Indeed what good would it do him to be swallowed by these tons of water? Better go aft, he thought, but as he turned, letting go his grip, a great wave swamped the bow and struck him with colossal force.

Smashed back, he hit a steel stanchion with a tremendous crack. Had his back been broken? He lay, stunned, unable to move. Seconds passed, and another wave tore him away and swept him across the deck like a piece of flotsam. He brought up against the railing — and then almost over it as the ship plunged downwards, but then bucked upwards at the last second.

Choking and gasping, he flailed, trying to get up by the railing, but without any luck. His every bone felt broken, his muscles made of water. He struggled to his knees but a third wave hurled him across the deck into another crate.

Oh Lord, he was becoming really frightened. Imagine! the first member of the contingent to be swept overboard. "Fight", he roared, "c'mon, get up and fight!" With a tremendous lurch, he got to his feet, only to be thrown sideways again when the ship lurched. He struck his head against a steel ventilator and blacked out.

In just a few seconds he came to, and saw a sailor bent over him. He clutched at the outstretched hand and somehow got up, hurting like blazes. Falling twice, they made their way back to the crew's quarters amidships. He sat inside the companionway, choking and gasping, while the sailor went to fetch a surgeon.

"I don't need a surgeon," gasped Jack, wiping his eyes. But then he saw blood on his fingers. In any case, the man had gone.

* * *

Back in his state-room, sadder and wiser, Jack allowed his blood to be wiped away and a bandage applied by a Surgeon Major, thirty-four, French-speaking, wavy hair neatly parted in the middle. "Just a scratch, Padre," he said. "If this is all I have to deal with on this campaign, I'll be a lucky man." He smiled reassuringly at Jack, who now felt very sheepish indeed.

"Thank you, Doctor."

"Eugene Fiset, from Rimouski, at your service. We're going to be working together quite a bit. Those field hospitals — hundreds brought back, wounded and dying from the battlefield, screaming in pain."

"Good Lord, I do hope not."

"War, Padre. Many of us will not return. Please, just say a prayer for me that I may be one soul who does." With that, the Major closed his small black bag and left Jack to himself. In the other bunk, Captain Forbes was groaning and retching, too sick to notice Jack's doings.

All the next day, the storm wreaked havoc with the boat and its passengers. Pretty well every one of the troops was sick, including Col. Otter who even had to relinquish his command.

* * *

Friday Jack found rather dispirited with its burial of Private Teddy DesLauriers, a 28-year-old Ottawa grocery clerk and member of the Princess Louise Dragoon Guards. Having imbibed too much alcohol during festivities ashore, he'd been helped aboard with severe *delirium tremens* and had given up the ghost.

Father O'Leary led the service as four stalwart friends carried the canvas-wrapped and weighted body of their dead companion up the narrow hatchway and with slow steps placed his body half way across the ship's rail. The rest of his heavy-hearted friends stood drawn up on the heaving deck, the spray drifting over them as they looked for the last time on their silent companion, covered in the flag he had just set out to defend. Jack crossed himself and offered up a prayer as the boards were tipped and down into the waves dropped the first member of the regiment to die on overseas duties, but whose soul, Jack knew, had been claimed by its Maker.

Later that night after the second sitting, Jack returned to his cabin to write his sermon for Sunday. Later on, Captain Forbes came in, and Jack glanced up, then returned to his writing. Forbes washed, got undressed and into his bunk. They had not spoken so far, so Jack was surprised to hear: "Keeping a diary, Padre?"

"No, I'm writing my sermon for Sunday. The Church of England service is Sunday at 11.30 in the morning." Jack put down his fountain pen, and paused. "You will be joining us, I presume? Or are you a Presbyterian? Their service is earlier, at 10.30."

"Neither."

"Roman Catholic?"

There was a pause. "I'm an atheist, Padre. I don't believe any of that truck about a kindly God. Had it drummed into me when I was little, but let it go pretty damn quick when my Dad died. I was six."

Jack shook his head. "Poor lad. So you were brought up by your mother?"

"Nope. This wonderful loving God you clergy talk about snatched her before I was a teenager. My grandparents were too hard up so they couldn't take me. Had to make do. Went out finally to work on the railway. When I was sixteen, I lied about my age to get into the military. Saved my life. I don't need no God to make me happy."

Now here was a challenge! Jack knew instantly why the Lord had placed him in this cabin. He had another three or four weeks to change the Captain's mind. But how to start?

To forestall further conversation, the Captain picked up a book and silence fell.

After a time he glanced at Jack. "What made you become a clergyman, Padre?"

"Well... at Bishop's University, I studied all the general subjects: philosophy, history, English... and one night, it happened."

"Just like that?"

Should he be truthful? Why not? "Towards dawn, I'd had a restless night, and... Well, I felt a hand on my shoulder. That grip was so very firm, almost as strong as if a giant had taken hold of me, but at the same time, gentle. Then I knew who it was and that I would be His forever."

"Just like that? Didn't you struggle? I mean, that was a pretty big decision you chose for yourself."

"No no, not myself, God chose it. And when He whispers in your ears, or He grabs you by the shoulder, I guess you have to just listen." Jack went on, "So I started on theology and church history; the more I studied, the more I knew my role in life was to spread His word and do His works, not only among the children of misfortune, but any who might have lost Him through no fault of their own." Jack hoped that was not too pointed.

"Padre, I still don't understand. Maybe this was the thing every family did in that province of yours? Have one kid in every family go into the church?"

"Could be a bit traditional among the French. But see, to be an Anglican clergyman, of course, you need a degree. On the

Coast, no one really got to University. My father was determined I would."

"A degree? To do good?"

Jack nodded; he was getting irritated.

"So were you always a do-gooder? And so you thought this was a way to do more good?"

Jack shook his head. "I was a bit of a hell-raiser, actually. I just never looked at my obeying this call in that way. I just got it, and I obeyed." He decided to go back to his sermon. "Sorry I can't explain it any better.'

"Well, thank you for being honest, Padre. But I'll also thank you for not trying to swing me round to your persuasion. I don't see any evidence of this precious all-loving Saviour you fellows go on about. Especially with this war coming at us."

Jack focussed on his sermon; to him the matter was now closed. And then he heard, "If you're so wrapped up in doing good, why are you coming with a regiment of men whose aim is to kill, wound, maim, and win."

Oh-oh. The captain had voiced a question that Jack had been suppressing ever since he had received this call to join up. The question did demand an answer — an answer he had so far not found.

"Got you there, eh Padre?" The Captain chuckled.

To be honest, yes, the Captain did "have him there." Jack struggled to find words. Why indeed had he let himself be swept up in the euphoria? Had he thought it through? Not really. "Simply, Captain, I just... Well, haven't faced all that. I did know I was needed at the front, rather than at my parishes in Quebec, which would not be facing danger on such a scale."

At least that might bring this conversation to a close so that he could get on with his sermon. But it was not to be. "Now all these bastard Boers," Forbes went on, "that we're going to South

Africa to try to kill and conquer, did you know that they are all strong churchmen? That they too believe in your loving God? Possibly even more than we do?"

Jack shook his head. "I haven't done as much research into our enemy as I might." Worse and worse, Jack thought. What am I doing, me, a young clergyman, now an Honorary Captain, pretending to help others?

The Captain persisted. "I took a course in Halifax before we left: 'know thine enemy.' The Boers do absolutely no work on Sunday, just as the Bible orders. They avoid any entertainment that we think of as fine in case it might lead to something your Bible calls defilement."

As the Captain paused, Jack hoped his denunciation was at an end. So very much to ponder on. The nature of war. What had he learned at university? They had touched on the subject, but for Canadians, such a peaceful nation, this was indeed a remote topic.

The Captain was relentless. "So Padre, if they believe in God, and there is one, and He's all merciful as you fellows like to preach, how come He's letting us go in and beat the daylights out of a bunch of farmers who also pray to Him for protection? Didn't Canon Scott say it was our moral duty to kill as many as possible? Even with Bibles in their hands and crosses held high?"

Got me there too, thought Jack. Then he blurted out, "You'll have to give me time, Captain." He smiled ruefully. "There's an answer, somewhere. Oh yes." But Jack still had no idea how to find it.

Chapter Seven

On Sunday, a couple of days after the storm, the Rev. Jack Alford held his communion service, as he intended to do during the voyage. He had decided to modify his exhortations to the men and concentrate on lessons from the four Gospels. As the vessel proceeded through the straits south of Newfoundland and headed out into the Atlantic, the swells became heavier and broader, but Jack made himself face up to the incessant rolling and pitching, for weeks of it lay ahead. He usually sought the bow, and so got to know others of the same mind. He would make his way forward through the enlisted men's territory, which housed bakers' quarters, cooks' galleys, two miniature rifle and revolver ranges, old hoisting machinery, seven horse stalls, carpenters' and armourers' shops, and so on. Apart from the long hours of dull, daily drill, the men made good use of their spare time in this limited space: sharpening bayonets or sensibly using coffee to die their brilliant white helmets brown, others writing letters or playing cards, some reading or discussing the coming war, like one big grand family. Yes, Jack thought, probably as brave a contingent of fellows as ever donned a uniform.

They were forging southward through heavy seas, the screw beating, the engines throbbing, the whole ship pulsating and trembling from stem to stern as she struggled along at two hundred and sixty miles a day. The mornings began, for officers as well as men, with a bath parade on deck when sailors hosed down the enlisted men with seawater. Breakfast at seven sharp and after a "smoke time," the relentlessly boring drill. Again after lunch more training, with a lecture by one of the senior officers at four, and then at 6.15, voluntary evening prayers. After dinner, often a lively concert was dreamed up by one of the companies, in competition with the others. After the last post at ten, Jack often found himself on the rear deck, muffled up against the soot and fumes from the smoke stack. He loved to sit back and admire the stars in their great dome of the heavens. He would dream of home, or try to sort out what duties he should think up. Often enough, he wondered how best to approach the young nurse. The four women ate together at one end of the officers' mess and it was difficult to cut her out of the herd.

Soon after they had entered the Gulf with the ship in complete disarray, Otter had placed a British regular officer from the Dublin Fusiliers as quartermaster in charge of the stores, and the ship began a more normal functioning.

One day as Jack headed toward the bow, Bible in hand, he passed this new quartermaster who had paused by the rail to watch the raw recruits training with rifles. On the ocean, huge nets of seaweed swam past, notwithstanding that the sea was almost as calm as a pond, allowing everyone to recover from their *mal de mer*. Jack stood with the Captain and watched the recruits: in the space of five minutes, two dropped their rifles and another knocked himself on the head with his weapon.

The Captain rolled his eyes. "What a bunch! Imagine sending the likes of them into a war!"

Jack nodded, but then added, "Most of them are pretty intelligent; won't take them too long. Though I have no idea why shouldering arms is so important. I should have thought learning how to fall on your face and fire at a moving target would serve them better."

"Oh that'll come, don't you worry."

After a pause, Jack congratulated the Captain on his new success as quartermaster, which occasioned a modest tirade: "Fruit and medical supplies are pressing deficiencies. And uniforms — do you know we're two hundred and sixty kharki tunics short? And we have a surplus of six hundred pairs of trousers!" Jack shook his head. How could the regiment have been sent off in such disarray? "And what is worse, our latrines and facilities below decks are quite inadequate. The food... well, I won't say anything about it, but water! It's so scarce I'm sure that later we'll be posting a guard over the taps. You Canadians have put together a right old mess. You'd never find that with the British army, I can tell you."

Jack was about to stick up for his country and its organization, but calmed himself. "Captain," he said, "we are all just so thankful that you have taken command. Just this morning I heard the men congratulating each other on their fine new quartermaster."

No need to go on, that mollified him and he made no more direct criticism of the Canadian organizational skills. And happily, so far, no mention was voiced of Jack's misadventure on deck, disobeying the ship captain's orders.

* * *

One evening at dinner, Jack noticed his bashful nurse staring into space. As she was getting up to leave, he rose and joined her. "So Sister, how are we doing these days?"

The other three pretended not to notice and went on chatting, though they kept one ear on the conversation. The sister simply shook her head, not speaking.

"Are we getting a little homesick? I've noticed other soldiers feeling that way. Perhaps you too are a prey to this?"

She nodded, close to tears.

He started to reach out and touch her hand as he often did when ministering to his parishioners on the Labrador. But here in an officers' mess, not wise.

Her mousy hair swept back over a long, plain face, but she radiated a warmth and vulnerability Jack found inviting. Slight of frame, he wondered if she had the toughness necessary to endure a battlefield hospital. He thought back to his lovely Lorna on the Labrador. He had rescued her from a schooner whose rough crew had subjected her to some dreadful goings-on. Unlike this nurse, Lorna had been tall, much taller than he and, in every sense of the word, strikingly attractive, with her jet black hair and strong dark eyes.

Many times over the last year he had thought of her. But each time, he had made himself put the image aside. They had spent a winter boarding in the same house, and had grown to be great friends. In fact, he admitted now that they might have been in love. But he had been too slow to acknowledge it, and she'd left on a schooner for Truro, her home. He'd written a couple of times, and her last letter informed him that she was now married and had just given birth to a lovely baby boy. So much for that. Next time, Jack thought, I'd better recognize love for what it is, and act on it. No time now to regret the vacillation on my part which had caused her to leave Labrador — but, he told himself, just do not let it happen again.

So now, hating to see one of the fairer sex in pain, he suggested they take a few moments of fresh air before retiring.

She seemed grateful at the suggestion and climbed with him onto the small deck above the mess, where they exchanged greetings and names — Kelsie McLaren, from Yarmouth.

"What did you think of that storm in the gulf, Padre?" Kelsie asked. "I hated it. And now we're heading out into the Atlantic. I fear this ship will never get us through another tempest. In

Yarmouth we all know about Atlantic storms. They're terrible. We've lost a lot of fishermen."

Jack nodded. "I think we all have our doubts... But then I say to myself, we don't really know enough about the sea and its ships, do we?"

"And there's the men..."

"They're not bothering you?" He felt himself stiffen.

"Well, not exactly. It's... We don't have nearly enough medical supplies. Not even enough smallpox vaccinations."

"Oh?"

"Yes, Doctor Wilson had me count them this morning, when the Quartermaster got after him for the third time. We're about three hundred short. What are the men going to do when we get to South Africa?"

"Can't the doctors pick up more in Cape Town?"

She shrugged. "Who knows? I hope so. But our head doctor said there'd be no time. Once we get there, we'll go right into battle."

"Well," Jack tried to sound reassuring, "let's just pray there is not a lot of pox going around."

"If there isn't," she looked at him with soft brown eyes, full of worry, "why bring the vaccinations along in the first place?"

Jack did not know the answer to that one.

"I guess I'm just worrying for nothing," she said. "It's my nature, I suppose." She faced into the wind and let it blow her hair. They both traced the quarter moon scribbling in foreign calligraphy on the inky waves. Jack acknowledged that he did feel comfortable talking to her. But what did that mean? "You know," he said, "you're not the only one with worries."

She looked at him sharply.

Oh dear, had he spoken without thinking? But then, she did seem interested. "You know, when I was exhorting the men in my sermon to do their utmost for Queen and country, I felt my words sounded pretty hollow. I just can't summon up that ringing oratory we all heard in Quebec City."

"I thought you spoke very well, Padre. I liked your sermon." When she glanced at him under the hanging lamp, he saw admiration and encouragement in her eyes. That quite heartened him.

"To be honest, I feel a bit leaden, too." Jack paused. "Probably the letdown after all those marvellous speeches. Now, facing the daily grind, I see I didn't bring enough books. I intended to spend more time studying. Of course," he added quickly, "I have a Bible and one or two others I can read."

"Yes, but aren't they boring after a while?" She frowned. "I haven't seen you on deck much."

"Well, I was going out a bit, but then, I guess because of my Captain's insignia, I found that every time I passed men just resting, they had to jump up and salute. I hated that."

"Why not take off your clerical collar. Is it mandatory?" she suggested hesitantly. "Then they might not."

"I checked with Forbes, my cabin-mate: he said the colonel's a stickler about form, as we all know. But no, apparently the collar's not necessary. So good idea: I'll wear an ordinary shirt like everyone else. Then at least I won't cause all conversation to stop when I come up. But we have to look smart when we move about — representative of Her Majesty, and all that. So I do have to wear a uniform, which includes the helmet, that they do have to salute."

They fell silent. Jack just enjoyed standing next to her in the semi darkness while the wind blew past. Perhaps the voyage might not be so bad after all.

* * *

The next afternoon in the bow, Jack met up with his companion from the Chateau Frontenac, George Dorsey. The grey ocean stretched flat before them to a thin horizon, above which an equally grey sky reached overhead with a jaundiced sun trying to break through.

"What ho, George. Got a moment off?" Jack's greeting was punctuated by loud rifle reports.

"Too many moments off, if you ask me. My boys are learning to shoot, under the gunnery sergeant. As long as —"crack-crack "— I keep hearing this infernal noise, I know they're busy. Certainly time they learned about rifles and such."

"Isn't it hard to hold target practice on board?"

"Well, they use a Morris tube — it's a liner for the barrel so they can use low-power & low-cost .22 ammunition in place of the .303. Oh, and it's also low-recoil, helpful for the new recruits."

"Now I've been meaning to ask you, George, if you brought any decent books?"

George nodded. "I have. But did you check the supply they got for us when we left?"

"You mean those dear ladies in Quebec?" Jack went on, "*Titus, Soldier of the Cross*, and some *Boy's Own Papers*; the *Wrestler of Philippi*, which I've already read, of course; *Richard Bruce* by the author of *In His Steps*; the *Gospel Trumpet*, which I tried to wade through, and Robert Louis Stevenson I've read. A bunch of romances but no Rider Haggard and not a set of Kipling, if you can believe it, save for one or two volumes of his least interesting works."

"I've got some books of poetry," George suggested, "and a survey of the Romantic Revival I'm studying for when I go back. That interest you?"

. "Yes indeed. And then may I interest you in a couple of my works on religion?"

"You know, Jack, I sort of stopped going to church after I was confirmed. Up to then, my parents made me go every Sunday, but I found those sermons so long and boring." He heaved an exasperated sigh. "I guess that's what finished me on religion."

"But George, you can find the most beautiful poetry in parts of the Bible. Listen to this." Jack flipped through it, as the rifles blasted away, and found a place he'd dog-eared for George, which he read out loud:

"My beloved is like a roe or a young hart: behold he standeth behind our wall, he looketh forth at the windows, showing himself through the lattice.

My beloved spake, and said unto me, Rise up, my love, my fair one, and come away.

For, lo, the winter is passed, the rain is over and gone; the flowers appear on the earth, the time of the singing of birds is come, and the voice of the turtle is heard in our land.

The fig tree putteth forth her green shoots, and the vines with the tender grape give a good smell. Arise, my love, my fair one, and come away. Song of Solomon, George. You should try reading it."

"Okay." George waited for a pause amongst the rifle noise. "What about this from Keats:

Season of mists and mellow fruitfulness,
close bosom friend of the maturing sun,
conspiring with him how to load and bless
with fruit the vines that round the thatch-eaves run..."

He had quoted it from memory, and went on for a few more lines among the resuming bursts of gunfire. "I tried it out on Dad, but he didn't go for it. Bunch of mush, he said. But in the autumn, I always think of it, down home on our farm. And now, this autumn, here we are..."

"Heading into a war..."

George shook his head. "Beats me how mankind gets into these scrapes. I'd much rather be back on that farm, to tell the truth. But this way, at least I get to see the world, earn some money, and then head home for what's going to be a good and enjoyable career."

Jack nodded and secretly prayed that it might be true: Let him not meet a sharp-shooter's bullet; let him have many more autumns before he takes his leave of this earth.

Looking past George, Jack saw Private Eamon McAndrews, the Cape Breton jokester. George turned as Eamon called out: "Hello there, Padre. Enjoying the voyage?"

"Private, don't you know regulations?" George barked. "Where do you get off forgetting to salute an officer?"

"Oh, George, never mind. Friends should greet me as their padre, not their superior officer. I don't deserve — "

"Jack, if old Brown catches us, there'll be another dressing down, which you want to avoid. You've gotten in enough trouble —"

He stopped to return the snappy salute that Eamon had given them both, winking at Jack.

"All ready for the fray, Eamon?" Jack asked. "We've been discussing poetry together." He noticed George seemed ill at ease with this friendly meeting.

"Passes the time, I guess. Now how soon do you think it will be before we strike landfall, Padre? Some of the fellas get seasick even when the sea's like a millpond. We sailors never bother, but them farmers — "

"Careful what you say about farmers, Private! You're talking to one," George exclaimed.

Jack couldn't tell if he was joking or being unnecessarily serious. "Well," he interrupted, "we're all off on our glorious mission together, fisherman, farmer, tinker, tailor, soldier, sailor, beggar man, thief."

"Dunno about glorious missions, Padre. I told you, some of us joined because of the three square meals and a decent roof. I never expected to be going out so soon to kill a bunch of Africans, no matter how bad they're supposed to be."

Jack nodded and drew in a deep breath.

"I have to agree with that sentiment, Private," George muttered. "But we mustn't lose sight of our mission, must we?"

Eamon nodded. "Yes sir. But there's so much talk of us beating the daylights out of the devils..." He seemed to hesitate, and then turned to Jack. "Sometimes in the night, I kin as easily see them devils beatin' the daylights out of us. What do you think?"

Indeed, that was the question to be asked. "Well, in warfare," Jack replied, "somebody wins and someone else loses. But we're doing our duty, supporting the Empire, an ideal ingrained in all of us very early." The last thing he wanted to think of was Eamon, or George, finding a premature grave. "Let's hope we all live to a ripe old age, Eamon." Jack smiled. "Now that seems to me like an easy cue for a few seconds of prayer? No harm in that — maybe a short silent supplication for an quick and easy victory?"

"I'd better get back to my company, Jack. Seems as if the shooting has stopped." With that, George took his leave.

Jack closed his eyes. Eamon was a stranger to church. But why not try?

When he opened his eyes and glanced across, he saw Eamon still sunk deep in... well, perhaps prayer, why not. A tiny pastoral victory?

They stood looking out into the waves, the day cloudy, a far-off fogbank menacing them, when Jack saw on his friend's face a new look that told of distress. "Anything else troubling you, Eamon?"

"Well, now that you bring it up, yes, Padre. Every time a bloody officer walks by, we have to spring to attention and salute. I've talked to me mates, and we agree Old Bill has to put some discipline into us, all right, we are a mangy bunch of bastards. But we drill hard, we learn how to shoot, we right-turn, left-turn, quick march, slow march, do all this here rubbish which, Father I tell you, might not be all that necessary when we lie on our bellies and aim at those bastards over there. But when we's takin' a rest, or shining' our shoes or maybe just having a doze, why leap up every time some bloody officer passes?"

"That does seem rather excessive," Jack remarked. He had heard that the men were beginning to resent Otter for his stream of orders, intended to instil discipline in men, most of whom had never received any form of military training.

"Excessive, you said it. What's worse, it's making me dislike the buggers, when some of them officers, like Lieutenant Dorsey there, are kinda human and maybe even nice. We don't want to get disrespectful — specially with us all going into battle together, eh? Why don't that colonel come out on deck himself, and see what it's like? He's always back in his damn cabin writing reports. Some say he's just trying to get in with the Brits so's he can join one of their regiments. As if there's something wrong with being a Canadian. The troops are calling him Black Bill!"

As he was speaking, another thought struck Jack. Why not stand up for these boys? But how? Well, at least he could make a stab at it.

Chapter Eight

From the moment he walked through the orderly room door, pith helmet under his left arm, Jack knew he was in trouble. The grousing of the men had surely reached the Adjutant's ears, and Jack saw that Brown was already in a bad mood, one he always seemed to wear along with his badge of rank. Jack found himself regretting his sudden impulse, but he'd taken the plunge and now had to make the most of it.

He voiced his concern at once. "I've heard that this particular discipline of saluting has been relaxed on other ships transporting the Imperial army. So Major, perhaps a little slack should be given our men at this point."

"That is really not within your purview, Padre," Brown stated. "You're supposed to be looking after men's souls, not their military performance."

"But shouldn't our colonel make it easier on the men who, after all, have volunteered to lay down their lives in the service of freedom? It may not be my place, I agree, but sometimes, the men need an advocate and isn't that what a padre is supposed to be?" It was coming out in a rush, which Jack regretted, but then, he'd become rather nervous. "We do have the example of the One who came before as an Advocate for the whole human race."

"Pretty grandiose ideas for some young curate just out of college and now elevated to the rank of Honorary Captain." Was that a sneer?

The look on the face of the Adjutant only built Jack's distaste. He wanted to fling back an insult, but held himself in check. "In these army manuals that I'm trying to absorb, I read that a commanding officer puts his men first, even before himself," Jack maintained firmly. "In any case, would you be kind enough to pass my concerns along to Colonel Otter?"

With that, and before any rude words could escape the Adjutant's mouth, Jack whirled and left, committing a rather ungraceful exit as the ship gave a lurch that threw him against the wall.

Oh yes, another enemy for sure.

* * *

For his sermon at his second service on Sunday, Nov 13th, he took as a text Joshua I, verse 7: "Only be thou courageous and very strong." He was saying it more to himself than the others. In fact, this voyage had begun to wear on him. He told the men to turn to their "true source of strength." Weren't they crossing the great ocean on behalf of the cause of liberty, equality and freedom? These impulses would sustain them on the long march, in the dreary night watch, and in the wearisome waiting. "The eye of your Canadian home is upon you," he finished, "the eye of the world is on you."

During the service, he noticed many looking over the port bow. And indeed, that morning they had seen the craggy rocks of San Antonio, the first of the Cape Verde islands, seven thousand feet high and twenty-two miles long. The service over, Jack doffed his surplice and joined the officers and men scanning with every sort of binocular and glass the oncoming landscape. Would they go ashore? The weather had turned a deal warmer and the sun was often their companion in the sky now, burning down on them, for they'd soon cross the equator and enter summer.

The islands produced coffee and bananas; Jack borrowed field glasses and made out some goats browsing on the hillsides. The ship ran down along the east side and soon got close enough for Jack to make out a couple of fishing villages in the breaks of the high, jagged, red rock that sloped sheer down to the sea. Their square white houses with black windows beckoned, but then the men had received orders: no stop-overs.

Sailing slowly past, the *Sardinian* soon came in sight of the next island, St. Vincent, with its decent harbour gracing a small coaling village. Heavy mountains scowled down on the many troop transports and cruisers lying at anchor. A small crowd had gathered on the quay, and Jack thought he made out the sound of distant cheering as they passed.

Back in his stateroom for the afternoon, Jack realized that he was at sixes and sevens. In a quandary, he realized that he had not yet found his true direction. One way to calm his thoughts he decided was to write a letter — how remiss he had been in keeping his family informed. When his departure had been approved, he'd just had time to scrawl a hasty note for his landlady to post, telling his parents he was leaving for South Africa. What must they be thinking?

Dear Poppa and Momma,

Here I am on the good ship Sardinian heading for the South African war. I guess by now you have heard a lot about the struggle. I have been made an Honorary Captain, which I hope will make you proud. No doubt you are wondering why I have taken up this challenge. Sometimes I wonder myself.

Snow must be all over the farm now, and drifting up around the house. I guess you're all nestling down in our wonderful old Homestead. I wish I could be with you, but I have cast my lot with these lads who will be needing my help in their hours of peril approaching all too soon. In a couple of weeks we reach Cape Town. I have often wanted to travel, and this was my chance. I cannot wait to see what the African continent will be like.

How does Lilian like teaching in Shigawake? Has Winnie gone off to Montreal to be a nurse yet? Mac is working in the woods this winter, I bet. You always said you wanted logs piled ready on the bank to float down to the mill in the spring floods. I hope Earle is studying hard so he can go to college, too.

Do not worry about me. I am well and happy, and love this new experience, though it's not all rice pudding. I expected I'd be seasick, but so far I'm fine. I shall write from the battlefield next month, in the Cape Colony or the Transvaal, when the fighting begins. A fine Roman Catholic priest, Peter O'Leary, has come to look after the French fellows, and a rather forbidding clergyman from Prince Edward Island to look after those from the breakaway churches.

I send you my love and prayers. Your loving son, John.

* * *

In the morning of November sixteenth, another ship, the *SS Rangatira* on her way from New Zealand to Southampton hove into view. A lucky encounter. Soon, Jack heard the Captain announce over the loudspeaker that letters would be taken over and thus posted from a British port. Jack was pleased to see his missive go off so soon.

The *Rangatira* also brought news from the front that was not good, having encountered another ship coming from the Cape. The British had faced more setbacks in the struggle, but this cheered the men greatly, for they knew that sooner rather than later, they could be thrown into battle.

For the crossing of the line on the next day, oddly cruel weather, cold and overcast like an October day, was interrupted by the celebration of whistles and the discharge of a large rocket from the captain's bridge. A holiday was declared and the men gathered around, celebrating.

Jack was approached by his friend from the sheds, the grizzled Corporal Ferguson. "Well, hello Corporal, haven't seen you around much, except for being a loyal attendee of my services."

"You preach fine sermons, Padre. I like to listen to 'em. So do all the boys." And they fell in beside each other as Jack wandered over to the rail where Lieutenant Dorsey was looking out to sea. The Corporal saluted him as was proper and they fell to talking.

Again today, Jack noticed the flying fish. Broaching the surface, flocks of them would go skittering for many yards, white forms flashing against the dark waves, like fisher faeries trying to break their spirits free from the freezing depths. Escape! They seemed to cry; such curious flutterings.

"Won't be much longer now, I hear," Jack said.

"Just as well!" The Corporal growled. Jack looked round. "You wouldn't believe what it's like below decks." He kept looking at Jack.

Lieutenant Dorsey turned to glance at the Corporal.

"I hope it's not too uncomfortable," Jack mumbled as the Corporal continued to look at him.

"Something wrong, Corporal?" George asked.

Ferguson shook his head, continuing to look at Jack.

Well, something's up, Jack thought to himself. "Corporal, if you have time now, why don't I come down and see your quarters before lunch?"

No sooner were the words out of his mouth when somehow he realized that the Corporal had been waiting for precisely that reaction. Indeed, he should have mingled with his men, much sooner.

The crporal muttered under his breath, "About time. We've been waiting for our padres to visit."

"What's that you said?" bristled George Dorsey. "Our padres do quite enough. Their Sunday services are first rate; evening prayer always fresh and interesting, with words that we need to hear. What more do you expect?"

"No, no, George, he's quite right. I have been neglecting my duties." Jack followed the Corporal to the companionway.

"Jack, there's no need for to you go down there," George said. "Everything's being done for them that is needed."

Jack glanced around. "But it's not the same accommodation as we officers —"

"No question of that Padre, we're in the army now, and the ship is only so big, eh?"

"The rank and file," Jack persisted, "have some very bright men, I've heard. Some could even be officers."

The Corporal broke in, "I been making a list. In the ranks we've got thirty-one university students, eleven teachers, thirteen lawyers, and twelve professional engineers..."

Jack and George traded looks. "Quite worthy men, no doubt about that!" Jack agreed. "Let's go check, George."

George hung back. "Jack, let it be."

Jack frowned at his friend, and dove on into the companionway.

"But I don't want you to get into more trouble..."

Jack stopped. "More trouble, George?"

"You and the Adjutant don't get on too well. Best not to push that too far."

"You think I care what the Adjutant says?" Jack's black eyes blazed.

"No, Jack, I'm sure you don't." George towered over him, looking concerned. "But you should try harder to keep in the good graces of the higher-ups. Makes for a more effective go-between, when you're really needed. On that battlefield, it might be important to have a powerful advocate."

"Aye," said the Corporal, turning to look up the stairs as Jack and his companion had begun to follow him down. "You watch how the brass is looking after us — I've seen enough already. And I've heard enough. Water scarce. No more washing. Some of my men not even issued kharki uniforms yet. What's it going to be like out on that veldt?"

Jack took note: the Corporal probably knew what he was talking about. He followed him into the ship's steel belly and reached the level of the troop deck. Jack looked around. The stench of food, fresh paint, seasickness, and the fug of sweat, almost made him gag.

Hundreds of hammocks were slung over the tables where the men ate. Much too close together, Jack thought, for in rough weather they'd bang into each other as they swung wildly in their meshes.

But an even greater shock came as Jack reached the second level. Here, the air was so thick and rank that Jack could imagine picking his way through with an axe. This vast birth deck was well below the level of water. In long stationery rows, these sleeping compartments had narrow passages with scant room to walk between. The men lay packed like eggs in a crate, and whatever air ventilation sent down into this black hole had to be conveyed by means of canvas air shoots from the upper decks.

Jack was further taken aback by the greetings from those soldiers who found the sun too strong and the deck too cramped, and so had come down for a rest. "Hello Padre! How d'ye like our dungeon? Padre, you should come down to see us more often! We all like your sermons, Padre." A warmth Jack now felt he did not deserve.

It was an oddly dispirited cleric who climbed those stairs, after having thanked the Corporal for this eye-opening tour. What have I been doing all this voyage? Jack asked himself. Why have I not spent more time with my men? Look at me, up there in my comfortable cabin, albeit with that confrontational Captain, eating my hot officers' meals in the mess — and paying no attention to the very men I've been sent to succour.

As they reached the top of the stairs, Lieutenant Dorsey said, "It's rough Jack, I know, but we all have to fit on this darned vessel, and it's by no means a real troopship. They're trying to do their best, I'd say. That Corporal Ferguson is a complete gem, though. I take my hat off to him."

"Well, make sure you tell him that," said Jack ruefully.

Chapter Nine

The next night, when the opportunity arose, Jack leaned across the table at dinner and said to Kelsie — and he didn't care who was listening, "I've got to talk to you, Kelsie. When you've finished, please join me on deck."

She looked at him, frightened. What on earth was he going to say? But he didn't care. He was so disheartened by his manifest lack of diligence, his selfishness, enjoying himself as if he'd earned it by years of army service instead of having just joined up. Not only had the visit downstairs chastened him, it brought to mind all sorts of indignities the men might be facing that he hadn't recognized.

He stood at the railing, waiting uncomfortably. The lanterns threw a low light across the loaded deck. Why was she taking such an age? Was she afraid to come? Had she decided that this sporadic relationship should go no further? Had he been neglecting her?

When she finally turned up, he wasted no time in pouring out all his worries

She listened, leaning against the railing, her feet braced on the iron deck as the ship rolled. She kept staring down at the glittering reflection of the half moon on the black waters, not looking at him. When he finished, she nodded. "And you know, Padre— "

"I think now, you should start calling me Jack."

"Well, all right then. You know, Jack, these boys, I don't want to add to your worries, but we're having quite a few of them in with burns on their bare legs from those steam pipes when they are doing those silly drills. The colonel's foolish orders for the men to go about in bare feet on that blistering deck, with trousers rolled up above the knees, is causing a good deal of sunburn, and with it, not a little suffering. I thought you would have noticed."

"I have noticed. I thought it was just temporary. One or two days."

"You haven't noticed very much then, Jack. It's been going on for a long time."

Silence fell.

"I guess I've pretty well messed up all down the line," Jack said. "I'm very sorry." His heart felt so heavy it might fall and smash into a thousand pieces.

Kelsie reached out, took his hand, held it, and then brought it to her mouth and kissed it. Her grey eyes stared into his sympathetically. "Don't take it so hard Jack. Now that you've heard and seen everything, you'll know what to do."

Her voice sounded warm and comforting. A little encouragement felt so nourishing at times like these. Had he been perhaps too hard on himself this last while? "Thank you Kelsie, thank you."

* * *

Jack went in once again to face his *bête noire*, Brown, who during the voyage had lost no chance in denigrating him, or casting aspersions on his experience, or his bearing as an officer.

He made an ungraceful entrance, the heaving of the ship hurling him against a wall. He had to brace his hands on the Adjutant's desk, an action his opponent took to mean he was being aggressive. Jack quickly straightened.

"I need an appointment to see the colonel, please, Major."
Jack stood at what he thought was attention.

The Adjutant's eyes narrowed. "On what matter?"

"Personal," barked Jack, ready for a fight.

Brown tried to stare him down.

Jack stared right back.

"Am I given to understand that you, as chaplain, are using
your position to get access to our colonel, busy though he may
be, and although he has given instructions not to be disturbed?"

"I'm doing just that," Jack said, and nothing more.

Again, Brown stared it him. Again Jack stared back.

Brown rose and went and knocked on Otter's door and
announced the Chaplain.

Jack walked in, doing his best to hide his inner panic that
recent days of army discipline had instilled. He used to feel
afraid of neither man nor beast, but now the prospect of con-
fronting the Commanding Officer of the entire regiment filled
him with apprehension. Brown shut the door behind him and
stood in the room at ease, listening.

Otter clasped his hands together, put them behind his head,
and leaned back in his chair. "I suppose you've come on some
pastoral matter, Padre?"

Jack sensed his superior was wary, but he also felt Otter was
not about to throw him into the brig.

"I wish it were a pastoral matter, Colonel, but I'm afraid not.
Which is why I am hesitant to bring it your attention. But I beg
leave, as your chaplain, to mention this problem of the men's
well-being, which you may not, perhaps, fully realize."

Jack heard an exclamation of disgusted astonishment behind,
but did not turn, watching Otter. In any case, he persevered.
"Your Standing Orders for the men, very well-intentioned, I'm

sure, to toughen up their bare feet and legs for the South African sun, is having rather unfortunate effects."

He saw the colonel lean forward, put his elbows on the desk, his shoulders hunch, and a grim expression form upon his face.

Jack pressed on, "You see, Colonel, some of the men have become badly sun-burned. There are also unshielded steam pipes that have injured others. I believe, however well meaning, that you might want to go easy on this particular order for a short while — just until the men heal. We want them in good shape when we begin battle."

"Is that all, Padre?" Otter snapped.

"Yes, Sir. That is all."

Behind, Jack heard Brown click to attention. He paused, looking at Otter, as neither spoke. Then Jack finished, "Thank you very much for taking the time to listen to me Colonel. I deeply appreciate it, no matter what your decision." With that he turned and left the room.

* * *

The next day, after evening prayers that the nurses attended, Jack fell in with Kelsie as she headed towards the mess. "And so how are the boys doing with their sunburned arms and legs? I've been concerned."

"And well you might be, Padre." Kelsie avoided looking at him. "As if there isn't enough to keep us occupied, with all the aches and pains from those awful drills. Don't I smell of liniment now? I've been rubbing it on them all for days."

"I still have a lot to learn about military conduct," Jack said. "I often find myself confused as to the good intentions of our officers."

The mess doors hadn't opened yet, so they drifted toward the side rail and leaned over. "Look, Kelsie!" Jack so wanted to talk to her about this latest *contre-temps*, but wasn't sure if he should.

Sleek forms sliced the waves near the bow keel, weaving their supple bodies to speed back and forth in a dolphin dance.

"Seen any whales?" he asked

"A couple of times. Spouting, far off." Occasionally, the dorsal fin of a shark, grim wolf of the ocean, cleaved the open sea like a knife.

"Such beautiful creatures, these dolphins," Jack murmured. "I've never seen them before." He paused. "You know, yesterday I saw a butterfly on deck. Its wings were moving up and down as though trying to keep its life flowing. A harbinger of a new continent, I suspect."

"Yes." Kelsie nodded, then shook her head.

"So," Jack went on, "I guess we will soon be in Cape Town..."

"Yes, and I'm not looking forward to it, Padre."

Jack grimaced. "Well, that butterfly did make me think, for a moment, of the souls that might indeed flutter up into an unknown paradise." They both fell silent.

She nodded. Then, Jack tried to sound optimistic: "Imagine, such a faraway and mysterious continent — ours at last. I don't suppose you've ever been, either?"

He glanced at her. He himself had even been aware that their voyage — and thus their new relationship — would be over... Had she considered that, too?

"That's when the killing starts," she said simply. "I've seen enough accidents in Halifax to know what we'll be facing. Our boys will get carried into hospitals, crying for help. I'll tend them all right, but I don't like the thought of my friends from the ship screaming in pain." She looked at him with her big eyes. "Jack, they're so young, even younger than me. How can any of us look forward to all this — having them butchered by savages they're going over there to wallop?"

She lapsed into silence, and Jack reached out. She came close to him. He put his arm round her. "I know," she went on. "I've come over offering my help and all that... But I just can't stop worrying. Rumours say the Boers are such fine marksmen... With those German guns of theirs, they'll pick off our boys from an awful long way away."

She's right, Jack thought, she's absolutely right. But on the other hand, although it meant facing dangers he did not relish, he still felt a growing excitement at drawing closer to this unknown continent.

"You'd think someone would at least say something to Otter," Kelsie said after a time, bringing the subject back to sunburns.

It was an opening that Jack still preferred not to take. "What perplexes me is why our second or third in command, Major Buchan or Major Pelletier, can't go in and tell the old boy what's happening. Does he have any idea of the havoc he's causing?"

She looked at him again, and he saw her steeling herself. "You've been told about it as well." Then she looked back at the sea.

"Yes." He still resisted speaking about his confrontation. "I expected a change, but..."

After a pause she went on. "One young kid was in, I'm sure he lied about his age to join up, anyway, he was grumbling loudly about the chaplains doing nothing."

Now that Jack did not want to hear. The good name of the clergy lay in the balance, so now at last, he had to speak up. It would relieve his distress. "As a matter of fact, Kelsie, I did go in. I faced Otter. I... I just didn't want to mention it."

"Why not?" She turned to him with an entirely different look in her eyes. "That was so good of you, Jack. I'll tell them."

"No, don't. You see, I got nowhere. I really expected a change right away." He shrugged. "And nothing happened. I failed."

"You didn't fail, Jack. You didn't. You tried. That's what matters." She paused, and went on as if to herself. "I will tell the lads. It's your good name, and I want them to know."

"Well, I don't want the lads to think ill of us chaplains." Though he wondered why the other two had not stepped in as he had. Or maybe they had? A lot more to this army business than just preaching sermons, he was finding out. What would the next hurdle be?

But in two days, Jack was pleased see that his request that the order be rescinded was listened to, and some form of normalcy restored.

And then, too soon for Jack actually, early in the morning, on Monday, Nov 29, 1899, a dull hump appeared on the horizon, scarcely discernible between the slate coloured sky and water: the flat-topped mountain which heralded Cape Town. And with that, the imminent approach of war.

Chapter Ten

Capetown! The ship steamed — far too lazily it seemed to Jack — towards the long low shore, past what Jack was told was a lepers' home on the parched, flat Robben Island, then seeming to crawl right under Lions Head on the top of Table Mountain. Jack quickened with excitement as he saw the harbour. Almost the entire regiment crowded to the near side of the ship, making it list slightly.

On the way in to the dock, they passed another troopship that turned out to contain soldiers from the Australian colonies. So here again, Jack thought, six other colonies in a soon-to-be dominion had produced a Militia and sent them on an even longer voyage to come and fight for Her Majesty, Queen Victoria, who reigned over Australia as well.

Although aching to get ashore, the regiment had to wait until the yellow flag was hoisted and a medical officer came on board to approve the ship for landing. Finally the ship came to moor at the dock and Kaffir (black) stevedores began to unload supplies. But the men still could not disembark, for orders came to spend another night in their cramped quarters.

After dinner, Jack loitered on deck, looking longingly out at the thriving city. Two of their four war correspondents were getting ready to disembark. Did orders not apply to them? Well, thought Jack, maybe chaplains are exempted also. He thought for a bit, and then crossed over to Stanley Brown, of the *Mail and Empire*, and another fellow, Kandinsky, who looked ready to disembark. He had stayed well clear of them during the voyage: with notebooks at the ready, he suspected they might be focussed on reporting the worst, rather than the brighter, aspects of the voyage. But now, perhaps no damage would be done.

"Mr. Brown!" Jack approached the friendly-looking writer who had grown a moustache during the voyage, perhaps to fit in better with the regiment. His inquisitive yet rather kind brown eyes suggested he might be an upright citizen. Jack was not so sure about the lean and hungry-looking Kandinsky, who had been tarred by the soldiers as a bit of a wastrel. "Do I detect your intention to go ashore tonight?"

"Why yes," came the answer from Brown. "We believe those orders have nothing to do with us. So, to better inform our readers across the Atlantic, we're going down that gangplank. Can't wait to set foot on this great new continent."

"My sentiment exactly," Jack said. "May I join you?"

Kandinsky scowled but Stanley nodded. "Of course, Padre. We're just going to wander around a bit, get a feel for the town, and perhaps end with a celebration drink." The last phrase seemed thrown out as a bit of a challenge.

"A drink would be just what the doctor ordered!" Jack grinned. "As long as we're not back too late... Like you, I shall take in the town with very curious eyes."

So it came to be that Jack, not glancing back but half-expecting a shouted command to return, hurried after them down the gangplank. Gingerly and proudly, he stepped for the first time on African soil.

As he trod the quay, he felt a surge of elation such as he had not known since Sir Wilfrid had shaken his hand at Spencerwood. At last, the African continent! What other Shigawaker had such luck? And who might have thought, when he entered Bishop's

University seven or eight years ago, that one day he would become a world traveller? Did he ever think, snowed in by blizzards on the Canadian Labrador, that he would soon adventure on tropical lands?

They turned off a waterfront street into the quaint old city thronged with dark-skinned, gaudily dressed Kaffirs, some refugees from the conflict to the north, and some slovenly, barefooted types in rags. Jack had never seen such variety: Malay and East Indians, Coolies, Soudanese, Arabs and Egyptians — turbans, fezzes, the woolly heads of Zulus and the slouch hats of the Cape "boys". Red electric trolley cars clanged past, their passengers sitting in open seats on top. Jack and the others took in every storefront, every passer-by. He enjoyed the rather grand public buildings that lined this main thoroughfare. Such a monumental style of architecture, he thought, must resemble European cities, particularly in Holland. Along the way, he noticed signs in Dutch as well as English. The colony had been an outpost of the Dutch East India Company until 1795, when the British seized it in the name of the Prince of Orange.

"I've never been able to get this South African history straight, Stanley," Jack confessed. "Mind you, I came at a moment's notice, and there were no history books on board I could find."

"All you need to know is that the place went back and forth between the Dutch, or Boers, and the British —"

"Until the Brits passed that Emancipation of Slaves Act. That's what undone 'em," Kandinsky added.

"Oh yes, in 1833," Stanley said. "I seem to remember a bunch of Boers trekked north, the *Voortrekkers* — "

"Five thousand of them," Kandinsky said. "Brought their Kaffirs with 'em. Crossed the Vaal River."

"Oh, so that set up the Transvaal," concluded Jack. "They wanted more land?"

"They wanted to get out from under British Control." Stanley sounded vehement. "But then in the Zulu uprising, 1877, they needed British help and so they lost their independence again."

"Got it back seven years later, though, at that Convention in London," Brown said. "But all the while, Germany was siding with the Boers. Didn't hurt of course that they discovered diamonds in 1867, and gold near Kimberly a year earlier."

"That's for sure." Jack was grateful for them piecing it together, now that he was actually here. Parts of downtown Montreal, he thought, displayed the same magnificent frontages, but he found these more interesting. Old Quebec City still held his heartstrings: nowhere else could be as attractive as that place he now called his second home. But this city here could at least claim the magnificent Table Mountain dominating its whole scene.

They squeezed back as a hansom cab trotted past, a Kaffir under a wide hat perched high on the back seat, snapping and cracking his whip like an expert as he wheeled two officers carelessly through some mud-packed, some stone-paved, streets. The three of them walked past rows of waiting carriages, brightly painted and gilded, rear danger lamps flaring red. Jack smiled at their names: Dashing and Bold, Napoleon the First, Swift and Sure, and so on.

One building, a newspaper office, rang bells to announce special war bulletins, and groups hastened to see what might be the latest. Jack took in the native drivers and porters, some in turbans, others in high-pointed straw hats rising like pagodas, and a group of Kaffirs guffawing at three jaunty young officers who strode past.

Finally, they entered a saloon that didn't look too costly. In front of a long counter, soldiers, civilians and sailors all stood drinking deep the health of the Empire. This bar, they soon discovered, circulated wild rumours and even wilder gossip about the war, as did most others.

And what a week this last one had been. Jack and his journalist friends Kandinsky and Stanley learned from the bartender, a short bearded fellow with an unkempt apron covering his squat frame, that things were not going well for the British: the Boers had Ladysmith and Kimberly under siege, he told them, as well as Colonel Baden-Powell's force at Mafeking. True, the British General Gatacre had successfully occupied Bushman's Hoek, but the Imperial forces had been forced to fight for every foot of ground in all their battles, suffering great losses. So far not one shot had been fired in the territories of the Boer Republics.

"Well, I suppose that augurs well for the Canadians," Jack commented. "Means our boys will get into action pretty quick."

"Yes," Stanley said, "at last we'll have something real to report." He nudged Kandinsky.

They spent the next half hour listening to, and trading, all sorts of rumours. The somewhat partisan bartender told them that in this rather divided city, some people were hoping for a pro-Boer uprising in the British territories of Cape Colony and the Natal. Stanley countered this with the news of the *Sardinian*'s thousand fighting men, all raring to do battle for their Queen.

Stanley proposed a second round of drinks, and Jack nodded. "But that'll be the last for me."

"The fighting is still a long way North," the bartender told them as he poured their beers. "You won't see any of that for a good while yet."

"The quicker we give those Boers the whipping they deserve," Stanley declared, "and the sooner we get back to Canada, the better."

"Amen to that," echoed Jack.

The bartender looked at them askance. "It may not be the

Boers who get the whipping. They beat the blazes out of the Imperials — what do you think they'll do to a bunch of rag-tag recruits from Canada?"

"My worry exactly," echoed Kandinsky.

Jack was taken aback to hear of skepticism about the ability of soldiers who'd shared with them a month-long sea voyage. "I, for one, have every faith in our lads," he snapped.

"Those Boers, they have the advantage of the Germans' guns and munitions," the bartender countered. "They know how to make a gun, I'll tell you. Soldiers have been in here talking about that six inch Long Tom — and those pom-poms: sixty rounds a minute, shells the size of your thumb, and four times the range of a rifle bullet! Oh yes, and their Maxim guns are much better than ours, from what I hear."

"Rumours are flying everywhere. You just wait," Stanley said. "We were told our boys have a nine inch gun —"

"A lot of use against roving bands of kommandos," the bartender sneered.

"So the Boers are not alone? The Germans are supplying them?" Jack had heard something about this from Kelsie, but it still shocked him.

"O'course. Everyone knows the Germans are backing the Boers," the bartender snorted. "They send down arms, they're doing everything they can. Don't want any spread of British influence in Africa. Age-old rivalry, o'course."

"Not so age-old, my friend," Stanley countered. "That dastardly Kaiser has wound it up a lot since the departure of Bismarck."

"You mean to say Boer bullets," Jack felt his ire rising, "made in Germany, will be killing our Canadians?"

"You're right they will," said the bartender, moving off to bring drinks to another group of soldiers rowdily demanding attention.

"Imagine going back home with a beaten regiment!" mourned Stanley.

"Those who are going home..." added Kandinsky.

"Well, I have every intention of making it through,"Stanley replied. "I think that goes for the padre here too, doesn't it Father?"

Jack nodded. "Yes indeed. No bullets will stop me doing my duty, even in the front line."

"I wasn't talking about being finished off," Kandinsky interrupted. "I was talking about choosing not to go back."

They both whirled. "You're not?" Jack asked.

"No sir. Why do you think I took this job cooped up in those awful conditions on that boat? Because like you fellows, I felt a surge of pride? No sir. I wanted a new life." The drink, Jack saw, might have loosened his tongue. "I've left behind a wife, sure, and I promised to send her money. But like all the others, she'll find someone else pretty quick, you watch. I'll be only too glad to get rid of her. All this talk of sweethearts and wives crying? The one thing I'll tell you is: most of them will be laughing themselves to sleep — in another man's bed."

Now this kind of talk Jack had not heard along the Labrador, nor in the tightly knit villages in Quebec. He was, quite frankly, shocked. But he held his tongue.

"I know, I know," said Stanley, ever the pacifier, "several recruits I interviewed intend to start new lives here."

All this was news to Jack. Should he have listened even more to his men on the voyage? But to egg on Kandinsky and learn more, he said, "Well, you may not be alone, Kandinsky, but you're certainly rare among these folk."

"I don't give a damn what the others think, nor you, Padre. There's some with lives so rotten, we'd do anything for a change. We cry out for it. You grew up with a silver spoon in your mouth. Most of us didn't."

Stanley shook his head. "You're wrong about that. They say Jack here was a poor farm laddie."

That reply got Kandinsky more worked up. Jack wondered how to pour soothing ointment on the bitterness.

Stanley tried. "Well, Kandinsky, you'll be well quit of that rag you write for in Montreal." He had intended this as a way of placating him, but in fact it just spurred him on.

"That rag, it might not be not up to the level of your high and mighty *Mail and Empire* back in Toronto," the swarthy journalist said, but from what I've heard, I wouldn't be working for them either. Bloody slanted paper, switching around everything you write, telling you what to do..."

"They certainly do not!" Stanley said. "We have all the freedom we need. I write whatever I please."

This friendly drink was turning into quite a verbal brawl. Jack gulped his ale and made ready to leave. "Boys, boys, you're both here to write about our gallant lads who have crossed the sea to vanquish some misguided beasts attacking our noble Queen. So let's keep a sense of proportion! Kandinsky, you're at liberty to stay here afterwards, of course, and we both hope you'll find a wonderful life in this good land. And Stanley, surely you're going to be fêted on your return after all those fine accounts, which I haven't read, of course, but which I know will be quite enlightening."

"And you, Padre," Kandinsky looked at him, somewhat mollified, "you were preaching that rubbish as though you believed in it. I do find you convincing. I went to hear you twice."

"Oh," asked Jack, "you've come to my services?"

He was about to go on, when Kandinsky cut him short: "Only to report what you said as a duty to my readers. Not because I belong to the C. of E., no sir, I was brought up Catholic, my parents are from Europe, and a hard time they had of it. But you gave me no reason to slander you, because I would've. That's what the readers love — misadventure."

"No they don't!" snapped Stanley. "My readers like heroism, bravery under fire, cheerfulness in the face of hardship, all the finer qualities of mankind."

Kandinsky sneered. "Arrgh, you think your readers are any better than mine? No sir, you just don't know them, and I do."

Oh dear, thought Jack, this is never getting any better. "Lads, shall we wend our way back? We might discover something interesting on the way. This bar, we've dredged for all the information we're likely to get. And it's bad enough hearing about the German nation, and how quickly those ruthless Boers are using European armaments to beat our plucky Imperial troops." He stood up.

Kandinsky nodded, and downed his pint; Stanley left half his on the bar and slid from his stool as well. The three of them waved goodbye to their somewhat confrontational bartender, and made their way back to the *Sardinian*.

Once on board, Jack stopped before going into his stateroom. The moonlight made everything almost as clear as day, and the scene was one he'd never forget: the harbour crowded with shipping, huge troopships and men of war. On shore, myriad lights sparkled from the city. Jack stared up again at the steep, scarred sides of Table Mountain, its top capped with fleecy moonlit clouds. He was not the only one awake; everyone was much too excited at going ashore the next morning to sleep.

He leaned back against the steel bulkhead, watching and thinking, his mind now full of Kelsie and the friends he had made on the voyage. What would the future bring to them — a long life ahead? Or a lonely grave in the sandy desert. He prayed for them silently, and then made himself retire, to be ready for the morrow.

Chapter Eleven

Thursday morning, November thirtieth, Jack disembarked with the regiment to an enthusiastic welcome from cheering crowds, and marched up through the town, along Adderley Street to the Green Point Campground, four miles away. On this, his first parade, he quickly got into the rhythm, swinging along with the best of them, carrying the heavy pack into which he had switched most of his belongings. Finally they reached an immense plain of kharki-coloured dust under the shadow of Table Mountain, and pitched their tents. Although the chaplains had marched together, by mutual agreement they joined their separate companies for tenting, Jack with H Company from Nova Scotia, Fullerton with G company from New Brunswick and Prince Edward Island and Father O'Leary with the French in F Company from Quebec.

While settling themselves four to a tent, the men were issued kharki uniforms, together with greatcoats, puttees, three days' rations from the stores and large jack knives useful for eating, as well as other chores. Jack was delighted to get his British Issue of a chaplain's insignia: a Maltese Cross raised in relief on a flat metal base, so the badge looked square from a distance. The men had fun learning to put on the puttees, thick woollen bandages about three yards long to swathe the legs from shoe to knee. Besides being hard to get right, Jack found them to be deucedly warm. Of course, he thought sarcastically, why else select them for use in a hot tropical country facing an unpredictable enemy who won't send a postcard warning of his next early morning attack?

The next day, the men went into town for their one day off, which saw a good deal of merriment, drunkenness, and visits to certain nameless establishments, which were doing a flourishing business. The serious business of war lay ahead, and to make matters more exciting, they had received orders to entrain the next day for the North. Jack's first concern was for Kelsie and the other three nurses. He had heard the upsetting news that they might not be coming with the battalion into the high desert to meet the foe.

After some inquiries, he found that the women had been billeted in a hotel in Cape Town, whither he went before even treating himself to lunch. As he was leaping up the steps who should he see coming out but Kelsie herself.

"Jack!" she cried. "What are you doing here?"

"I came to find you, of course," Jack replied, "just as soon as I heard you might not be coming up into the interior."

"No." She paused. "We just heard ourselves." She looked a little crest-fallen.

"So... this means goodbye for the moment," Jack ventured.

She nodded.

He felt a wave of affection, looking at her soft, lovely curls falling about a plain face, which it must be said contained a long nose. A bit chunky, like himself — well, solidly built — which would probably stand her in good stead during the long hours of physical work nursing. She wore the regulation tunic of a Canadian nurse: a kharki "bicycle skirt" with a blouse equipped with shoulder straps and service buttons, and her kharki hat sported a little red cockade. As with Jack, a thick brown belt encircled her waist and she wore similar leather boots. "I had been wondering how I would get to see you," she murmured.

"Do you know where you're going yet?"

She nodded. "A hospital in Wynberg. It's a suburb of Cape Town, very nice, they said. A lot of the wounded from the front are expected. They need us there." She again looked as if tears might appear. Then she pulled herself together. "I'll do my best. But I thought I would be looking after our own boys. I've gotten to know quite a few. That's why I came, Jack, to care for Canadians."

"In the weeks to come, may your wish come true."

"But still, I don't like to think of anyone being so badly hurt he has to be brought by train all the way back to Wynberg. Let's hope this old war comes and goes, and no one gets hurt." She actually smiled, and then giggled.

Jack joined in. "Oh yes, if only that could be true," he said. "Now tell me, have you heard from your family? By the way, do you have time for lunch?"

"Thank you, no, I have to buy supplies, and then we're going off. And yes, I get the odd. All is well there. But come with me now if you like."

They set off down the street together. "We've been asked to try and equip ourselves. So I'm going to find some liniment, and whatever other medicines there are. I'd like to get a good scrubbing brush box, little things, but they'll make a big difference."

What a wonderful nurse, Jack thought. She had definitely been growing on him, but that was the way of things in wartime: you meet, and you part.

"Now Jack, look out for yourself, won't you. I've heard tales of chaplains going out onto the battlefield to help the wounded, and getting shot themselves."

"Well, I do expect to be going out under fire. But for some reason, I'm not dwelling on that now. On the battlefield, fear might well be my own worst enemy, but I'll face it then. Right now, let me put danger from my mind."

They stopped at an apothecary where she bought a number of items. They found a couple more shops, and she gradually filled her large pouch. They walked back slowly, Jack carrying her bag like an old friend.

"Funny, I've heard it said," she mentioned, "in wartime you get closer to a person in a much shorter time."

"True." Jack wished he could find words to express what was in his heart. "Maybe I'll be posted to your hospital, and then we can work together."

She nodded. "That would be nice. Though they've warned us against becoming too attached to anyone. You see, one could just be torn in a million pieces by seeing soldier after soldier pass away, even while we're looking after them."

They were silent as they walked.

"Enough of all this sombre talk," Jack said, after a while. "Now, since you work in Halifax, why don't we think of brighter things. There is a train, you know, comes all the way from Halifax to Montreal and it stops in Matapedia. That's the junction for the Gaspe. I've even heard talk, and a lot of it, that a track may be laid down to Gaspe in the next while. Apparently they're making plans already. So it will be easy —"

" — for me to come and visit you!" she cried. "How I'd love that. You've told me so much about your old homestead. Won't it be fun walking back over those fields you told me about, and looking down into that valley where your grandfather built his first cabin in the New World."

Jack's mind went back to his farm, and dwelt there: such delightful thoughts, walking back with his little waif — well, no, this tough, wiry nurse — but to him, still a fragile creature who might well benefit from a long walk over his fields.

"And you must come yourself and take the train and see us in Halifax!" cried Kelsie. "You'll love my little sister Orla. She's four years younger than me and she sticks to me like a limpet. I've written her already about you. She's quite religious, too. You know, I'll be back working in my hospital there as soon as this ghastly war is over. You must promise to come."

"Of course I shall," Jack agreed, "of course. I'd love to meet her. And all the family."

The two of them continued walking, relishing those delightful pleasures, which both of them, in their heart of hearts, knew would end up being so unlikely.

* * *

Bedding down in a tent on Green Point was no novel experience for Jack, who was used to sleeping out in the open. But this hard baked ground had a different feel from light crunchy snow with pine branches spread upon it. And having to get ready for sleep in a small tent with three others was also new; he'd been joined by George Dorsey, now nicknamed Big George, and two other lieutenants, Robert Willis and Harry Burstall, also a giant of a man. They managed after a bit of a struggle to erect the tent, but knew that soon they'd be doing it in a flash. This night, however, the troops had been carousing, so little was said before heavy sleep claimed all four.

Friday morning saw them striking their tents, packing, and marching off to the Cape Government railway station, passing the summer residences at Somerset Road, this time through ever more vociferous crowds. When the men drew up at the end of the march, Jack and the other two chaplains manoeuvred closer to hear His Excellency, Sir Alfred Milner, the Governor-General of the Colony. He wished the soldiers a pleasant trip and a happy and speedy return, which seemed to Jack a rather fatuous send-off for men about to risk their lives for the Governor and his Colony.

Two trains had been commandeered. As the men mounted the carriages, the ladies of the town distributed sandwiches, tobacco and canvas water-bags. Jack shared a compartment with other officers, slightly cramped, but after all the excitement of leaving, he was able to sink into his own thoughts.

As the little narrow-gauge train moved out from the station, he had a fine view of the City Hall against the distant Table Mountain. Soon, they trundled along past the marshlands of the Cape Flats, and then through a most beautiful succession of farms, gardens, orchards and forests. Orange trees, just past their blossom, glistened in the sunlight; vineyards with newly formed clusters stretched in regularity; orchards of figs and apples gave place to bits of forest, usually pine. In the distance, Paarl Mountain came into view, probably thirty miles away, and then they wound through beautiful wine lands stretching from the railway to the Hex River Mountains, enormous ranges, bigger than anything he'd seen in Quebec Province, for sure. At appointed stations, the men were served with coffee biscuits and bully beef.

Much later, the little train began to climb the winding mountain pass to reach Touws River Station and finally, at the top, the plateau of the high desert.

When Jack woke the next morning, out the window he saw the endless landscape of boulders and scattered low bushes: all the dreariness of the Karoo desert — broken admittedly by mounds, or "kopjes" as hills were called hereabouts. He also spotted distant islands of green centred by a windmill, which showed that farmers could tackle this desolation and carve out large, irrigated properties. Occasionally they passed a Kaffir kraal with its mud huts and naked youngsters, and hundreds of goats plucking a living from the stunted growth of the veldt.

Jack's eyes widened. What on earth was that — trotting along beside the train catching bits of bread thrown by soldiers? Two spindly legs, round, feathered body, long, long neck, two huge eyes above the big beak — an ostrich of course. The first he'd ever seen.

My Lord, it ran fast! Up to forty miles an hour, he'd heard. After a few minutes, it lost interest and stopped. And in the course of the trip, Jack saw others, mostly alone, some in twos or threes and a few in a flock. Certainly new wildlife for him to contemplate en route to death and destruction.

Towards evening, the African sky offered Jack a most glorious sunset, wispy clouds overhead and, on the horizon, heavy bunched-up, blood-red cumulus, auguring the battles to come. Again Jack examined his conscience: how on earth could his sermon on the morrow justify an exhortation to go forth and kill enemy soldiers — farmers whose windmills he'd seen, perhaps, and rather like his own family. Well no, he argued, not like them. They did deserve a whipping, having challenged Her Majesty. Or did they? Would not slaughter be a bit harsh for simple men taking up arms to defend their own country, as that Quebec shopkeeper had maintained?

No no, they were rebels, savages who must be taught a lesson. After all, didn't the British Empire stand for certain freedoms? He'd heard enough in Cape Town to know the Boers treated the black natives, Kaffirs, like an inferior species, almost like animals, with none of the rights that Her Majesty would bestow upon them. How could religious-minded farmers be so harsh to these original inhabitants? But then again, what did he know of actual conditions hereabouts? Wasn't the Zulu Uprising only a couple of decades ago?

Back and forth between these two poles of thought flew Jack's brain all day long as his train sped through the inner plateau of the Karoo desert, and sleep finally claimed him.

Sunday morning around four a.m., the train pulled up and the men sleepily disembarked at the junction of De Aar, 4, 180 feet above sea level, with a population of six hundred. The town consisted of a straggling line of cottages, a hospital with three hundred and fifty wounded, and a fat little cemetery. The officers were quick to point out that this new vantage point was well suited for defence, for they could take advantage of the many small hills, those kopjes that ringed the town, where now nine pounders and howitzers dominated the skyline. At last, forty-four hours north of Cape Town, Jack had reached a real battle zone.

Before the sun was fully up, they marched over a rotten bridge that spanned a stream that Jack thought might better be termed a sewer, and got to a dusty campground next to the 2nd Battalion of the Duke of Cornwall's Light Infantry, and pitched their tents

No church service. Jack didn't know whether to be pleased or annoyed. After that cramped journey, he was in no great mood to preach, but on the other hand, the rhythm of Sunday services would be most beneficial to the men. Everyone more or less dropped down and slept, taking advantage of their morning off.

Just as well, for at noonday the most pulverising sandstorm tore through, blasting the tents with blinding, shifting sands. Jack fought the onslaught, but finally had to lie flat, like the others, handkerchief over his mouth, on the lee side of a crate of ordinance. The sand stuck to his sweaty face. It put Jack in mind of those good, old-fashioned Labrador blizzards, but these grains of fiercely stinging sand did not melt on contact and found their way into every portion of the clothing. Try to eat lunch in those conditions? No, food was a mockery; water and biscuits had to suffice.

Not the picnic everyone had prophesied.

Chapter Twelve

Three days of punishing high temperatures, sandstorms, ever-lasting thirst and unchanging routine tormented Jack and his fellows until, at last, an order came to entrain for Orange River. The next day at dawn, Jack noticed the enlisted men being loaded into open cars. As an officer, he'd been assigned a compartment in a covered carriage. But he remembered his conversations on the boat and decided to travel with the enlisted men. He walked past the open carriages and spotted his fisherman friend, Eamon McAndrews, who he hadn't talked to for a while. So he crammed himself into a hard wooden seat between his friend and other privates.

Moments after Jack had settled, who should come past but Adjutant Brown with a couple of officers, inspecting the carriages before the train set off. Arriving opposite Jack, he stopped dead. Jack met his gaze as he took in Jack's uniform sitting among the enlisted men. The others stared as well. Jack felt three pairs of eyes on him, and smiled graciously.

Brown gathered steam to blast an invective, but the train gave its peculiar whistle; the two officers finished their inspection and Brown had to follow, obviously seething.

Jack relaxed. "I suppose all this inactivity is driving you crazy, Eamon, like the rest of the men?"

A tough bearded corporal in the seat ahead joked, "If he don't have enough to do, I'll fix that pretty quick!" He gave a hearty laugh, and Jack saw at once that it was Ferguson. "Corporal, I didn't recognize you in that beard!"

"I got so sick of shaving in cold water, Padre, I thought I'd take on the look of a Boer. Maybe I'll be able to sneak up on 'em quiet-like, and knock off a few."

"You big ruffian, don't you have anything else t'occupy that bleedin' empty head than choking the life out'a us all with those damn drills?" Eamon quipped. Jack saw they had developed an easy camaraderie.

"I know enough to shoot a Boer between the eyes. That's all I need." The Corporal laughed again. "Now Captain Alford, how d'ye end up coming to sit with the likes of us? You should be up there in a closed carriage with the rest of them. Did you not see the look on the Adjutant's face?"

"Corp, you know how deeply I care about what he thinks!" Eamon grinned with the others. "And maybe from here, I'll be better able to instil in the lads a love of the Almighty, and even a few of His Ten Commandments." Jack finished with a wink at Eamon.

The soldiers around joined in the merriment. "You'll never instil nothing in our Ferguson, Padre," Eamon joked. "He's the toughest one in the army. Oh yes..."

"And we're even proud to have him as our NCO," another private threw in.

"But don't let him hear you," Eamon said, "or he'll — "

"Bloody right, he'll..." the corporal croaked. "He'll see you run around the train three times for your bravado!" The others didn't know whether to laugh or be silent.

"And when do you think this blasted inactivity is going to end, Padre?" Eamon asked. "I missed our church service last Sunday. Did you cancel it? Or did they?"

"Oh, they did, for sure. Just to let me off the hook!" Jack

grinned. "But next Sunday, I have to give you a double-barrelled sermon to make up for it."

They all laughed again.

After the men had settled down, some drifting off to sleep, Eamon whispered, "How'd you make out with that nice little nurse, Padre? She seems nice, but I would have gone for the prettier one, that one there in charge."

"Beauty is only skin deep, Eamon," Jack repeated for want of something better, but chastising himself for mouthing such a cliché. "Well, I was sad enough saying goodbye. But we might end up serving in the same hospital, looking after the few — very few, I hope — Canadians felled by Boer bullets. For the moment, she's better off down at Wynberg. She did say she'd rather look after Canadians than the British who are apparently coming down by the trainload."

"Aye," Eamon murmured, "them Brits ain't doin' too good. I guess they'll need the likes of us. We'll show them Boers a thing or two, when we get into it!"

"I pray you are right," Jack mumbled dubiously.

"You don't sound like on the ship. Your sermons then was sure full o' fire!"

No, he didn't, true. Perhaps the bartender's words had rattled his composure. The Boers did have better armaments, and were savaging the Brits. But Otter, who had shown little regard for his men on the ship, might now prove to be a great marshal in battle. This thought made him feel better. "I'm quite sure that we Canadians will acquit ourselves with great valour, high skill, and unique bravery, when the time comes."

That settled the conversation for the moment and as Eamon fell silent, Jack found himself drifting off.

Visions of his sweet Kelsie returned. How was she bearing up under the stress of the Wynberg Hospital, with its trainful after trainful of wounded? He should write her when he had time; she had often entered his thoughts since their parting. Enough of that, he said to himself, and forced his thoughts off to the Gaspe and his Old Homestead, now under snow. What a snowball fight he'd had with Mac, when they were youngsters! With a stroke of luck, he'd knocked the tuque off Mac, and then his younger brother had charged him and they had both fallen back into the snow. He found himself smiling and drifted off to sleep.

* * *

The packed train chugged through the desert heat, soot from the engine choking Jack in this open carriage, especially as they rounded curves. But for the most part, the rails ran dead straight — and thus were fraught with danger. So easy for Boers to cut the line, thought Jack, or indeed gallop up and ambush them. Yes, they were coming ever closer to Boer territory.

At noon five hours later, still not having eaten, they arrived at Orange River. But then, Jack found himself and the others forced to stand, sit, even lie, baking on the sand under a scorching sun while their officers haggled. Jack raged against this uncalled-for delay — apparently centred on which of the two regiments was to advance, theirs or that of the Gordon Highlanders, who had been waiting here. In the end the Highlanders won, poor souls, soon to be decimated at Magersfontein under Lord Methuen, not thirty miles away, in what would be known as the Black Week.

Jack marched with the men to the campground of the Scottish regiment, who had left it in a right old mess. And once again, the African weather displayed its turbulence by drowning them all in a blinding rainstorm as they tried to pitch the tents. Torrential rain did happen on the Gaspe, but nothing like the suddenness and force of these downpours.

Orange River was no place of luxury, either. The enemy were

in force not many miles away, so the lads had to keep ready for a night attack at any moment. Having eaten almost nothing and sopping wet, they all retired on thin bed sheets laid over puddles on the stony ground. To make matters worse, at this altitude, a blue and freezing moon rose, casting a chill over any attempt at sleep.

Jack was growing more and more annoyed at the inefficiencies of the supply lines. On arrival here, they had found no water to drink save in a murky trough. The boarding house across the tracks had some, but Jack was suspicious of that. He saw other men so thirsty that they got down on their hands and knees to drink from the rough trough like animals. Jack also knelt to take a look. Cloudy and hot; what a perfect breeding ground for germs! What should he do? He took a little, just to moisten his lips.

Finally, he strode to the nearest Captain who was standing by himself and demanded to know why fresh water had not been provided.

"I'm sorry, Padre," the Captain replied. "As you know, we're supplied by the Imperial Army. Probably some sort of slip up."

"Well, this had better be the last one, so far as water is concerned!" Jack had lost his clerical sang-froid, for sure. "This is a desert here. The first thing we all need is water."

"We're well aware of that, Padre."

"You are? So why are we faced with that hot muddy liquid full of germs? It's... it's just not right!"

The Captain nodded and shrugged. "Wartime, Padre. Lots of things happen that are just not right." He turned away sorrowfully.

The men who had drunk at the boarding house came down sick, for the Boers had thrown a dead sheep into the well to poison the water, before the Highlanders had arrived.

The next morning, December eighth, over a breakfast of

hard tack and tea, gossip abounded: either they were off at once, or Boers were on the attack — all manner of rumours voiced by all manner of passers-by. But it ended up with the men ordered to build, of all things, a railway siding.

Troops, Jack thought, come to fight. Now being asked to be labourers?

He wandered over to watch a couple of hundred soldiers digging away, laying sleepers and stretching great lengths of heavy iron track.

He stood, taken aback, then all at once threw off his helmet and jacket and pitched in. But after working for ten minutes, Jack saw his cabin-mate from the *Sardinian*, Captain Forbes, stamping towards them. Oh-oh, he thought, trouble. He looked down at the earth he was levelling, and just kept working.

"Rolling up your sleeves, Padre?"

That's a switch, he thought and grinned as he lifted his heavy pick. "Only to make you realize we chaplains are good for something."

"Bully for you."

"However did they rope you into this little enterprise?" Jack kept swinging his pick.

Forbes squatted down. "I told you, before I joined up, I did a little work on a rail crew out west. No one else here seems to know anything."

"I know nothing of railways either," Jack grunted. "We don't even have one yet on the Gaspe."

"Any and all advice is welcome." The Captain rose and repeated it louder for everyone's benefit. So he does have a humanitarian side, Jack thought, gratified.

As they dug with picks and shovels, Jack found himself working beside Pvt. McAndrews again. "How do you like this 'going to war' business, Eamon?"

"Sure beats being shot at, Padre. But the time will come for that too, eh?" Eamon broke off and looked up.

Above them stood Adjutant Brown. "What's this, what's this?" the Major snorted. "Padre, will you never learn?"

"No, never!" Jack retorted. He made no pretence of hiding his dislike. Six weeks in uniform had not tamed him. Eamon moved away.

Brown reacted as if struck, but controlled himself. "Chaplains don't belong in work parties. Honorary or not, you are still a Captain... Now why don't you come away out of that trench, and behave like a proper officer?"

Jack stood up, thinking. How should he handle this?

Behind the Adjutant, he spied his friend Lieut. Dorsey taking off his officer's coat. Placing his helmet on the folded jacket, Big George walked calmly over and joined Jack in the trench.

Two other lieutenants followed suit. Further away, a captain joined the work.

Dorsey glanced up at Brown. "Come join us, Major. Nothing in the book forbids officers to do hard work, from time to time, not even an adjutant." He grinned and picked up a shovel.

Jack knew his friend was risking insubordination, but with everyone now following suit, Brown just sneered, spun on his heel and stalked off.

They all had a good, though smothered, laugh and on went the work of building the siding and platform.

By the end of the sweltering day, which Jack hoped he'd not have to repeat, they found out that Lt.-Col. Girouard, of Soudan fame, had arrived from Cape Town. This Canadian served with the Imperial forces and had been appointed military head of the railways here. Jack and the soldiers were drawn up as he came over to inspect their work: three quarters of a mile of track laid, and 150X15 feet of platform built. Addressing them in a loud voice, he congratulated them on a job exceedingly well done. He was on his way up the line and would most certainly bring news of their wide range of abilities to Field Marshall Roberts.

All very well, thought Jack, but why not give the men what they came for, a rousing good battle?

Chapter Thirteen

That night as Jack fell onto his thin ground sheet under canvas, he heard the news: they were off the next day to Belmont, where the British rear guard was encamped.

Promptly on the morrow, they entrained and travelled the short twenty miles north to Belmont. Again, no city, just a few sad buildings. His regiment marched out to a farm and then marched right back again. Finally, they encamped beside the railway station, with its projected roof and long platform. Nearby, an empty hotel had been vacated by its owner, a Mr. De Kock, interned by the British in Cape Town as a Boer inciter. At one end of the platform, a derelict shack served as a poor excuse for a shop, opposite a goods shed with holes in the roof.

This first night in Belmont, the regiment all had to sleep with their boots on, ready to turn out at a moment's notice, with half a hope and half a dread of a Boer attack. They had set up a picket on Scots Ridge, the largest Kopje, from whose top, it was reported, they could see the flashing message signals from distant Kimberly, where Cecil Rhodes, the former Cape premier and diamond magnate, had been surrounded by the Boers on November twenty-fourth.

The terrain around was littered with the bodies of dead horses and men awaiting burial, giving rise to the horrid stench of decomposition. Scarcely three weeks before, General Sir

Redvers Buller, then Britain's commander-in-chief in South Africa, had undertaken to clear the enemy from this one crucial line of communication, the railway. So General Lord Methuen had marched his eight thousand Imperial troops forward to find the Boers here on three stony kopjes, the only defensive position in the eighty miles between Orange and the important town of Kimberly. His brigade of guards attacked under cover of darkness. But the maps were faulty, and when dawn came, the guards found themselves still some distance from the nearest kopje. "Suddenly," a witness said, "quick vivid jets of fire ran along the crest of the kopje like jewels on a coronet," as the Boers fired.

The British infantry had to clamber on hands and knees up sheer sides covered with rough thorn bushes and scratchy brush. The Boers calmly leaned over the breastworks and picked off the pith helmets as they appeared; a short, crude, bloody affair.

The guards finally did seize the hills, but hundreds of Boers trotted away across the veldt, untouched by artillery or cavalry. Some three hundred British were found dead or missing and only half as many Boers. The enemy were said to have been using dum-dum, or soft-nosed bullets that expand, and Britain protested in official letters — the first of such allegations. But throughout the war, both sides were to accuse the other of their use.

After breakfast, Jack knew that the many grisly burials would begin, with him officiating. But first, he decided to look around a bit. Up the hill he went, passing the bodies of six men and seventeen horses lying in a heap. At one pile of rock, he stopped. A curious stone? He stepped closer. No, the face of a half covered Boer! Staring bleakly out from under its burial cairn. As he climbed, he saw feet and arms sticking out of the earth. All around him lay other reminders of the battle: scattered shrapnel balls, broken belts, snapped bayonets, smashed rifles, spent cartridges and lost equipment. This eagerly anticipated war, he was beginning to see, not only cluttered the ground with brave animals who had patiently served a Boer or British cause, but with shattered human remains, too. And even after the fatigue parties gave them decent burial, the air still bore their penetrating perfume.

So finally, the real truth of war began to drill its dreadful message into Jack. Where were the parades, the bunting hung along routes of cheering crowds, the eloquence of speakers and the encouragement of the clergy? Was this all that remained after man attacked man with unparalleled ferocity? What new insights were gained, what new ground won, what stride forward had mankind made? None whatever. So what was he to make of all this? Very disturbing. He climbed harder trying to put these new insights together, or out of his mind entirely.

When he stopped to survey the countryside, he saw, down among the carcasses of dead mules and horses, what looked like pinched, black pigmies. Dwarfs? Priests? He blinked. No, just little old men, lurching from side to side as they moved. Having borrowed binoculars for the climb, he raised them to his eyes. Quickly, he dropped them.

Not dwarfs, not priests — but vultures! Great, ungainly vultures. And what a feast they were having!

He looked up and saw others gathering. The arrival of a gun party disturbed the gorging and the birds flocked upwards as well: great black bodies and gaunt, bald heads held aloft on their broad wings. Shivers rippled up and down Jack's back. Putting aside his initial disgust, he realized that without them, the desert would become unliveable. This contagion that bred pestilence, they devoured; this stench that filled his nostrils, they removed. See them as "friends", he decided, cleaning up the mess that we humans in our ignorance have left behind with our indiscriminate bombardments and murderous weapons. Vultures left just bare bones to glimmer in the desert sunlight as reminders of human folly.

* * *

For two long weeks, the regiment was kept in a state of readiness for any imminent attack, but the only battle they fought was against the elements. The Karoo desert — named after a small prickly thorn bush — offered a harsh environment, one that Jack and his companions found exceedingly unfamiliar. Give me snow and blizzards any time, he thought, rather than this infernal summer heat with those blasted sandstorms and sudden devastating downpours. Even the tent poles, made of iron, blistered the fingers of anyone foolish enough to touch them at midday. And the men soon discovered a new enemy: lice! Not long before these mites infested everything and everyone.

One night, Jack sat up with a start. He'd lain outside the tent, watching his pipe smoke curl upwards to the myriad stars, so much more crisp and vivid than on the Gaspe. On the horizon, a low crescent moon now shed a little light. But what had he just felt? He jumped up and shook the greatcoat enwrapping him. Out fell a good-sized lizard.

"Did you creep in for warmth, you little blighter?" Two days ago, sitting on a large boulder to drink his tea, he'd been fascinated by their antics. How fast they moved — in the blink of an eye, they were gone. None in the Gaspe, that's for sure. But here, every size and type. Later he came and stood by a ring of soldiers who had staged a gladiatorial contest between a tarantula and a scorpion. Should he try to stop it? Did the combatants have feelings like dogs and cats? Oh well, it did make the men's long hours move more quickly.

For two weeks, neither Jack nor the others were given water for washing, not even their faces. And as a consequence, no way to wash clothes. But that morning some water had been scrounged, not too clean but acceptable. So while the men were drilling, Jack sat in the entrance of his tent and did his wash.

A movement caught his eye, and he looked up. Through the empty camp stalked an ostrich. How tame! This ungainly bird, however, finding the campground virtually empty, wandered over and stood looking down at Jack for a good few moments.

"Good morning, Mr. Ostrich. How d'ya manage to survive in this odd dry environment? I don't see how you do it. Better you than me, for sure. Give me the green fields and brooks of Canada any day." And so he chatted on while his new companion, hearing the friendly voice, ambled forward. Then it leaned down. Jack shrank back. It stuck its beak into his soapy water and drank. Good Lord, thought Jack, that'll make you sick — and you'll spoil my wash! But then, I guess ostriches survive by drinking anything, so long as it's wet.

Eight feet above him, the bird turned its head sideways, and looked Jack straight in the eye. Jack flinched. It stooped to pluck his soapy shirt. "Hey!"

The bird lifted it high in the air and shook it, showering Jack.

He let out another yell. The ostrich took off with the shirt, emitting its hoarse, sonorous chuckling. Jack leaped up to chase it, but then bent and threw a couple of rocks, whereupon it stopped short and turned to stare at him.

Oh-oh, thought Jack, now he's coming back to attack. A good deal taller than Jack, it had black feathers on its back and white primaries on wings and tail. The legendary kick from those powerful legs, two toes on each foot, could finish a man. Its bare neck was pinkish and from the small head, two large eyes stared at him with a fierce intensity.

Instead of an attack, the bird turned and, dropping the shirt, strode disdainfully away. Jack sighed and went to retrieve his shirt.

* * *

More trains from the north passed with the wounded, bringing news of what was later touted as Black Week, December 10-15. It began with Major General Sir William Gatacre setting out from Stormberg in a bungled attempt to fight his way through to Malteno. His exhausted force tramped all through the night, lost its way and, not knowing where the Boers were, attacked the wrong kopje. They were soundly beaten; the infantry retreat degenerated into a huge rout. When they got back to safety, they also found they had left six hundred men behind on the slopes of Kissieberg kopje. Those British troops had to surrender to the Boers — what a disaster!

The day that Gatacre was completing such an abject page in the chronicles of war, Methuen set out from the Modder on the last lap of his bid to relieve Kimberly. His route lay throughout the Magersfontein hills. To take these hills, he sent out four thousand men in a solid rectangle. Eventually they stumbled upon the Boers who had hidden themselves in unlikely trenches dug at the base of the hills. Thousands of rifles were directed on the Highlanders at point-blank range and in less than a minute, hundreds were killed or wounded. The Imperial brigade was turned into a panic-stricken mob and their fine leader Major-General A.J. Wauchope lay dead, not thirty miles from Belmont.

The news of Methuen's defeat was given out in London on the Thursday after Monday's news about Stormberg. Thirteen thousand of their finest troops had been defeated in the open field. It struck England dumb. But more was to come.

Buller's army had set out to cross Tugela river and march towards Ladysmith. But the Boer's agile leader, Louis Botha, had entrenched his forces around Colenso, where they dug in. Cleverly concealed in hidden trenches, they had not been affected by Buller's bombardment. So once again, the British marched into the arms of Boers whom they could not see and whose strength and position they knew not. The Guards at the Modder, the Highlanders at Magersfontein, and now the Royal Artillery at Colenso, all were sadly decimated. The impact of all this upon England was devastating.

The Royal Canadians, however, saw in these defeats their chance to prove themselves. But when would they get to do it?

* * *

Christmas day arrived. Jack celebrated communion at nine, which was greeted by the men with some satisfaction in anticipation of a splendid meal afterwards. They knew orders had gone down to Cape Town for a blessing of plenty. But it was not to be. Seven chickens and two ducks were all that fed each company of hundred and fifty men. Jack grew even more annoyed at how "his" enlisted men were treated while officers got their surfeit.

A continuing dearth of good, fresh, clear drinking water exacerbated this discomfort. Whoever was responsible, Jack concluded, was just not doing his job. This time marching straight to the orderly tent, he asked to speak to Adjutant Brown. Was Jack beginning to relish this animosity between them? Well, why not? It kept him occupied, and gave him someone on whom to vent his frustrations.

"Major Brown, I have to report, sir, that the men are very dissatisfied with what was provided for their Christmas feast!" He was ready for a fight, and Brown surely saw that.

But the battle did not materialise. "I'm sorry Padre, but all the different regiments sent agents down to Cape Town to requisition supplies. Apparently our own man did his level best, but was unable to get ahead of those Imperial scoundrels, if I may use the term. And then, some equally dissolute groups raided our train and got away with even what he did manage to secure. It's all part of fighting on someone else's land, I suppose. Do let the men know we all wanted better for them," Brown ended with a wry sad smile.

Well, that did rather take the wind out of his sails; Jack turned and went back to his rounds of the troops.

* * *

A moon rose, full and harsh, and sailed across the clear sky while Jack lay listening to Big George wax lyrical about his family. "Martha and Mary, three and five years old," George went on, "Annie got her parents to look after them while she taught school, because I was in university. We named them after your biblical sisters, Padre." Jack snuggled down as best he could on the hard ground, head on his greatcoat, and began drifting off. Their other two tent-mates had gone to the central area where they all talked long into the night. "When I'd come home from class, I'd share what I'd learned at university with Annie. Like you, she loves to hear poems. Funny, I learn them quickly, even after I've read them only a couple of times..."

Jack heard a pause, and mumbled "Uh-huh" to encourage George, lest he'd thought he'd fallen asleep.

"You know, Padre, she's so beautiful, Annie. She looks after me like a prince. But I do all I can to help her, too: wash the dishes, oh yes, and I put the girls to bed — Martha and Mary love nothing more than a bedtime story from Poppa. I'm even trying poetry. Nursery rhymes for Mary, who's the younger."

Jack roused himself enough to murmur, "Lucky girls..."

"We've got a big bedroom in her parents' house where Annie corrects her homework and I do my studies. That's just the very best time, us together, her preparing lessons, me reading books for my classes."

The pause needed filling. "So Big George, why did you decide to join this force?"

"Well, I joined our local Militia to get a bit of spare cash. I love farm work, but going back to farm to help Poppa — no point. My two brothers, they do all the work that's needed. So here I was at military camp and I guess not a lot of the fellows were in university, so they put me up to lieutenant as soon as they decently could. More money again. And then this came along. For her part, Annie didn't like the idea of me putting myself in danger. But it seemed, from all the talk, that it would be a short war, and not very dangerous." He gave a snort, which turned into a chuckle.

"Nobody thought conditions would be like this," Jack agreed. "If only we had decent water, and good healthy food... But then, I suppose as they say, war is war, and you have to take what's offered."

Other evenings, George pushed Jack to talk about his own life. So he spoke about his sisters, especially Lillian who had come to teach with him on the Canadian Labrador. "Now she's back home, but she's thinking of going west one day soon. Must have a bit of a wanderlust like me." He told him about Winnie, going to be a nurse, and Jeannie, the youngest and prettiest. "My older sister, Mariah, married a fella a while ago, Joe, building a sawmill down in the Hollow, as we call it. That's where my grandfather built his first cabin. He was British, you know. Came over on a warship called the *Bellerophon* about a hundred years ago. You know, I often wonder why Poppa never talked about it. Maybe because Grandfather spent all this time just surviving, just getting our farm started — keeping alive in those times was not easy." He lapsed into silence.

"Go on, Jack," Big George prodded.

Jack realized that over his short life of ministering, he felt more comfortable listening than talking. But George had revealed so much these nights, he felt he should respond. By now they had become close, making up for a need normally filled by families, or a sweetheart.

"Our fields stretch right back north beside The Hollow. When we finished haymaking in the head field, we'd jump on the load and lie back, looking up into the sky: such great clouds on the Gaspe, with the creaking of the old wheels as the oxen trundle along. Always a cool breeze off the bay, and if it rains, boy, not like here, you see it coming: cumulus starts building early, huge castles..." He paused, lost. "I have a little brother, Earle, eight, he can pitch hay up with the best of them. He milks our three cows all by himself now. And there's Eric, the baby." Again Jack lost himself in a reverie, and then heard a snore. He smiled. Turn and turn about. We talk each other to sleep. Fine way to go.

Chapter Fourteen

At the end of December, a new British Garrison commander, Lt.-Col. T.D. Pilcher, rode into town, just like one of the old-time sheriffs. He told them the Royal Canadians had indeed done a great job of entrenching the camp, fortifying it against possible attack. So, time for a raid or two.

Sunday morning, after Jack gave his service at dawn, the usual time nowadays, Pilcher organized a group of men from the Queensland Mounted Infantry and the Royal Horse Artillery stationed nearby, and he picked C company (Toronto) from the Royal Canadians — chosen, the other men complained, because Otter hailed from that city. On New Year's Eve the raiding party headed northwest for Sunnyside, where Boers were rumoured to be encamped. The rest, including Jack, remained in camp, subjected again to endless drills, and boredom.

When Col. Pilcher returned, Jack got his first real sight of a Boer war party, forty prisoners. They seemed slovenly: heavily bearded under their slouch hats, no uniforms, of course, just dressed in every sort of getup worn by farmers hereabouts. Their haunted eyes and slouched shoulders showed them to be a defeated lot. But these were the men who had successfully beaten the Imperial Army over and over again. Amazing, thought Jack.

Earlier, Big George had brought back four Boer prisoners who had been working on their farms. "And they was tough looking buggers, too," he told Jack, as they watched the men march to a compound. "They left their wives and children behind to work the farms. Willingly they came, you know. We only brought them in to see if we could find out anything."

"Dirty dogs," mumbled Jack. He and George turned away to have lunch at the mess under a large canvas.

"Aye, dirty they were, but not in any sense you mean — just from working in their fields. How the hell they grow anything here, I have no idea. Hard life!"

"I guess that's what produces such good soldiers. Beating the Imperials time and time again." Jack took out his water bottle and drank. He'd filled it that morning from the special supply of water handed out from a tank car that had finally arrived from Cape Town. Never enough water — they were always thirsty. Often after rainstorms, the troops fell down to drink out of the muddy puddles — water that Jack would not even let his dog drink on the Gaspe.

"Dunno why they seem incapable of giving us decent water." Big George shook his head when Jack offered his flask. "After all those good ladies waving handkerchiefs and crying for their sweethearts leaving — little did they dream we'd be abandoned when it came to basic necessities."

"Exactly, basic necessities," Jack agreed. "So those four were sent off in chains to Cape Town, I suppose?"

"Not at all. Otter sent them back to their farms." They sat at the wooden tables with others, waiting to be served by orderlies.

"What!"

"For sure. They weren't fighting us. Do you know what the word Boer means?"

"I think someone told me. Farmer?"

"You're right. Farmers all. Just like my own family. We farm in New Brunswick, they farm here."

"So they've just gone back?" Jack asked.

"That's right. But first, they promised they wouldn't do any more fighting. They took solemn oaths. Where I come from, a solemn oath is pretty good."

"So we can rely on the Boers' morals? Those same fellows who have been attacking Her Majesty?"

"Those same fellows, Jack. Maybe they weren't sympathizers of the British — no sir. But they just wanted to stay and work their land, and not be ruled from London. They wanted old Paul Kruger to stay in charge, they told us. You should have heard what they said about Rhodes and that lot."

"Well, we've come all this way to fight for her Majesty," Jack paused as a plate of stew was placed before them, "and it is our right, as Christian soldiers, to do what we can to win."

George looked at him. "I'd say you're right, Padre. But they think of themselves as Christian soldiers too, you know. Hard to tell what a man is meant to think."

* * *

A week later, Pilcher, by now their hero, decided to go off on another sortie. This time, he picked another group, which happily included H Company from Nova Scotia.

Jack decided that if he was ever going to see action, he'd have to fight for the chance. So he got to Pilcher and, after saluting, asked if he might accompany them.

"So you want to come into battle, eh Chaplain?" Pilcher scratched his head. "It would mean extra supplies... I'm not sure you're worth it, old boy."

At least he spoke honestly, thought Jack, and replied in kind. "Colonel, suppose you run into trouble. Suppose some of our boys are wounded, or indeed killed and need burying? Then you'll find me a very valuable asset. I can bury the dead as they might expect burial back home in Canada. Would you deny them this? — when you have a ready volunteer standing before you?"

Pilcher put his hand to his chin, and rubbed it. After a moment, he nodded. "Yes, Padre, seems a worthy investment. But..." he paused, "are you up to the march?"

"Sir, as I've said many times when I first volunteered, I was posted to the Canadian Labrador, and there endured — "

"The Labrador?" interrupted Pilcher. "If you've served up there, you can endure anything. Come along then, and make ready."

And so, excited but fearful, Jack went off to fight his first battle.

At daybreak the men were ready to start, and the procession wound past the eastern kopjes of Belmont and onto a road that led right into the Orange Free State, the first time that Imperial forces had entered Boer territory. In their kharki, hot puttees, pith helmets, some with puggarees (strips of muslin worn over the helmet to protect the neck) they marched over a desert dotted with anthills, honeycombed by burrowing animals and covered with stones the size of skulls. The landscape stretched to the horizon, but when Jack looked down he discovered the sand strewn with colourful small plants: crimson tufted flowers like heather among the silver grey scrub, and other pale plants he did not recognize.

At last, Jack was coming face to face with Boers in mortal combat. Was he up to it? Without a gun, how would he feel when his comrades got shot, perhaps killed, right next to him? But the thrill of battle was taking hold.

Luckily the day was cloudy, but Jack still found the march too hot and, in fact, exhausting. Mounted scouts spread out on all sides to keep an eye on the kopjes, fifty to two hundred feet high. Jack and the Company marched seemingly forever through prickly bushes, over the harsh terrain strewn with rocks, nothing on the horizon to relieve the tedium save for a few interesting cloud formations in the sky. Hard going.

At last in the distance they made out a windmill nestled in the centre of a rising slope of trees: Witdam Farm, the home of the Orange Free State leader, Commandant Lubbe. Soon scouts came racing back to report they'd seen three Boers galloping away on horseback. So no immediate engagement.

When they arrived, they discovered that the Kaffir servants had just prepared a bounteous meal: joints and knuckles of veal or mutton, heaping dishes of rice and barley, and large boiling pots of tea and coffee. Enough for twenty or thirty Boers, who apparently had left in a great hurry. The Kaffirs, of course, were only too delighted to serve Her Majesty's men. Just an hour before they had been serving their taskmasters, the Boers, who were not always kind to Kaffirs.

Jack and his friends were quick to take advantage of this lavish spread. As he gorged himself, Jack looked around at the farm. Built of local stone, one storey high, it spread out, protected from the desert sun by shade trees, mulberry bushes and pomegranates. Stone walls divided the enclosures, and behind the barn and henhouse, a number of kraals (Africaans for corrals) decorated the sloping kopje.

After the much appreciated meal, Jack sat on the stone veranda to enjoy the cool air and talk with his tent mates, Harry Burstall and Robert Willis, each in charge of a section of H Company. But this pleasant interlude did not last. A scout came galloping back around half past four to report that the enemy was in sight, approaching swiftly over the desert.

Everyone leaped to their feet. Pilcher quickly put together a striking force of two hundred and fifty men and lined up the infantry.

Then came the further news that the farm was surrounded.

No time to waste. The soldiers raced to disperse themselves to their stations and await orders. The Royal Horse Artillery took up a position on the right and the mounted infantry proceeded to the left, while on each side of the farm and at the back, the Canadian Maxims took up stations, rapidly lugged to the top of small kopjes. Half of H Company under Lieutenant Willis supported those guns while half of the Nova Scotians under Lieutenant Burstall hurried to dig trenches.

Jack stayed within the confines of the building with Surgeon Major Fiset, both ready to go out and tend to the wounded. At any moment, Jack expected a party of fierce Boers to sweep through an opening in the circle of hills and to blast them all with a whirlwind of death-dealing lead. The correspondent, Stanley Brown joined them inside.

Moment by moment, Jack felt the suspense mount. The big guns got ready with their rounds of shrapnel, and the mounted scouts ranged about, keeping an eye on the approaching enemy. Jack wished he'd had a rifle; as it was, he just fingered the small cross around his neck, his only weapon, as he heard the approaching thunder of hooves over the veldt.

Nearer galloped the fierce Boer commandos, about six hundred of them, it had been estimated. Around Jack, the men tensed and gripped their rifles.

Nervously, Stanley, Jack and his friend the surgeon, nestled down, hoping the stone walls would protect them.

The command went out to make ready to fire. The artillery crew loaded, and stood poised.

Tense, apprehensive, Jack lay below the window with Fiset, waiting for the hail of bullets that might end their lives. Let it all be over soon, he prayed, let our men acquit themselves royally; let only a few be killed.

Then, as quickly as it had appeared, the menace vanished. A

scout galloped in, crying, "Hold your fire! They're ours."

Jack and Stanley rose, as did Fiset. They brushed themselves off cheerfully and went out to get the news.

An Australian force of Victoria Mounted Rifles had been taken for Boers: they were on horseback, wore droopy hats, grey uniforms wrapped with leather bandoliers. At five hundred yards, they certainly looked like Boers. But this possible catastrophe — when they might have shelled their own comrades — had been avoided.

Back at the Lubbe Farm, the Kaffirs prepared yet another meal. They killed a beef and Jack and the fighters all enjoyed a savoury supper, including lots of fowl. After having eaten his fill, Jack rolled himself in his greatcoat and lay out under the bright stars to sleep, thinking of his Kelsie, far away in some crowded hospital.

The next morning, reveille blared out at four a.m. and by six the column was able to move out before the sun got too hot. They brought with them twenty horses and about twenty-five head of cattle and all the contents of the Boer leader's house on an immense wagon drawn by an ox team of fourteen lovely longhorn beasts. They arrived at Belmont in the evening with their booty to the cheers of the other men.

Chapter Fifteen

After the two forays, the omnipresent boredom of the stay in Belmont weighed on the Canadians. And to make matters worse, Jack was told by the Adjutant, who seemed to have a special gleam in his eye, that the three chaplains' pay had once again been disallowed, no authority having yet been received for the payment of officers sent out for instructional purposes. Like O'Leary, Jack decided for the moment to grin and bear it. But when he heard Major Macdougall was off to Wynberg hospital on sick leave, he penned a short note to Kelsie. He only half expected it to reach her, for perhaps by now she had moved closer to the lines of battle.

Jack began meeting any train heading south in case he could be of use or give pastoral care. When a train going north pulled up, a short, square-shouldered gentleman in his mid-thirties got off. That large, slightly bald head, heavy black moustache, round face with its dark twinkling eyes — it struck Jack that this man here was the most famous author alive, Rudyard Kipling!

Jack walked straight over to meet the great man, feeling at the same time surprisingly shy and timid.

The writer greeted him. "Well, good morning Padre."

Jack made his introduction and found out that Mr. Kipling was on his way to the front to observe and perhaps report. He appeared delighted to discover that Canadians were quartered here, for he had done extensive research in Newfoundland —

"although those beastly American papers, they keep referring to my work in *Captains Courageous* as having been done in New England."

Jack told him, not too eagerly he hoped, that he had read his wonderful *Jungle Books*, then given them on to his younger brother Earle and his sisters. They'd all read *the Barrack-Room Ballads* and Jack knew some by heart. He'd also heard of the soldiers' charity, the "Absent Minded Beggar Fund", named after a Kipling short story title.

The author seemed pleased at the recognition, and offered Jack a clay pipe from the supply weighing down his pockets. But Jack confessed he smoked a well-matured briar and had no need; he recommended that Mr. Kipling present some to the other enlisted men.

Once the troops recognized him, he caused an even greater stir of excitement. He wished them well, and hoped that one day, his son would be old enough to join in such commendable forays. Then as the train began to pull out, he leaped on it, though with pockets still bulging, for most of the men also smoked briars.

Jack was tickled pink to have met him in the flesh, another experience he would never have had back in the Gaspe.

* * *

Indeed, every day, trains passed by loaded with troops on their way into battle, while the RCR remained inactive — subjected to more drilling, heat, sandstorms and rainstorms, building trenches, reinforcing walls and stone works, preparing for the ever-present danger of a Boer attack. So a sports day was declared for the following Sunday to enliven camp life, and Jack volunteered for H Company's football team, having played well at Bishops. How he looked forward to a fine practice! In foot-races, the Canadians would be pitched against the Australians, everything from a hundred yard dash to the long cross-country.

On Thursday, the men were excused drill so that they could train for the games, and they chose a deserted area outside the camp. But H Company's team was diverted by three or four ostriches pecking their way towards the "playing field."

"Look what we got!" cried their elected leader. "What about a bunch of feathers for the womenfolk back home."

"Yes sir," the men shouted, and in a body approached the flock, cautiously at first and then, as they came closer, all broke into a run.

The flock scattered, and seemed to take delight in dodging the men who were scudding about trying to catch one. Men tripped, pushed each other out of the way, fell on the sand, quite a free-for-all. Finally George, the biggest of the team, managed to grab hold of one and get a twist on its neck. The others descended and started to yank out the prize feathers. Jack wondered, was this a fit occupation for a clergyman: robbing a bizarre bird of its only covering? He held back.

The bird gave a tremendous kick, which sent another man reeling backwards clutching his stomach in pain, whereupon they all let the bird go.

Big George came up and offered Jack one of his three feathers. "Something for that sweetheart you haven't told me about, Jack."

Taken aback, Jack paused, then replied, grinning, "No such sweetheart, but I have a wonderful mother; she'll be delighted, if I can just find a way to get it to her." An ostrich feather. Imagine coming back from a war, a battle zone, and presenting your mother an ostrich feather.

They stood around, laughing and joking, when Jack saw an orderly heading for them with a serious expression. Oh-oh, he thought.

The orderly came up and saluted Jack in his old worn playing clothes: "Sir, report at once to the Colonel!"

Me? thought Jack. What have I done now?

* * *

Jack now faced what he thought must be the hardest decision in his life.

He had just come out of Otter's tent, where his commander seemed harassed in the extreme, struggling to finish the paperwork flooding his desk. During the short meeting, orderlies and enlisted men kept coming to and fro with more papers, asking questions and generally creating an impression of chaos.

"Chaplain Alford, I've had rather bad news. The Chaplain of the Hussars has been taken ill, and so has the other fellow, I forget his name. That leaves no one of any faith at the Orange River Field Hospital. A message just came in asking for me to release one of our three. As you are," he coughed, "perhaps our most important, being Church of England, I'm asking you if you'd mind returning there for a bit?"

"And not follow the troops into battle when they go?"

Otter was peering at the latest dispatch, sighing heavily before looking up again. "What? Oh. Yes of course, that's what it means. Well, are you up for it, Chaplain?"

Jack was nonplussed. What could he say? "I really came over to be with the troops when they faced the enemy..."

"I know I know, but our worst enemy right now is this blasted fever. Can't get rid of it. Do you know that twenty percent of our force is down? We're below strength by a long shot. Well? I'll have transportation for you in a couple of hours."

Jack stood silently again, and then found himself saying, "Yes sir."

"Thank you, Chaplain. Good luck."

Jack stood outside the tent as more orderlies pushed past. He'd had his three minutes. And now, to the future: hospital duty. He walked slowly back to his tent and there was George, writing a letter. He looked up.

"I've just been ordered," Jack said, "back down the line to Orange River Junction to look after the wounded there."

George watched with his brown eyes as he tried to absorb the news. "You mean, you won't be coming with us when we go to the front? But what will we do?"

"Let's just hope no one gets wounded, or... Anyway, you'll have Father O'Leary." By now, Fullerton had been seconded elsewhere.

George shook his head. "Terrible news."

"Well," Jack said, "thank you for saying I'm needed." He could not hide his dejection.

George dropped his eyes. "It won't be the same in the old tent. And who'll be waiting — to come out under fire if we ever catch a bullet, or worse, to ..."

Jack looked at him. "...to bury you? Well, I know that's not going to happen, so you have no worries there."

"You do? You mean that? You have a real feeling about it?"

What could Jack say? He was very afraid that, yes, that's exactly what might happen. But he brightened. "Absolutely, George, you'll be coming back, I know it."

With that, George gave a little smile and turned to his writing, while Jack proceeded to gather his belongings. It would be a sad parting but likely he'd soon be with these men whom he had grown to know, and indeed love, possibly before they did go off into conflict. At any rate, his was now a very different battle.

* * *

Jack sat, fuming, on the rough front boards of a bullock cart — going at the pace of an ox was no fun at all. The two large and mangy animals wandered along yard after yard, looking neither right nor left, yokes on their shoulders, like wounded veterans themselves. How uncomfortable in that hot noonday sun. However did the loads of wounded make the trips from battlefront to hospital in such vehicles? The cart was splashed with blood.

Arriving in Orange at nightfall, he was assigned a tent vacated by another who had gone back to the front. Much better to face hospital fresh on the morrow, he agreed with the commander, a rather harried young major clearly over his head in administrative toil.

The next morning, Jack surveyed the field hospital, a collection of tents with anywhere from five to ten men in each: some on knee-high cots, others on rough ground sheets, most suffering from various stages of typhoid. His mind churned. So our fighting lads, coming to defend her Majesty, end up here living out their last agonies from a fever that should have been avoided. Awful.

Most of the doctors were posted near the battlefields and so here, Jack found only two, both overworked and harassed.

He introduced himself to one: "I've come," Jack said, "to minister to the men's spiritual needs and —"

"— and to bury them, I suppose," remarked Dr. Jenkins, a heavy-browed and rather hawk-like individual with glasses, who nonetheless seemed to retain some warmth in his fatigued body.

"Yes, to bury them too, I suppose." Jack shook his head. "Do we lose many?"

"One or two every day. We do our level best," he told him in a pukka British accent, adding that they found it difficult to achieve much real healing. "We use Listerine, or another purgative. Or starve them for a week — that's the cure of choice right now, although I'm not sure I agree. Unfortunately, we're rather short on morphine."

"Well, if there's anything I can do, I mean anything, to make it easier for you, do let me know."

"Thank you, Padre. Our army regulations permit only orderlies to tend the wounded. Even when I was down at Wynberg, those wonderful Canadian nurses you sent were not, according to army regulations, even able to bathe the poor wretches. That will have to be changed if we are ever to fight another war — which I sincerely hope will not happen."

Chapter Sixteen

The first few days at Orange River Junction, Jack was rushed off his feet; so many wounded, so many devastated by fever. He found the orderlies a mixed bunch: a few slovenly, a few astonishingly conscientious. And trains kept bringing more and more, some from the Royal Canadians: those too sick for front line field hospitals and not up to the long journey down to Wynberg. British and Australian forces were both treated here and, to his surprise, a goodly number of Boers.

That decided him. He should make an attempt to minister to these supposed enemies. But not without trepidation did Jack enter the Boer compound. He had heard they were a godly lot, but how would they take a clergyman from a different denomination?

After a few words with the supervising orderly, he went in to the Boer compound. He withheld any disgust he might have felt at these evil-smelling brigands from distant farms. They all had the longest beards and haunted eyes, but they did bear pain with great fortitude.

His first patient proved not a success. "Good afternoon, my good man," Jack said. "Is there anything I can do to help?"

The elderly farmer turned his head and fixed Jack with fevered eyes. "I'll have none of your papist nonsense, thank you. We have our own pastoors. And I have the strength of the living

God within me. I pray to Him every hour of the day. No need of the likes of you." He turned his head away.

Oh well, on to the next. Already he calmed himself with the image of a citizen soldier, a farmer, driven from his quiet life into the thick of battle, leaving a farm wrestled from the recalcitrant desert by the work of many generations. Why would any Boer not want to preserve that? And indeed, protect it from invading armies?

So he tried this approach with the next cot, a sturdy and obviously hard-working farmer, his arm a stump from the elbow down. As Jack sat, the farmer turned and a frown creased the heavy brow.

"I presume you're a farmer?" Jack began by way of introduction. "I come from a farm myself."

"You don't look like it."

"Well, I did get to university — the first student from my area, a farming and fishing peninsula in the Gulf of St. Lawrence. So you and I both did the same hard and often dirty work."

"Not likely. Here, Pastoor, we have Kaffirs. They muck out the cattle and they cook our meals. You do that for yourselves." The large face broke into a grin, revealing some decayed teeth. "Y'see, we know how to treat Kaffirs in this country."

Jack was taken aback. "Perhaps if you gave the natives proper schooling —"

"Educate a Kaffir! That's you English all over. The only education they understand is the stick. God Almighty gave us dominion over them so they could help us make a better living — and they benefit from that, too. No damned nonsense — we keep them in their place. You fellows insist on equal treatment? They'll drive you off your land in a flash. Look at those Zulu Wars. You Imperials come here, interfering and telling us how to live, wanting to take away our land. You're as bad as they are. Take that message back to your commander." With that, he rolled over on his side.

Jack felt like heading right for the door; why help such a breed? But again, he remembered the Lord's words: every man, oh yes, was made in His image, hard as this was to stomach in this case. So he made himself persevere.

After meeting the same treatment a few times, Jack came to sit beside a wounded lad who looked about sixteen. He was shivering, but not with the enteric, Jack thought. Had his wound become infected? His leg and his arm were bandaged. He looked up at Jack. "So you're a pastoor?"

"I am," said Jack, "and a Christian like you. I'm trying to do my best to help anyone suffering: anyone who might like to hear of Our Lord, or perhaps welcome another drink of water, or just someone to talk to."

The boy nodded, his face twitching with pain. "Am I going to live, Pastoor?"

Jack smiled. "Oh most certainly, my lad. I've seen men with much worse wounds going home to lead good, productive lives on their farms. You see, I come from a farm just like you."

"I come from a farm, Pastoor, but what I do now? My vader was shot, and moeder was killed when they shelled the farm. We defend it against those British trying to steal our land. And now they've got it."

"They may have it now," answered Jack. "But my boy, as soon as this war is over, you'll be able to go back, because the British are not concerned with farm land — just with your government. They want a different type of administration, installed under Her Majesty. They, and I must say I, believe that this may bring even more freedoms and, indeed, emancipation for your Kaffirs.

"So you don't think I'm going to die, Father?" the boy asked plaintively.

"No, I certainly do not. And I'm very sorry about your mother and father, that's one of the beastly things about war, I suppose."

"But you support it, don't you Father?" the lad asked.

"I have asked myself that... many times, son. What's your name?"

"Pieter Lemmer."

"Well, Pieter, I think my answer right now is that I have come to help the wounded and bury the dead. It's not a question of being on one side or another, but of being on the side of healing."

Well, Jack thought to himself, that was well said, and probably well believed, too. One's spoken word often mirrors one's soul.

"And tell me, Pieter, where is your farm?"

"We're up by Ladysmith, sir. It's a fine farm, hard work in this dry land, as my vader always said. But we make do, we have trees around us, we have a lot of oxen and cattle, and we do well enough. But it's too big for me alone."

"Don't you have any relatives?" Jack asked.

"I have an uncle: Oom Gideon. His last name is Prinsloo. He wasn't well liked by my vader, or any of our branch. You see, he and his family went with other relatives on their side to live in the British colony. He might be in Cape Town. I don't know if he wants the life of a farmer now. But that's the first thing I do, when I get better. I go find him. But I have no money..." The little lad held back tears.

"Well, Pieter, that's something I could try to do for you. Gideon Prinsloo?" Jack wrote down the name, and the last address that the lad could remember. He promised that he would do his best to seek him out and bring him the message.

And so Jack moved among the Boers all day, taking requests, helping those who welcomed him and avoiding the others.

Being the only clergyman, he also had to bury the dead, a

daily occurrence, and do his best to attend to the woes of the officers and men, many of whom, on their deathbeds — even though it was a little-used C of E rite — wanted to confess their sins. Thus Jack heard a good deal more about the vagaries of the human character than he had ever known.

Of course, as he moved among the wounded, little by little he began to notice some anomalies. What about the treatment of enteric fever? And how did the doctors deal with bullet wounds and shrapnel?

"Mauser's a fine rifle that those Boers use," explained the younger of the two doctors. He was just out of medical school and had adopted the military moustache; his round baby face belied a fierce intelligence. "Good clean hole. I've seen men shot through their arms, their bodies, and the exit hole was not much larger than the entry. You know, those dreadful dumdums, they take half a man's body with them when they exit. But these Mausers, they're clean and precise. There's even, in some cases, not much bleeding. We've been able to save a goodly number of lives. Though if the bullet strikes bone, it will tumble and make a bit of a mess."

Jack nodded. "And I hope our own bullets are also easy on the Boers?"

"From the Boer casualties we've seen, I'd say so. But of course, the majority of the men here are suffering from enteric, the real scourge of armies for the last hundred years."

"Is that so? I have no experience of military history. In Canada we've not fought any foreign war."

"In the Soudan, 1885, forty percent of the men died from enteric; in the Crimean War, four thousand five hundred dead of wounds but over seventeen thousand from enteric. Over in your part of the world, in the Civil War on the Union side, some ninety thousand dead of wounds — but double that from disease."

Jack was astonished. "Then why haven't they vaccinated everyone?"

"Vaccination's only recently been discovered. Not enough time, or the will, I suppose. I do know that in England the men were offered it, but only on a voluntary basis. Once they observed the reaction, extreme and painful, though it just lasted a day or two, most of them opted out. They may have some vials in Cape Town, but by then it's too late. No good vaccinating someone who's already down with it. We're even running short of castor oil. That's what we do: a thorough purging followed by Dover's powder. Or sulphate of magnesia, in drachm doses, frequently repeated. I don't know what we're going to do with the next trainload."

"Then you'll revert to the other treatment: starving them."

"Yes, however improper I believe it is to starve a follow who's only eaten hardtack and bully beef once a day before he gets here. They'll die of starvation before they die of enteric, but that's the prescription we're ordered to use."

It seemed to Jack rather draconian. And he'd heard of other shortages too.

"You see, Padre, I have a lot of ideas about what we could do, even now. But the higher-ups, they don't want to hear from an uppity young doctor just out of university."

Jack's interest grew. "Such as what?"

"Well, have you noticed how men go out at night to relieve themselves nearby? The latrines, fifty yards away, are too far. Now if you placed slop buckets just outside, to be emptied in the morning, this would avoid men relieving themselves in the dust. That dust blows right onto our food, into our tents, and the flies love it, too. That, I believe, might have an effect. Those damned higher-ups in the regular army pay so little attention to hygiene. That's the real shocker, because in war nowadays, disease is the real enemy. Proven over and over again."

Indeed it was. Talking to the young men, day after day, hearing their ills, watching their woes, sitting with them as they passed away, his temper built. He had to do something. Finally at five o'clock, after a long day of rounds beginning at daybreak, he went to see the officer in charge. Kept waiting outside the tent, Jack sat on a barrel in the falling sun to gather his thoughts.

When at last invited in, he greeted the commander who, though harried, was cordial. "I hear you've been doing a fine job, Padre, attending to the burials and helping the wounded."

"Doing my best, sir. But I've had an opportunity to see and hear details of what the doctors need. If this were rectified, it might improve the men's well-being."

"You know, all of us are under such a strain," the Major said. "I accept your offer of information with the best of spirits, but that's what the orderlies and doctors do all day, come in here to complain."

Jack shook his head. "I'm sure they do, sir. And I'm sorry to be one of them. I don't suppose, frankly, there's a place for someone as uneducated as I am about the doings of a hospital."

The doctor peered at him. "Your reputation has preceded you, Padre. I was told on good authority that you're not afraid to go in and say what you think to whomever it may be."

Jack gave a weak smile. "Well, I'm afraid that is true, sir. I guess I was born to be a troublemaker."

"Then I have an idea for you." The older man studied Jack. "How would it be if you got involved in our administration? The doctors here are run off their feet, as doubtless you've noticed." Jack nodded. "All they can do is try to keep our wounded alive. The orderlies, too, what with the men having fifteen or twenty bowel movements a day, are badly overworked. So I have no one I can send down to Cape Town." The Major paused, then nodded.

"Tell you what: draw up a list of what the doctors need, and I'll endeavour to get you a pass for the railway and find some money."

"Well, I have no funds myself, that's for sure. Not even a cent since leaving Canada. The government will, I feel sure, issue such orders, but nothing yet."

"No problem at all. In Cape Town, you'll manage to find everything we need, I'm sure. Somewhat *ad hoc*, but that's how I'm learning to get things done around here. Oh, and Lt.-Col. George Ryerson, the Commissioner for the Canadian Red Cross, is there now. A fine man, he should advance you some funds, so do try to connect. And then you might visit one or two other hospitals on the way back, such as the big hospital at De Aar. After that, I've been told you may report back to your regiment."

Well, this was a new twist. Jack thanked the officer and left. Indeed, another challenge.

Chapter Seventeen

Jack set off on the long train ride to Cape Town. Although the train sped down the incline from the Karoo desert, his journey seemed to take forever. More and more did he look forward to seeing Kelsie, building their meeting in his mind as he was wont to do, convincing himself that chances were good he'd find her at Wynberg. There, of course, he would make contact with Ryerson as well. The trip seemed full of promise, though he decided he must return as soon as possible to rejoin his regiment, which would likely be facing a firestorm.

On arrival he hurried to the old Tudor Hotel on historic Market Square, where officers in transition were billeted. He was also concerned about the young Boer: How would he ever make contact with young Pieter's uncle? But the hour was late and Jack had to retire, along with anxieties about how he'd possibly fulfill all the obligations and then get to see his Kelsie, who had the uncanny knack of populating his dreams these nights.

The next morning, Jack dressed and went downstairs to the elegant dining room, a far cry from what he'd been used to. Several officers from various British regiments were sitting about, tucking with relish into the eggs and sausage, tomatoes on toast, relaxing and smoking cigars. The tall, latticed windows admitted a soft morning light through the gauze curtains, and the plain dark mahogany tables glittered with cutlery that swam on their smooth surfaces like icebergs on a midnight sea. Jack sat and took a drink of the fresh, clear water — such a treat — when who should he see entering but Kandinsky, the correspondent.

He lifted up his newspaper, but not quickly enough.

"Ah Padre, what are you doing down here? May I join you?" Without waiting for a reply, Kandinsky came over and sat, waving an arm to attract one of the many Cape coloured, or mixed race, waiters who appeared quickly to take his order.

"Well, this is a happy occasion," Kandinsky said, beaming.

Jack frowned. What on earth had happened to the man? Indeed, an altogether different and cheerful mood. "I should ask the same question, Mr. Kandinsky. What brings you here? Happy to be removed from the battle areas?"

"If you can call that pigsty up in Belmont a battle area. No, I've been down here about a week, digging for news, any news. All one can report from Belmont is disease, rats, lice, drill, nothing our readers want or need. But..." He paused, as the waiter took his order. "In the meantime, believe it or not, I seem to have found a job on the *Argus*. Fine newspaper, established fifty years ago."

He did look self-satisfied, Jack thought. "Have you now? Well congratulations!"

"Thank you." Kandinsky slurped down his fresh water, which had appeared with the waiter. "The Montreal paper sent me in here to see what I could pick up from the Imperials... Damn Boers, they're a hardy lot. Tough to beat. But the Imperial troops here are building up like the devil. You know," he leaned forward, "one can pick up a lot of gossip, a lot of background one doesn't find up there with our abandoned troops."

Jack nodded. Even on his way from the station, he'd noticed the town more crowded than before.

"I was surprised to find out, Padre," Kandinsky finished his juice and wiped his mouth, "from a fellow correspondent, that the thieving beggars seem to have some modicum of honour."

"How so?" asked Jack

"This fellow told me — oh, you've heard of Winston Churchill, of course?"

Jack shook his head. "Why should I? Up country, as you know, we hardly get any newspapers."

"Indeed, and why would some word of a young British war correspondent escaping be of interest? Well, lemme tell you, I met him last week. He'd been captured by the Boers when they ambushed his train."

"And then they let him go?"

"No siree! I'll fill you in: the Boers rigged the tracks, boulders of course, derailed the trail, and Churchill went out under fire with a few others to roll the blessed things off the tracks so the train could keep going. That's how he got captured. But they did succeed in getting the train going."

"Good for him." Jack leaned back as a waiter put a plate of eggs in front of him.

"Now this is the point: that Boer commander, once his captives were properly drawn up, was most polite. He greeted them with a very gentlemanly speech."

Jack began eating as quickly as he could. The sooner he was out of the dining room, the better.

"That Boer commander — he addressed his prisoners, and said he regretted the unfortunate circumstances. Now listen. He complimented the British on their defence, and..." Kandinsky again leaned forward. "...he trusted his rifle fire had not annoyed them unduly! In fact, he even added that he hoped they'd understand its necessity!"

Jack absorbed that. Unusual behaviour for a scoundrel, he thought. But it would fit in with a farmer's integrity, certainly.

"So what do you think of that?"

"Most impressive."

"Sure impressed our Churchill, I can tell you." Kandinsky helped himself to a piece of Jack's bread, on which he slathered butter and took a large bite.

"Some half-witted farmer, never been off his land, spends all his time with pigs and cattle, and then behaves like a gentle-man." He shook his head, not noticing how this last remark upset Jack. "But they work hard to scrape a living out of this godforsaken land."

"And so if Churchill was captured, how did you happen to meet him?"

"Made his escape! Damn brave, I'd say. Whole of the Orange Free State out looking for him. Found his way on a goods train to Durban, and by boat down to Cape Town. Got into all the papers, I can tell you. When my bread comes, you'll take a slice, of course. Now what are you up to, Padre?"

Jack explained his mission, without adding many details. "Do you happen to know where I might find this Prinsloo fellow?"

"The local outdoor markets. Excellent source of gossip, I've found them. Not far from here you can visit one." He gave directions to Jack.

After his hearty breakfast, Jack headed for the market in question. He passed by the Castle, a huge pentagonal building with arrow-like wings at each corner, reminding him somewhat of Quebec's Citadel — certainly the old stone walls were almost identical. There, he found the market and wandered in. Much like those seen in Quebec City, he decided. Farmers from the Isle d'Orléans, a few miles down the St. Lawrence, would gather on Saturdays to display their fresh produce. Here as he walked among the stalls, he found similar displays of potatoes, carrots, turnips and suchlike vegetables, along with peas, corn, and so on. Of course now, February, it was summer in South Africa.

He stopped at one booth and asked about the small display

of the eggs he saw, and inquired if he might buy a good many for his hospital up at Orange River.

"These are just for our customers," the woman replied, her grey hair piled under a bonnet, an apron covering a plump body. "Anything that has to do with the troops, you need to talk to our wholesaler."

"And how do I do that?" asked Jack.

"You'd have to see my husband. He'll be back in a couple of hours."

He tried at another booth where, as with others, he received the same evasive answer. Not so easy to walk in and order supplies! Perhaps they suspected him of being an undercover agent. So after a touristic look round, he headed for the army depot. He reckoned that for the more important foodstuffs, the central Quartermaster would arrange it all, as suggested.

Once there, he found which of the many officers suited his problem, and at the appointed desk, waited while the Quartermaster dealt with a tall and unusually thin Boer, fairly well dressed. He found them discussing something to do with the agricultural sector. So, in a pause, he asked if the Boer knew anything about a former farmer by the name of Gideon Prinsloo.

He could see the man sizing him up. "I might. Why'd you ask?"

Jack explained his errand: a Boer lad he had met in the Orange River Field Hospital wanted to get a message to his uncle.

"That might be possible," the tall Boer answered warily. But after taking a good look at Jack, he went on, "If you wait at the corner of Riebeek and Bree streets around seven this evening, I shall try to meet you."

At the appointed time, Jack stood on Riebeek, and soon the tall Boer came up, introducing himself as Johannes Kamp. "I believe I can take you to the fellow. He wants to hear more. I suggested we meet at a tavern. If you'll come, we can offer the fellow a drink."

So Jack followed Johannes along this main street until they turned down Buitenkant Street and entered the Perseverance Tavern, a rather disreputable looking bar.

"May I buy you a drink?" asked Jack.

"No thank you, Pastoor. I know you fellows of the cloth never have any money. I've made a somewhat decent living supplying the Imperial troops. Though it's not always easy... What will you have?"

"A beer, please."

As they leaned on the bar and talked of farming in the Cape Colony, Jack suddenly found himself spun round. He faced an enraged fellow with red eyes, bearded, and very drunk. Before he could see what was happening, a fist thudded into his jaw and down he went.

The bar erupted in chaos.

Groggily, he looked up to see above him the wild-eyed oaf, who yelled out, "You let one of them Imperials in here again and I'll set the bar on fire."

"Steady on!" Johannes grabbed the drunken wretch and, assisted by another, hauled him to the door. "That's a pastoor you hit!"

"I don't care what he is, this is an Afrikaner tavern, we'd don't need the likes of Imperials coming in here telling us what to do — taking our land away from us!"

With a mighty push Johannes and his helper thrust the man into the street, sending him sprawling into a puddle. Johannes came back, adjusting his clothes, while Jack picked himself up.

"I'm sorry, Pastoor." Johannes looked Jack in the face. "Did he hurt you?"

Jack shook his head. "Just a bit dazed. But that was a mighty punch. Must have been a boxer." He managed a weak smile.

Seeing Jack was all right, the customers went back to their drinking; it seemed a fairly usual occurrence in this particular tavern. The bartender came over to apologize. "That Hendrik, he's a troublemaker. This is a good tavern. We serve anyone." He offered Jack another beer as a peace offering.

After conversations had settled a bit, Jack asked, "So, Johannes, are there lots of Boer sympathizers hereabouts?"

"No one likes their land taken away." He took a draft of his ale. "Even before the war started, we could see problems coming. A few of us came over from the Transvaal into Cape Colony." He seemed about to go on, but then closed his mouth.

Jack nodded and took another slug of his new draft, then turned as Johannes looked over his shoulder and brightened.

A short, heavyset man with the requisite black beard came up to them. His eyes kept darting around the room as he greeted Johannes, and then he looked hard at Jack.

"You'll have a beer, I think, Mr. Prinsloo?" asked Johannes.

"Drop of Scotch," grunted Gideon Prinsloo. Nothing was said until the bartender brought the Scotch, which he threw back in a jiffy and placed the small glass back on the bar. Johannes motioned with his head to the bartender, who filled it again. "So how is my nephew?" Prinsloo asked finally.

"The lad's been shot, or perhaps it was shrapnel. But he's doing well. Won't be too long before he's back on his farm, which I understand you know?"

"Aye," replied Prinsloo. "Although I haven't been there for four or five years. I moved my family into the Cape Colony — for which I got no thanks from the rest of them. A lot safer in these times; I have four children to think about and a hard-working wife. We found a small piece of land, not very productive, so I'm down here, doing whatever I can."

Johannes chuckled. "I hear 'whatever you can' happens to

turn a pretty penny, Gideon. No one can get an egg without your approval."

Jack registered this, and then looked at Gideon, who shrugged. "Eggs are perishable. The British send their main supplies from England, but eggs," he grinned, "they cannot import." Then he looked at Johannes. "From what I hear, you're not doing too badly yourself."

"I get by," Johannes agreed enigmatically.

"So I guess, to get to the point," Jack said, "young Pieter would like to know if you could come and help him on his farm. You see, now he's an orphan. Parents killed in the war. He should be home within a month."

Gideon Prinsloo shook his head. "Too bad, I liked them." He sighed. "Well, no question of me coming in a month, Pastoor. Too much to do here. But it's a fine farm, and once this war is over, I'd be honoured to bring my family to help run it."

"That's good news," Jack said. "If it hasn't all gone to rack and ruin by then..."

"Those damned Imperials, forgive my swearing, Pastoor, but they think nothing of destroying a fine farm when they feel like it. I don't know what they'll do when it's all over. The farms they've destroyed will produce nothing. Then what will they be getting?"

"I'm sure they don't want to take over, exactly," said Jack. "I'm a Canadian, of course, but I've not heard of the British trying to take over farms. It's the government they want to change."

"They want the gold. They want the diamonds. The farmers can go to hell." Prinsloo swore and then gulped his jigger of Scotch, and put the glass down for more.

"Is there some way," Jack asked, "that you could scribble a message for me to bring to Pieter? He trusts me, but it may be a long time for a lad to wait until this terrible war is over: months, maybe —"

"More like years," Johannes interrupted

"Nothing easier." Prinsloo signalled to the bartender for pencil and paper and, as they were talking, wrote a short paragraph for Jack to take to his nephew. "I always liked that lad. He's a decent one. Played with his cousins, my children, you see, they loved him too, fine generous lad. His parents and I stopped being on speaking terms, but the children didn't know that."

With that accomplished, Jack felt he could move on to finding his Kelsie. And she'd probably be able to get her commander to introduce him to Lt.-Col. Ryerson.

He hired a carriage, and they trotted off through the outskirts to Wynberg: a charming little British suburb with rows of houses and neat gardens with climbing wisteria. But on reaching the hospital, he discovered the four Canadian nurses had been moved up the line towards Kimberly. With hopes shattered, Jack felt more or less defeated.

However the Director of the hospital was most helpful. He not only knew Ryerson, but also how to get in touch with him and promised Jack that he'd have some word the next day.

As Jack turned to go, the Director called him back. "I almost forgot. Here's a letter that someone left for you."

In his carriage trotting back to the centre of Cape Town, Jack read:

Dear Jack,

I just have a feeling that you will be coming here somehow, so I'm leaving you this note because tomorrow I am leaving for upcountry.

Because this is war and we never know if we're going to meet again, I wanted to tell you how much your friendship and wise counsel meant to me on the boat.

You have often been in my thoughts since then. Funny how a person stays with you, even when he's far away.

I think of the times we stood at the railing on the boat, and of our last meeting in Cape Town.

I guess there is not much point in writing when I don't even know if you'll get this. But if you do, please understand you brightened up my life when I needed it. For sure, when we get back, we must meet again, either in Halifax or in your beloved Gaspe.

Your friend, Kelsie.

Chapter Eighteen

On the long train ride back to Belmont, Jack found that Kelsie's letter had given him lots to occupy his thoughts, a welcome release from wartime vicissitudes. Clearly, she was expressing her liking for him. He wished he'd been a bit more forthright in his note to her. But then, it probably never reached her. So what now? Try to find her? Of course, but his duty came first. Would they run into each other? Surely, at some point. And what then? Well, better wait until then to decide. But one thing was sure, she needed him, and he himself wanted to look after her — perhaps even for a long time to come.

But first, he was anxious to see Big George Dorsey again, and young Eamon; he wondered how they were getting on. But his orders had him first stopping in De Aar. When at last he arrived, he alerted the hospital commandant as to what he might expect by way of supplies.

"We've already had crates of sulphate of magnesia, thanks to you," the officer told him.

"Thanks to Dr. Ryerson," Jack corrected. "He made it possible. I just moved it along."

Jack offered a short evening service, and the next morning was able to find out the latest news. Lord Roberts, the new Commander-in-Chief, had paid a surprise visit to Belmont and General Kitchener inspected the men, and declared them ready.

The Field Marshall had announced that the Canadians were to join a newly constituted Nineteenth Brigade under Major General Horace Smith-Dorrien, a protégé of Kitchener. This time, he told them, they would see all the fighting they'd ever want and in desperate and difficult conditions over harsh terrain.

In order to help relieve the beleaguered British fortresses at Ladysmith, Kimberly and Mafeking, Roberts had decided on a different strategy: strike directly at the Boer capitals of Bloemfontein and Pretoria.

On Sunday, February 11th, the RCR had left on a march to Graspan, where they had a short spell of sleep under the stars.

At five in the morning, the brigade had then begun a twelve-mile trek to Ramdam. There, they joined a large military offensive of over thirty thousand men, plus five thousand native drivers managing twenty thousand mules and oxen and some fifteen thousand horses, all set to snake across the veldt in the hottest month of the year.

Heavens, what news! Jack felt he must get with them as soon as possible, now that they were facing their first major engagement of the war. After breakfast, he headed off by train for Orange River, desperate to catch up with his unit beyond Belmont.

When he arrived at the Orange River Field Hospital, he checked in with the officer commanding, the one who had sent him down to Cape Town. He reported fully on his doings and received welcome compliments. He set about visiting the wounded, and again was greeted by the ghastly sights of war: fever, exhaustion, wounds and death. He was accosted by a convalescent with a bandaged arm — a corporal, in the best of spirits. "Padre! Welcome back!"

"Thank you, Corporal." Jack couldn't remember his name, but the corporal introduced himself and after some talk about his fresh wound, went on, "Padre, last week, imagine our surprise when they gave us eggs for breakfast!"

Jack smiled. "Well, I'm glad they finally — "

"Not they, Padre, you. We heard you was doing it. Down at Cape Town. Good for you!"

"Well, I only saw that they — "

"We toasted you with our fresh breakfast water. Next time, could you try for fruit juice?" The soldier laughed at his own joke and nudged Jack. "You here for long this time?"

"No, I must rejoin the regiment. Just as soon as I've done some ministry here."

"Me too, I want to be with the lads." He shrugged. They both knew that the corporal would be here for a good while yet.

Jack went on his rounds, and soon found the cot where young Pieter lay.

"Well, Pieter," Jack said, "you look as if you're feeling better."

Pieter turned, and his eyes widened. "Pastoor! I never think I see you again."

"You decided I was all talk and no action?" Jack smiled. "Well, I've got something to show you." He reached in his pocket and pulled out the paper on which Pieter's uncle had written an address and his agreement. "There we are, Pieter, your Oom has written a note. He can't join you right now. He's the one helped me get all these eggs for us here. He seems to be making — for himself, and so for you and your farm — a pretty fine income."

"He is?"

"Oh yes. And he told me to assure you that he will come with his family and help you, once this nightmare is over. So, you may find it hard for a time, but in the long run, your worries are over."

"Oh thank you, Padre!"

Jack could see the news had done more to help young Pieter

recover than all the medicines in the world. After exchanging a few words of comfort, Jack moved on.

He wanted to leave early in the morning and so worked well into the night. Before finishing his rounds, he came upon a familiar form. There on a cot lay his cabin mate from the Sardinian, Captain Forbes.

As he knelt he saw all the signs of enteric: the rising fever, headaches, and a stomach-ache. Diarrhea had not set in yet, nor the delirium that often accompanied the fever in its second week. Usually the disease ran its course for a month, but a proportion of sufferers did not survive; one never knew.

"Well, Captain, indeed a sorry state of affairs! Did they bring you all the way here?"

Forbes turned and saw Jack. "No, I was in Belmont trying to commandeer more transportation." He nodded, holding his stomach. "So now what? You'll try to cram thoughts of heaven down my throat?"

"No," Jack said with a tired smile, "I have discovered that talk of an afterlife doesn't sit too well with lads who are in pain."

Forbes nodded. "Good for you."

"But let me try to help... Can I get you anything to ease your pain, Captain? Or shall we talk a while? You will find me a willing listener."

"I got no talk in me." He made a face. "I haven't slept for days. I know I've got to sleep, I know it helps, but I can't seem to. Maybe tell me about that province of yours, filled with Frenchies." He groaned with pain. "How about giving me your reasons for liking it?" He writhed, then asked for water.

Jack rose, went to the orderly table at one end, poured a glass of the precious, clear liquid from the tank and brought it over to Forbes, who drank.

"Well first off, I don't minister much to the Frenchies, as

you call them; my parishioners are mostly English. Not easy for them, being alone up there in northern Quebec. You're from Nova Scotia?"

Forbes nodded. "Halifax. Never been to Quebec. Is it nice?"

Jack made himself comfortable on a camp chair beside Forbes. "Well Captain, our woods are lush and green: hay, wheat, oats, all come on their own. You just spread the seed and they grow. In fact, all the water you'll ever want, we've got." Jack found himself warming to his subject. "And our lakes, so still, so beautiful. Around the edges, I've seen foxes, deer, often moose, come and dip their noses in the clear surfaces to drink their fill."

Forbes nodded, and relaxed as if being told a bedtime story.

"The streams that feed those lakes are homes to mink, otter, sometimes beaver. Many's the time I've seen them splashing about. Trapping season, they hide, of course. You know, I used to go camp at the edge of a lake instead of staying at some parishioner's. I'd watch the moon rise over the lake and listen to the loons with their unearthly calling. Spirits of departed ancestors, the Eskimos say.

"In the morning, dawn, that's when it all comes alive: I'd see across the still water deer bring their fawns to drink, so delicately do they nuzzle the water before sliding off into the woods. And then of course, there's the splash of trout leaping for flies. Just drop in your line and there's lunch in ten minutes! Heavens! How I loved to fry those trout crisp golden brown, slather them in farm butter and brew myself up a strong cup of tea. What else would a man want?

"And our clouds! Such wondrous shapes, oh yes, romping high in that vivid blue sky. Every so often, they'd rear up and clap their hands in thunder, and open their hearts in a downpour to feed the forest and nourish the crops. Marvellous province, quite marvellous." Jack lapsed in the silence and glanced down.

The Captain was fast asleep.

That's one way to care for the wounded: paint them word pictures, take them by the hand and lead them away from their agony, away from conflict into a loving world of home and family. And for himself, oh yes, very curative. But tomorrow, the fray.

Chapter Nineteen

Jack waited impatiently on the railway platform for a train heading north. But the first to arrive was heading south, loaded with wounded and with rumours of a major engagement being fought at Paardeberg Drift. It disgorged its veterans, and upwards of a hundred men began their agonised trek over the few hundred yards of desert to the tent hospital. Jack helped one man who was bent over, clutching his stomach; another beside him bled from an arm that hung lifeless.

Then he heard, "Padre! Good to see you."

"Corporal Ferguson!" He handed his soldier on to an orderly and threaded his way back to the limping man.

The corporal still had not shaved; his long black beard resembled those of the Boers, but now so did his haunted eyes and almost vacant expression. Terrible things a war does to a man, Jack thought, no matter on whose side he fights.

Jack started to press him for news but the corporal needed no pressing. Obviously hoping for someone to listen, he launched out: "Padre, you don't know what we've been through. First, that march with ole Black Bill to catch up with Smith Dorrie at Graspan, and that next day with 'em all to Ramdam — blasted kharki, it wrecked your skin between your legs, stiff, chafing, and those damn useless shoes... Mine were gone even then." His bottled up feelings poured forth. "We all carried our rifle, bayonet and a forty pound kit, including a greatcoat. We needed water and supplies, so we had to follow a bunch of oxcarts, over-loaded of course, stopping and starting, breaking down. Twelve miles that day over a dusty veldt, temperatures well over a hundred, I swear." Ferguson winced and motioned Jack over to one of the station benches.

Jack helped him hobble across and they both leaned back against the stone wall of the terminus.

"Well, by the time we reached Ramdam, mid afternoon," Ferguson's voice was dry, raspy as sandpaper, "we was just so, so thirsty, I can't describe it. To make it worse, you know what they gave us for lunch? Salt pork and dry biscuits! Like a bunch of animals, we herded around that dirty dam up there. And then, along with them mules and horses, we lay on our bellies and drank — water at home no man would wash his hands in."

Disaster, Jack thought; if someone as tough as the corporal was now beat, what about the others?

Like the haunted sailor in the *Ancient Mariner*, Ferguson pressed on. "Next day, Wednesday, we left Ramdam at four thirty in the morning, thousands of us — on reduced rations if you can believe it. We made Watervaal Drift about mid morning, dead tired. My poor feet was burning, blistered all over." He shook his head, and leaned back, eyes closed. "Ten minutes after we arrived, we had to go on fatigue, shoving transport wagons across the Modder River and up the opposite bank. We'd had no breakfast, well, a bit o' coffee and biscuit before we left Ramdam. No dinner at noon, either, we worked right through till we shoved that last overweight wagon up the hill." He paused, lost in the awful memory, and his shoulders sagged.

Jack sat fascinated, but also horrified.

"Well at least we'll get supper, we thought, and a good rest. But didn't we have to get right back at it and lug over them big naval guns? Such big brutes, we attached ropes, five hundred of us, I'd say. So we didn't flop down till eight — too late for supper, we just fell asleep, hungry and all."

Jack couldn't stop an exclamation escaping his lips.

The corporal, in spite of his tale, forced a grin. "Yep, and one thirty in the morning, I had to roust out the men and start marching again, still not a bite!"

"Unbelievable!" Jack paused as an orderly came down the platform with a big bucket of water and a cup, giving each a drink of water. "So how far did you have to go then?"

"Eleven miles this time. We stopped by the Modder again and at last got to eat, a bit of bully beef and biscuit. Then I did picket duty all night, without a wink of sleep, 'cause I knew the other poor fellas couldn't. I heard firing from the front, but the hills blocked me from seeing any.

"Came in from picket duty at daybreak, and Padre, that whole camp was under arms, ready to march. By the end of that day, we reached Jacobsdal. I couldn't 'a walked a step further."

"Jacobsdal, that's a good way up the line. Towards Kimberly?"

Ferguson shook his head. "That's northwest. But us, y'see, Roberts wanted us heading for Bloemfontein, a good way East."

"What's it like, Jacobsdal?"

"Fine little town, maybe twenty-five hundred people — well... before the battles. Their church, big stone building, full of Boer wounded, and our wounded as well. You know, they had Boer doctors and nurses — just great at treating us all, too."

"So you stopped there? They fixed your feet?"

"No, no hospital for me, I thought, I'll rest here, and then go on with the lads. Didn't want to let anyone down. I laid around a spell with boots off, but when I went to put 'em on, couldn't walk a step! So I cut out the backs..." He shrugged. "They felt a bit better.

"Four times we had to fall in on false alarms. Transport broke down and we got nothin' to eat — again! So they said we could catch any sheep or goats. Our boys caught a goat, yes sir!" He gave a hoarse laugh. "Skinny as anything, but we got it cooked and you know what? Got another order to fall in right away — and we had to throw the damn thing out."

"They wouldn't even let you eat first?"

"No sir, pack the kittles! But just as soon as we lined up, another false alarm. Lord, we were tired, but the lads caught a sheep this time. Cooked it and we got her half eaten and lay down — dead ready for sleep! Most of us, we'd only had an hour or two in three nights, and doing the hardest kind of work. But at two in the morning, Saturday, we'd just laid down when — listen to this — we got another blasted order to bale the blankets and fall right in again!

"Now sir, you try struggling over that veldt by moonlight, steering clear of thorns, stones, humps, well they were termite hills, I guess, and other stuff in the dark. We stopped at four in the morning, just by the muddy Modder. We was so tired, I didn't even loosen my tunic, just dropped like everyone else, out cold. General French was having a brush with the Boers just a mile ahead. But we got nothing to eat again till five in the afternoon, and then it was only tea and biscuits."

Played out, the corporal needed help. Jack went to rise, but Ferguson held him back: he had more to tell.

"Loud were the lamentations and many the curses, you can imagine, when we were told to march that evening at six. My feet was done, finished. The fellas, they went on to Paardeberg Drift but I got sent back. Couldn't do nothing else. See, look." He lifted a leg and hauled off the remnants of a boot. The other was heavily bandaged.

Even without looking Jack knew what the corporal and his squad must have endured.

"Next morning, no breakfast in sight, so another fella and myself, we struck for the river. Got across to a field hospital and managed to get dressed by a doctor. Awful mess around there, hundreds lying about outside, all kinds of wounds, and doctors in shirtsleeves, but not nearly enough, dressing them.

"Next day I started for De Aar by mule wagon and travelled all night. In the morning at Klip Drift, we changed bullock wagons, but Padre, we had to lay there, underneath them for shade, all that burning day long. We only travelled at night so off we started, rough it was and freezing — cold rain soaking us to the skin. Others, worse wounded than me, you could hear them yell, what a time they was having, for sure." Ferguson trailed off, closed his eyes, and lapsed into silence.

Jack was stricken himself — what a tale and a half. As an orderly hurried by, Jack grabbed him, made him see to the Corporal, and went on to minister to others as needed.

He could not imagine sending troops into such an important battle, under these conditions, after so many horrifying days on the march. Surely, troops fought battles after they were rested and well fed? He found it hard to grapple with the truths that this conflict was beginning to force upon him.

* * *

After a traumatic day of helping soldiers to their hospital cots and generally organizing what he could, he foresaw he'd have to spend the night, for more trains would be arriving the next day.

But first, at dawn, burial duties. A young Bugler led him to their latest burial site. Head spinning with dreams stirred up by the first hard news of the campaign, he allowed himself to speak without thinking. "I suppose, Bugler, like most of our other boys here, you have been aching to get to the front for the real fun."

"Fun?"echoed the Bugler, a tall adolescent with short blond

hair and blue eyes. "I'm perfectly happy back here, Padre, even though I have to blow at these never-ending burials. Up there with them Mauser bullets whistling, watching your best friend shot, brains spilling all over you, no sir, I..." He stopped as the words choked in his throat.

"I'm sorry, I spoke without thinking," Jack affirmed.

"You know, Padre, I came here, all happy and ready to fight for Her Majesty," he said. "But what I've seen makes me sick. Last time I blew the call for a charge, it near stuck in my throat — sending so many fellas I knew to their deaths: sons, husbands, and lots of lonely fellas never even knew a woman. All for good Queen Victoria. I wonder if she knows what damage her bloody government is causing, the lives it's wrecking."

They reached an already-dug gravesite and waited for the oxcart with its lifeless burden.

"I wouldn't blame Her Majesty for all this," Jack said. "I do believe, from what I hear, the Boers might have brought it on themselves."

"Aye, but there's not a few fellows talking about the diamonds and gold they have hereabouts."

"Well, we're on duty now, Bugler," Jack replied, reflecting that his job was to keep the morale up as best he could. "We should put thoughts like that out of our minds. I'd rather wait till I get home and do some proper thinking in the calmness of my rectory. Such sentiments here may just kill our initiative and help the enemy. I believe now we must win, and get as many as we can back home safe."

The young Bugler eyed him. "As you say, Padre, we have our duty, and we'll do it. But me, I got no quiet rectory. What am I going to do in the Old Country? Keep blowing, I guess — thankful I got this job and a warm barracks, and pay I can send home to me Mum who's scrubbing floors. T'weren't easy to learn all them bugle calls: we got almost two hundred. My favourite is 'Lunch' — what you know as 'Come to the cook house door, boys.'" Of course, Jack did know that one.

At last the oxcart lumbered up and orderlies lifted out two bodies. Wrapped in simple canvas, no question of coffins, they were lowered into this grave dug by the burial party the night before. A cross had already been erected, and Jack knelt to check their names, carved in the wood by friends. Then he rose and began to read the Burial Rite from the Book of Common Prayer.

* * *

When the next trains carrying the wounded from Paardeberg arrived in the station, Jack was there to greet them. Those who could walk needed help to reach the field hospital, and those who needed transportation, he began to supervise. The doctors were back at the hospital making ready for this new onslaught, and the job of organizing arrivals seemed to have fallen upon him. He grasped the reins of organization easily and even developed a knack for getting things done without treading on toes. In fact, most responded well to his taking charge and his many encouragements.

When the last little train of the day came chugging into the station and its carriage doors emptied out the wounded, Jack glimpsed a familiar face in the back of a cart rumbling by.

"George!"

The body stirred, lifted its head over the sideboards, and brightened momentarily. "Jack!" Then big George Dorsey sunk back, silent.

Jack felt an icy hand clutch at his heart. Big George had been wounded, and badly. Jack had always feared that this day might come. But now, the face of war had taken on a new and even more personal look.

Chapter Twenty

That night, Jack made straight for George's bedside. Lifting a lantern near and putting his campstool beside Big George's cot, he touched his hand.

His eyes opened, though his stare was fuzzy.

"So they got you, those bloody Boers."

George nodded. "They got me good, Padre." He grinned weakly. "But you found me..."

"Has the doctor seen you?"

"Just been. From the look on his face, not much he'll do for me. He gave me something to drink and a potion to help me sleep." He was silent for a while; the effort of speaking tired him. "Got an orderly to dress my wounds. See, I got hit in two places. Leg and stomach."

"I've seen a lot of wounded here, George. A leg wound such as yours, which didn't break any bones, they'll get fixed in no time, you watch."

"I know that, Padre, it's the stomach they worry about. Shrapnel ball went right through. Did some awful damage, the doctor said."

"Shall I fetch water?"

"No Padre, listen, I've decided. One thing I have to do. My daughters, when they grow up, they'll have to know how I went. Because they'll have to stop another war like this. They'll have to speak up. Their generation, they can't have this happen. What we faced. Annie, she's got to tell them, when they get of age. It's all I can leave to them now, and the other farming families around us. Boys like me, growing up. They can't be let go. No war ever again. See, I'm finished, Jack. It's over for me. But you..."

Jack winced. He prayed it be not true. "The newspaper dispatches will reach Annie, she'll know. They'll hear — "

"No!" George reached out to grip Jack's hand. "No, Jack, not general stuff. *My* stuff. Write it down. My last words..."

"Now now, we'll have none of that kind of talk; we're going to get you better." Jack tried to sound encouraging.

"Does that mean you won't write?" Jack could see the brown eyes go dark and his life force ebb.

"Yes, yes, George, of course I'll write. Every word." Keep that spirit alive, give him a hope — the one thing that saved so many patients clinging to life. "I'll be right back with pad and paper, I'll get it from the orderly room, you just watch."

When Jack returned, he had scarcely sat when Big George began. "I'm starting with Paardeberg, because that's when we..."

"Won our big victory, I know George, everyone's talking about it. You're all heroes."

He smiled weakly. "You'll send it to her?"

"Better still, George, I'll take it, I'll deliver it in person. You've given me your address. But look, you're going to make it, I'm sure — "

"Jacko, no need for that. I'm going. Just, get it down... I'll talk slow."

Jack replied, after a pause, "All right, Paardeberg..."

George nodded, collected his thoughts. "We got there, worn out after the marches, after the lack of food, like dead, in fact, but then we heard the first shooting, about two miles ahead. No time for tea or coffee — they gave us a shot of rum, and we struck out to find the enemy.

"First, that Modder. We had to wade through. Stretched ropes, slung our rifles, put everything in our pith helmets and we took that river, chin high. The current, Jack, it was so strong — horses and riders, they got pulled under, and down stream; transport wagons, mules drowning.

"Well, we got to the bank and headed for the firing line on the double. Not long before we had to drop, those Mauser bullets came whistling, thick as hail. See, the Boers were hidden behind rocks and bushes on the banks, so we'd hardly seen one all day."

"You were all alone, you Canadians?"

"No no, we were mixed up with Black Watch, Seaforth Highlanders, a few of the Gordons. The Cornwalls, about three hundred yards behind. We lay there, pinned down, all day in that heat. Then about four, we heard the Cornwall's colonel call 'charge'. They fixed bayonets and started the rush. As they passed us, their colonel called out, 'Come on Canada!'"

"So we up and joined in. The Boers ran off, but stopped on the higher bank and poured on such a rifle fire! Just the flat desert we had to cross. Halfway to their trenches, I saw the colonel of the Cornwalls shot, right through the forehead.

"I ran on till the men ahead o'me went down and I saw we'd never gain the position. Too far, through that deadly fire. Bloody madness, his order. I dropped and scooped out some sand to kind of hide in. I lay still so's not to attract attention, but fellows around kept up their awful screaming. That sure drew the Boer's fire — from three sides of us, right up till dark. I expected my ticket every second, Jack...

"Those three daylight hours from our charge till dark, so long... So many right close by, wounded, what a noise: screaming, some dying, some praying out loud, others cursing their luck. Such a row. And the smell! You soil yourself when you're hit, eh?"

Jack could just imagine the carnage, some of which he was seeing here in the hospital. No longer the grand celebration, the big send-off, the bands and the cheers. Just blood... and death.

"Those stretcher-bearers, Jack, they worked out there on the veldt, all day long under that hot sun, the bullets flying past, and them binding wounds, getting last love messages... But Jack, so many fellows died without a soul to hear." A sigh escaped him. "And we kep' on fighting, firing, holding tight, right through that intolerable heat, until we saw the slopes of the nearest kopje washed red in the blood of the dying sun. Sixty-seven casualties."

George lay back, his energy — fired at first by the excitement of his remembrance — now deserting him. Jack sat, looking down.

"After dark, I crawled back on my stomach, gosh, four hundred yards or more." He shut his eyes. "Haven't even gotten to the second, the main battle, but..."

Jack nodded. "Don't even try to talk about it now." He rose. "I'll be back, George, I'll be back tomorrow. With my pencil. Sleep now; do you good. And I'll be back."

Was that a wisp of a smile crossing Big George's lips? His breathing grew slower, as he fell asleep.

* * *

All that night, Jack, himself wounded in soul as they in body, ministered to the injured, some on stretchers, some on the ground, all in pain: a picture that would hang forever on the walls of his memory. Boys and men, sixteen to forty-five. At one cot he began to kneel, but saw that the fair-haired boy had breathed his last, a grimace from the horrible wound frozen on his face. Only a lad, maybe sixteen, dead before he had even entered manhood.

By his side, a soldier lay with both legs shattered above the knee. Would he rather live or die, Jack wondered. What must it be like to lie, day after day, looking into such a dark future, knowing you would always be a burden. Pain brought no groan from his pale, feverish lips, but tears began to trickle down his sunburned cheeks. He moved his head and covered his face with his hands, ashamed, as Jack knelt. He reached out to hold the man's hand, bowing his head and praying, more for himself than the soldier, "Lord, give him courage... Let me take what strength I can from this hero." He spoke a few words of comfort and rested with him, scarcely sufficient, he knew, but sharing the pain.

One glance at the next body was enough. The now unbandaged hole on the side of his forehead spoke of a leaden messenger that had called him to a painful ascent into the great Beyond, before Jack could even comfort him with prayers. By his side lay another who would never more behold the light of day: some Mauser had shot away his nose and right eye, while the left was so injured, yes — probably in one rending, blinding, stinging flash — he'd been sent to walk in darkness. The man lay on his back with a stained bandage round his head as groans heaved from his lungs. How could these men ever say, "Thy will be done"? But Jack knelt, and prayed with them a good spell.

All was not silence in the tent. Across the aisle, one wild soldier lay in the grip of delirium. His voice, now loud and harsh, now soft and gentle, muttered as a child by his mother's knee: "Now I lay me down to sleep..." Then in some drunken argument, he poured forth such oaths that Jack involuntarily covered his ears. Then he loosed words of wonder as he wandered down some river path: phrases to a sweetheart probably awaiting him, but who would never see him again. As Jack went over, the man stretched out his hands: "I'm coming." Jack stopped short. No more delirium, no more pain or suffering — "I'm coming, Lord!" he yelled, "I'm coming!" And that moment, the Lord in all mercy took him off to a happier realm.

Jack came out of that tent, and who should he see, with arm

bandaged, sitting in another tent opening, having a smoke —
Eamon McAndrews.

"Well Eamon, they got you too?"

"Aye, a Mauser they said. Paardeberg. The second battle.
That was some fight, Padre."

Jack knew what was required: let them speak their pain. "Can
you tell me about it, Eamon?"

He nodded, stubbed out his cigarette, and leaned back.
"Well first, you had to make it through that first one. Bugler
Williamson of C company — he was the fella, Padre. After that
damn stupid colonel yelled, he stood up out there right in the
open and he blew the charge, long and loud — it sure drove us
forward, we had t' leave our wounded where they fell. I tripped,
and just as well, cause right overhead I hear them pings of bullets. Ahead, they kep' their rush, protected by some magic, it
seemed, Padre..." He paused and blinked back a tear. "And you
know, some pierced that terrible hail of death and still they lost
out, right at the end, gone, my cousin among them. To get to
their trenches, Padre, you had to charge a quarter of a mile! Over
veldt just as flat as our skating rink in Dingwall, not a mound
between us anywhere, for sure. You'd a asked me to go even a
hundred yards, I'da' said, not possible."

"Do they know yet how many...?"

"Twenty killed and maybe sixty wounded in that first battle.
Sure and 'twas a heavy-hearted regiment lay down that night.
We all said prayers for them fellas who, though worn out, just
that morning had jumped up when they heard reveille, ready
for the fray and now, poor buggers, rotting out there on the
hot sand..." He opened his eyes, turned to Jack, and proceeded
to light another cigarette. "What we went through for another
whole ten days, out on that veldt before the second battle. Such
icy rain, time after time, and that cold..."

Well, this desert plateau was a mile high, unlike anything he'd known at home, Jack thought. "And the dead, did they get buried?"

"Father O'Leary, bless his soul, he'd been up all night under those fusillades, roaming, searching for wounded... Yeah, he performed burials. Bunch of graves down by a growth of trees near the river. I helped dig a big one, Padre. Seventeen bodies, they put em down, side by side."

Yes, thought Jack, Peter O'Leary, good for him, God bless him! But still, he felt a real pang of guilt for missing it himself.

Chapter Twenty-One

Jack couldn't leave. Eamon McAndrews still sat in front of his tent, smoking: drawing so deeply on his cigarette as though the smoke were his breath of life. Jack squatted, leaned forward, cupped some sand in his hand and let it flow through his fingers like the blood that had ebbed from so many veins. Should he keep listening? Could he? He made himself. Had he himself crossed that Modder with the men, might he have made their endings any easier? No time for those thoughts now. The men needed a listener, and a listener he would be.

In the low light of the lantern, Eamon went on, "Pompom Tuesday,"

"Pompom Tuesday?"

Eamon nodded. "We lay out that day under a scorching sun, aiming at whatever moved. But Padre, when they got out their one pounder, a Vickers Maxim, twelve one pound shells in a belt — rattled off in that many seconds... The pom-pom! Sounds like that, you know."

He lapsed into silence. Jack had heard talk of this terrifying gun. But not from a man who had endured it himself.

"Terble, Padre, it was terble. Took the spirit right out of us. How could we win against that? We lay there, baking, thirsty — dying of thirst in fact, and we wondered... what can we do? That pompom just kept right on, firing. I thought, thank God I'm still alive. After a bit, I learned to count twelve and I'd poke my head up and let the bastards have it again. But I hope never to live another day like that. And so cold at night — you've heard the talk? At three in the morning, it passed right through your sopping wet flesh, it grabbed at your innards..."

Jack nodded: he'd heard of the repeated storms that had burst over them during that awful week before the second battle. Wet and deathly cold, the soldiers lay below lightning flashes followed by violent crashes of thunder, lighting up battles below with shivering electric extravaganzas. How chill that wind must have blown...

"Hungry all the time. Your whole system cried out for some fish, or vegetables, and salt. And all the time, relieving ourselves, time after time, however you could do it without being shot, dysentery, diarrhea — well, we all suffered."

Jack shook his head.

Eamon stubbed out his cigarette and stretched. "Now water, of course we had plenty of that," he said, with a snappy crispness.

"You did?" Jack frowned.

"Let me tell you about our water, all right, Padre? The river — they drew it from the river. And we was well below that there Boer laager, as they called their camp. And by and by, I guess when them Boers could no longer stand the smell of their rotting carcasses, well, they threw their animals into the stream! So our water had, well, sort of a sweetish taste."

Jack grimaced.

"Oh yes sir. Later, I would stand on the bank and count thirty or forty dead horses or oxen... their hair rotted off, blue I guess with decay, and gangs of our soldiers working to move them on... so many carcasses, so rotted they broke in pieces when they pushed them off the rocks." He paused, and grinned. "Well, Padre, then," he paused again, "then the water had an even sweeter taste."

Jack could hardly believe his ears.

"And then," almost triumphantly, "afterwards, when I heard a pile of dead Boers, well, ninety in fact, were hauled out in one day as they floated down, that's when that beverage got pretty tasty, Padre. I could almost hear my mum say, "One lump or two, son?""

Jack felt sick; he needed to light his briar, too.

Eamon coughed and frowned. "Better hit the cot, Padre, can't face it any more — because after what, a week or ten days? Monday afternoon, yes, word came of the big night attack."

"That was it, then, the second battle?"

Eamon nodded. "That's when it came: the big Battle of Paardeberg."

* * *

The next morning Jack arrived at Big George's tent, and peered in. George lay still, his wound newly dressed, a rough blanket over his body. Had he ceased breathing?

Jack came over, sat down, and placed a hand on George's shoulder. The farm boy stirred and opened his eyes.

"Not long, Padre... before I go meet my Lord."

What could Jack say? Better not disagree; leave all him all his strength for telling the rest of his tale. "I've come with my pen, George. I'm ready."

George gave a barely perceptible nod. Jack could see that he was summoning up all his energy.

"Look, George, you don't have to tell me now, I can come back. I've heard part of the story, I've made notes — "

"No no," he gasped. "I've got to tell it, Jack. They've got to know. For the future..."

Jack put out a hand to calm him, and leaned forward.

"We'd been on a kopje, we called it 'Starvation Kopje' for

two days and nights, and we were all so hungry. Around six on Monday, we marched upstream." He paused, gathering himself. "At eight, we went in single file through pretty heavy undergrowth till we got to our forward trench. We lay down and got what sleep we could. At two they woke us up, and we had to fix bayonets... That meant one thing..." His eyes glazed and Jack wondered, could he finish this? Was he leaving now? Was this it?

Then his head turned and his eyes focussed again. "The rear rank got picks and shovels. Over the trench we went. Pitch black. So we grabbed a holt o' the next fella or his rifle, so's to keep ranks, eh? And we crept forward, quiet as possible. Never a word 'cept for whispered commands."

In spite of himself, Jack felt the excitement grow. He was right there beside Big George, and said so.

George nodded. "We kep' goin', we knew some of us would never come back, but we kep' on. The fellas behind, they followed, picks and shovels at the ready, rifles slung. What was going to happen?" He winced and closed his eyes.

George's voice grew louder: every spit of energy was rising into the telling. Was this shortening George's life? But George had given him a writing job to do, and do it he must.

"Well, without warning, the Boers started shooting. They poured on such a pile of lead right into us. Murderous, Padre, right as we were advancing. That's when I got it in the leg. Burned like hell. We all dropped. The bullets," he mumbled, "the bullets, they was everywhere, coming at us, I heard them snap through the air and ping off the rocks. They went past us, they struck, I never seen the like, Jack."

Nor had anyone, thought Jack: unique in all Canadian experience.

"Everyone hugged that ground so tight. Behind us, we heard the fellas digging in like crazy. Volley after volley, right through us. Unearthly, Padre, the crack of those flying bullets and the thump of those Krupp guns. Like the furies after us. I just lay and waited for my turn to come, but it didn't."

George lay quiet for a while. Jack reached out and smoothed his forehead with a cloth, bathed as it was in sweat. Big George gathered himself.

"Word came from the rear, the boys had dug a trench deep enough. We wriggled back, under all those bullets.

"The stretcher-bearers, in the dark, they grabbed the wounded, hauled them back there too. Gruesome, Padre. By a flickering candle, Fiset, he was right with us, doing his best. Had to blow out the candle because it drew action." George motioned and Jack gave him a sip of water. "You heard it all, Padre, the loud prayers, the cursing and angry screams... I even heard blood gurgle up and cut one poor fella off. Awful, even now, just an awful nightmare.

"Well, we kept firing, I'll tell you. My leg was hurting, by now, oh yes, it hurt like hell, but I wasn't going to let them know that. I kept putting my head up and taking a shot wherever I saw the flash of a gun. I got a few of them... And then some damn piece of shrapnel from a Krupp 75 ripped into my stomach. That was it.

"I stayed, numb, hurting like the dickens, but firing when I could, in that trench till dawn broke. Then we could see — my Lord! Jack, we were so close — probably fifty paces. So we waited for the order to charge with bayonets. I knew I couldn't, I couldn't move, or even stand. But I was ready, I was so ready..."

He seemed to lose his train of thought. His breaths were getting shorter. Not much strength left. Jack prayed that he could get it all out, not only for Annie and his farmer friends, but to relieve his soul.

"And you know what? Someone shouted. Look! A white rag

tied to a rifle barrel! Waving. Jack, waving! From a Boer trench. Surrender? No — watch out, could be a trick! But them Boers started coming out, man after man, they threw their rifles on the ground. Padre, we'd won."

Tears gathered in Jack's eyes as he finished writing.

"We'd won, Padre."

"Yes, Big George, you won. Everyone knows it. And I've got it all here. Written down." He wiped his face. What an ordeal. Just hearing it.

These last words seemed to let George relax.

Jack put down his pen and turned his head to look down at his friend. For some reason, George also turned and looked up at Jack. Their eyes met.

For one enormously long moment, Jack stared into those eyes. How deeply he looked into that soul! George longed to remain on earth. What a vast and utter despair at never seeing his beloved Annie again! Nor his little girls. That look said everything. Then thankfully, George turned away. And then was still. Deathly still.

Jack dropped his eyes, folded the paper, mumbled a short prayer, touched the rough, lifeless hand for a long moment, and rushed out of the hospital tent. He hurried, for some odd reason, out into the darkness, any darkness. Going down an incline, he tripped, fell into a shallow donga. He remained motionless, and tears started down his face.

The harder he tried to stop crying, the more they came. How he hated to say goodbye to this friend, yes, hated it. And this whole horrible war. He'd been holding himself in for so long; he'd tried so hard to stop the pain from reaching into his soul and twisting his heart. He had a job to do, after all. But one young lad after another, some teenagers, some his own age, some older, all going off to meet their end...

He crouched, curled over, rocked forward till his head touched the ground, and let a wild yell escape his throat. Chaplain Jack just let himself go.

What was it about this war? Why had it all started so well — and then ended so badly? And not even ended. It was still going on. So much more to face. So many more on their way out of this life and into the next. And all for what?

How he wished he were back in the Old Homestead, in Shigawake. How he longed for his safe parishes in Northern Quebec. When someone was old they died and you attended the family and you preached at their burial. But day after day this sorrowful ascent of youthful souls, one after another, and you doing your best to help them — it was all too much. Finally, just much too much.

He pounded the earth, tense and angry. Then he stayed frozen. Oh God, he prayed, why put me through this? Why?

At last, he found himself relaxing. He rolled over on his back and stared into the sky. There, the comforting Southern Cross marked the heavens with its celestial benediction. Blessing him too, he guessed. Yes, we all have our wounded ways to walk. And walk them we must. He lay for a long time, and then, taking a handkerchief from his pocket, dried his face, coughed, and sat up.

Back to the tent, back to duty, and back to the war.

Chapter Twenty-Two

Jack buried Big George the next morning outside Orange River Junction, and tried again to rejoin his regiment. But trains kept on coming with their loads of damaged humanity. Who should Jack see next, alighting on the platform, but his friend, Stanley Brown, the correspondent for the *Mail and Empire*. Stanley had marched with them, eaten with them, slept with them, and Jack knew he'd have news. "Stanley," he called out.

Stanley brightened. He hurried over, held out his hand. "Padre! Good to see you. How have you been making out down here?"

Jack shook his head. "Sorry state of affairs."

"I guess you wish you'd been with the boys."

Jack nodded. "But what a need for me here: so many lads passing in their last days on earth. Some even their last moments."

The two friends walked along the platform. "But what are you doing here, Stanley? Giving it all up? Going back?"

"No siree. I just wanted to see how our Royal Canadians are doing in hospitals back in De Aar."

Jack offered to show him around, but Stanley asked, "You don't happen to know where a man can get a bite first?"

The two walked to the canteen. Over a mug of tea and some hard tack, Stanley launched into what he'd seen, recently, especially after the surrender. Jack got out his pencil. "Funny me taking notes and you doing the talking. But you see, I promised Big George I'd get down this account for his family."

"George Dorsey? How is he?"

"Buried this morning." Jack paused, squeezed his eyes shut. Stanley nodded in sympathy.

"But not before I heard his side of Paardeberg, Stanley. What happened after that white flag went up. Were you there?"

Stanley nodded. "Once they surrendered, I was allowed to go forward." Stanley broke his hard tack into his tea, fished out a chunk and popped it in his mouth. "At first I wondered, is this really over? This terrifying procession of death? Can our boys finally draw a deep breath, without it being their last?

"Then I saw the enemy come up from below ground, Jack, like the last trumpet had blown the great reveille. Out they scrambled: dirty, ragged, ill-fitting clothes, as if called back from the dead. As they marched past I saw the true Boer: shambling along, casting sharp glances right and left from under his old felt hat, drawn well down. I picked out some blonde foreigners, maybe a Swede or German...

"And mingling with these whites, those poor black devils, unwilling slaves, for sure, carrying their bundles. Imagine, Jack! This crowd of gaunt, dishevelled beings who defied for ten long days and nights the finer discipline of the great British Empire! And for every life that left their ranks, they'd taken another for sure."

Jack was about to interrupt, but the words came flooding out. "I went out with a burial party. Two bodies lay not far apart: one, beautiful in its calmness. Serenity on every feature, Jack. A smile hovered on the half-parted lips; not a frown troubled that worn brow. As I gazed on the face, I saw nothing but happiness. Filled me with emotion: he'd known no fear, and I thought, if that were death, who can fear to die? I could have watched for hours that beautiful stillness, that peace."

Having finished his soggy hard tack, Stanley took another gulp of tea and sat back, and shook his head. "Then I turned to see another on his back on the blood-stained sand, hair matted with gore, pain gashed across his face. Chills ran down my backbone, I swear. I tried to yank my gaze away, but no, I could not. Why did one death appear so calm, and the next so hideous?"

He pulled himself together, downed the last of his tin mug of tea. "You know of course that this surrender of General Cronje happened on the very anniversary of Majuba Day, on February twenty-seventh?" Jack nodded. He knew that on that day nineteen years before, at the Battle of Majuba Hill, the Boers had humiliated the British army and thereby gained their independence. "At last, the stain upon the British forces had been gloriously blotted out by our Canadian boys. A knock-out blow to the Boers."

"Let us hope so," echoed Jack fervently, though he suspected it might go on and on.

"I went ahead and explored that *laager*, Jack me boy. What a stench! You know, 'twas practically a bunch of homesteads, all under the ground. In those trenches, we found such a conglomeration of household goods and munitions: beds and mattresses, blankets and cooking pots, rifles and cartridges, corn meal and flour, women's dresses, children's playthings... Oh yes, and sewing machines, believe it or not, and bibles and hymnbooks scattered all over. Everyone had a tin trunk, you know? Painted in gay colours.

"Above ground, they kept the big trek wagons and such, but they were burned and battered in heaps from the shrapnel. Covered in lyddite explosive, too — even the earth had a jaundiced appearance, you know, all yellowy. They'd lived and fought from those rabbit warrens. They had women down there too, Jack, oh yes, the General's wife, Mrs. Cronje, she'd been there.

"I got back in time to see Roberts welcoming her husband, the Lion of the Transvaal, sort of a low, thickset fellow in his short, rough overcoat and wide-brimmed hat. He took it off and I saw his partly bald head and newly trimmed whiskers. A broken man; well, he's now sixty-five. You know, Jack, he showed no interest in the meeting, even when Kitchener congratulated him in front of us all for having put up a jolly good fight — quite unstinting praise for what General Cronje had achieved with his farmers, untrained as they were."

"Now the British are sending him off somewhere?"

"Yes, St. Helen's Island, I believe." The train gave a long whistle, and Stanley leaped up. He wanted to get to De Aar too, he told Jack as he turned to run for the train.

Jack waved him goodbye. Then he carefully folded up the notes of Stanley's and George's stories. Not to be lost, nor ever forgotten.

* * *

After a good many more days ministering to these wounded, Jack got to join his regiment in Bloemfontein now that Roberts had occupied it. His first morning there, he went to report to Col. Otter's office in town. He had heard and indeed now could see in their faces how his regiment had been faring all the long way here, sleeping under old blankets while the storms kept raging; the water still bad and rations scarce, which had taken its toll on the men. They now had seen battle with their naked eyes, fought with their bodies as well as their minds, endured so much, and had become the best of hardened troops.

He became aware of his own neat uniform, worn but still

intact, as he saw how his troops themselves now were dressed: some in clothing from a dead Boer, or shirts with no buttons, trousers with no knees, or torn or patched with anything that could be scrounged, shoes mostly finished. And as well, he noticed something else. Were they reacting differently to him as he passed? Where was their former warmth? Their greetings were now almost non-existent. He put the thought from his mind. They'd been through so much and had not seen him for almost a month, that's all.

When Jack came to the orderly room to speak to Col. Otter, Adjutant Brown greeted him with a false show of affability. "Well, Padre Alford, how nice to see you! I do hope you had a nice rest while the rest of us engaged in some rather difficult warfare."

Jack looked up. "Not much of a rest, I assure you, Adjutant, but I believe I was helpful in my own small way."

"Oh, I'm sure you were the most tremendous help," he said, "back there in the rear, enjoying the town's pleasures..."

Such an unkind cut, Jack felt an urge to lash out and smack the fellow in the face. But he had trained himself to accept the usual barbs with a clerical dignity. "May I see Colonel Otter to report what I have been doing?"

"Of course. I'm sure Colonel Otter would be delighted to hear about all the little joys of life we've all been missing. Just something to lighten his day perhaps?" Adjutant Brown turned to knock on the inner door and announce Chaplain Alford.

Jack went in to find Otter as busy as ever. He looked up, nodded, and went back to his papers.

"I thought perhaps you would like to know what I have achieved, Colonel."

"No need to worry, Chaplain. Father O'Leary upheld all the best virtues of the chaplain unit. He was with us through thick and thin. He roamed that battlefield in the dead of night, tending to the wounded; he even on one occasion brought me news of the enemy's position. He was a marvel, so as a chaplain, you need not worry. You have been well represented."

Jack looked at the floor. "I did what you asked, sir. I tended the wounded and buried the dead. An awful business. But I also managed to get a few other things done. The commander at Orange River asked me to take on some administrative duties. I have them written here, if I may present it to you, Sir."

Otter nodded.

Jack went forward and laid the paper on his desk, and then saluted. "Is there anything else? Otherwise, I shall get back to my quarters."

"No, that will be all, thank you Chaplain."

Jack strode from the room, mind whirling: first he sends me away when I want to stay with the unit, and then shows no interest in what I've done. Is that the way of army life? Oh well, put it behind, Jack told himself.

He walked slowly back through the town, hardly noticing these unfamiliar buildings, and onwards about half a mile to the grassy plain where the regiment was encamped. He threaded through the tents, passing what seemed to be a party; no, a group doing their wash. But was he hearing aright? They were discussing him and Fullerton. Both had been absent for the recent battles.

"That's the kind of job for me," a young corporal was saying; Jack remembered the voice. "How would you like to be a clergyman, Fred? When fighting comes along, just get the hell out! Far behind the lines."

"No question about it, some fellas are good for nothing," a bass voice mumbled. "They lead a church service, but where's the good in that?"

"Now come along you two, when you talk about chaplains,

you're also talking about Father O'Leary, don't forget that." The speaker was younger, and fresh. "No one will ever forget him. No finer man ever walked God's earth."

"We're talking about the other two layabouts, Sonny," the Corporal said. "Off they go, back down Cape Town: bars and girls and everything that goes with it."

"Sure," echoed the bass, "at the sign of a dog collar, I bet them pretty whores down in Cape Town sure get excited."

"Damn right. Nothing stimulates a woman like somethin' she can't have."

"Who says they can't have it?" said the bass. "Who knows what them clergy got up to? That Padre Jack, quite a ladies man by his look."

"You still going to his service Sunday?" young Sonny asked. "A chaplain who doesn't share what you go through, then turns up to preach long after danger's past? That's not someone I listen to."

"Damn right," agreed the Corporal, "I'd rather turn Catholic, though it'd send my Poppa into an early grave. I like that O'Leary, I'd listen to him before I go to the likes of Chaplain Alford, taking off like that for Cape Town."

Jack had heard enough. He walked on, hoping they wouldn't see him. He'd followed orders, done his best, but in the troops' perception, just a layabout — a laggard who'd failed in his mission. Would he ever forget that conversation? Could he redeem himself? He felt so bitter — a new and unusual feeling for Jack: being regarded as a failure. And through no fault of his own.

Chapter Twenty-Three

The next day, Jack learned that mail had arrived from Canada and, luckily, an envelope for him. He shoved it in his pocket to read at lunch. It might help not having to speak to the other men.

Over his tin plate of stew, he pulled it out. How good it was here, in Bloemfontein to have a decent meal — well, decent by previous standards. Though nothing like the meal his mother would be preparing.

Dear Son,

We were pleased to get your letter from South Africa. The girls have been looking for news of your regiment. They figured out how to get their hands on some Montreal papers. They say you been having a bit of a rest. I imagine pretty soon you'll see real warfare. Make sure you don't get yourself hurt. We want you back in one piece.

Not much news here. Your brother-in-law Joe Hayes has big plans. He's started on a dam in the Hollow because he's planning on setting up a saw mill. He got a bunch of the boys to cut trees and haul them to the river bank for floating down in the spring. Your sister Maria tells me she's been feeding eight or ten workers as well as her children. I guess that's how he gets them cheap.

Harvey Manderson's old grist mill had a dam, but Joe wants his lower down. He plans on flooding part of the

Hollow. I told him fine by me. He hopes to saw boards for fish-boxes for Robins in Paspebiac. A new mill will come in real handy for Shigawake, too. No more hauling logs to Bonaventure.

Joe and Maria's had a new baby boy, and named him after our family name, Alford Hayes. Going to be a muddle, I guess. The other girls are fine. Winnie teaches up at the corner school, and Lilian wants to take off somewhere else to teach next year. She's got a wanderlust like you. Jeannie's too young to go but she's sure planning on it.

There's more talk of the railway coming. Pile of excitement for sure. Terrible lot of fellas coming to build it, I guess. But I'll believe that when I see it. They haven't even asked me for right-of-way across our Hollow.

Mac and Clare are both taking over the farm-work. Earle is doing more and more, and your little brother Eric runs around like he owns the place. Your mother spoils him terble. Next door, the Byers is fine — good, hard-working children they got there, and John's farm next over is doing good. I got to close now 'cause it's milking time.

Oh, you got a letter from some fella called Clayton on the North Shore. Says he's a full teacher now, and follows in your footsteps up there. Got a degree and all.

We look for news when you can send it.

Everyone here sends you best wishes. Come back soon.

Your father, Jim.

Jack had been so involved in the letter he'd forgotten to eat. And now the stew was cold. Oh well, he spooned it down with some relish, nonetheless. Always hungry, it seemed; the rations were hardly bounteous, even in Bloemfontein.

Now to work, visiting the hospitals. The largest buildings in town had been converted: Grey College, the OFS barracks, the Dames Institute and other suitable structures were all flying the Red Cross flag. A few of the many overseas nurses and surgeons with little red and white arm badges were attending the patients. These two weeks after Paardeberg, Bloemfontein had been swept by a massive and unanticipated epidemic of enteric fever. Far too many had been taken sick for the small medical staff and orderlies to cope with. Conditions in most hospital encampments were the worst Jack had seen so far. He soon found out that the incubation period for the fever came exactly at that interval between the many troops drinking from the Modder river and now.

And so Jack began his new rounds in one of the hospitals. After lunch, he got the surprise of his life. There lay old Father O'Leary. Well, at fifty, Jack didn't think of him as old. Old Poppa was sixty-five, after all, and could pitch up onto the hay-rack with the best of them, walk two miles back in the woods to cut trees, then walk out and milk three cows and get firewood ready at the end of it, all in a day's work. Tall, lean, with a big walrus moustache, Old Poppa was fit as a fiddle. But the men persisted in saying "old" Father O'Leary.

He wanted to go and see him, but would the little priest be angry like the others? After all, Jack had left the brunt of the ministering to him. Jack paused. He just didn't feel like another confrontation. But... this was a brother of the cloth, and obviously sick.

When he came up, O'Leary broke into a weak grin. "I been struck by the enteric, Lord help me."

"What a piece of work!" Jack sat down. "What are they doing for you, Peter?"

"At least they're not starving me. Doses of castor oil, and that blessed sulphate of magnesia. They say I'll make it through, but

I've seen some of the boys, and I know what I'm in for. Not that pleasant."

"Not pleasant at all, no, but with the help of the Lord, you'll survive." Well, Jack thought, at least he has his share of charity. "And I'll certainly attend your bedside every day, and stand in for any of these useless orderlies."

O'Leary smiled weakly, then clutched his stomach as another convulsion shook him.

To take his mind off the present circumstances, Jack continued, "I hear you were a big hero at Paardeberg. The boys are full of your exploits. We're all proud of you."

"Thank you, Jack. Too bad, you weren't up there with us. You should have been, but you had to obey your orders. I heard about that."

He dropped his eyes. "You heard? The men seem to think I'm a coward." He paused. "I was afraid you would, too."

"Don't say that Jack. You did your duty. I know that."

Jack sighed. "Nothing like seeing your chaplain out there on the battlefield beside you, dodging bullets. I guess I've let them down." Jack could not suppress the pain that flooded through him at the thought.

"Jack, you haven't. You did your duty, never you mind. The Lord is with us both."

Jack felt good at the unexpected warmth — a companion in arms who had some understanding of what he had been going through. So far the two of them had not had many substantial conversations: usually matters of administration — when to hold services, when to share hospital duties, whom to visit separately and that sort of thing. But now Jack felt another kind of closeness. His friend was in pain and he would do all he could to help. "Would you like me to write a letter for you, Father? To your family, perhaps?"

O'Leary shook his head. "My parents are long gone, Jack. I've got two brothers out there in Ireland, but you know, once you're in the Lord's service, you can't take a wife. I've had to learn to accept just serving the Lord alone, with no one beside me."

Must be hard, thought Jack, to do that all your life. "Well I've got a pretty big family back on the Gaspe. Yesterday I got a letter. So good to hear from them all." Jack sat silently, remembering his family safe and sound back there, and here he was, subject to the slings and arrows of an outrageous attitude from the lads, as some famous writer once said.

"You never told me much about them, Padre," O'Leary said. "Who've you got back there?"

Jack told Peter about his relatives, about his homestead, and about the Hollow, and his growing up. Odd they'd never exchanged this kind of information before.

"And what about a pretty little fiancée, Jack? Surely you've got someone waiting for you back home?"

Jack shook his head. He paused. Should he mention the sublime Lorna? He was about to put the thought out of his mind and then the words just started to take shape. He told the good Father all about her. And how he'd missed his one chance. Finally, how he had managed to get over it.

"Well, there'll be another one, I'm sure," said O'Leary. "But thank you, Jacko, for telling me. Takes my mind off my own troubles."

"Now look here, Peter," Jack said, "you know very well that they'll cure your enteric. Not a lot of fellows are dying of it, although they come pretty close." He cracked a smile.

"Well, Jacko, if it's His will I'm supposed to go meet Him, so be it. But like you, I think he has more work for me here."

"I pray so," said Jack. "Now I'm feeling guilty — so enjoyable sitting here with you, but a lot of other lads need my services.

Maybe the first thing I'll do is see some of your flock. How would that sit?"

Jack saw the old man's eyes glisten. "Mighty fine, just mighty fine, Jacko." He proceeded to tell Jack who he'd been seeing before coming down with this wretched disease, and told him where they were. Jack went off to do this new duty for Peter and his God.

* * *

It wasn't all that easy. Some Roman Catholic soldiers greeted him with suspicion, being fond of Peter and all he had accomplished under that blizzard of bullets, which of course Jack, to them, had avoided, and others perhaps warned by their leaders back home to have no truck with devils from the breakaway Church of England. In any case, the rest of the afternoon turned out to be less pleasant than he'd hoped. Most of the Catholics did their best to be polite, but with such a visible effort Jack felt it better to leave them alone. One or two did welcome him, and another even asked for confession and absolution. Jack did not know the correct words to use, but he sat and cupped his ear by the dying soldier's mouth and heard of some minor sin troubling the lad, a sin Jack felt better left unsaid, for it did no damage to his soul. And he told him so.

When the afternoon was over, he was about to go into the mess tent when he saw a group of soldiers turn away from him. Would it never end? He decided against eating and went back to his tent, got onto his cot, and pulled out his Bible. Perhaps between its covers he would find solace. But even turning the onionskin pages, his mind still churned up a storm. Torture indeed, and all the nastier for it being unjustified.

Chapter Twenty-Four

On Friday morning, now that Jack was in a proper town, the capital of the Orange Free State, he came up with the idea of having his Sunday service in an actual house of God. He knew that the authorities in Quebec might take umbrage at his decision, but after all, this was wartime. Might even deflect some of the hostility.

A Dutch Reformed Church was not far from the campsite. So what, he thought, if it hadn't been consecrated by a Church of England bishop, and so considered lacking direct linkage to the Apostle Peter, it was still a church. He made inquiries and found his way to the house of the leading elder. The door was opened by a tall, somewhat surly, Boer. By now Jack knew to make allowance for these different characteristics: none of the Boers were actually happy-go-lucky, cheerful souls. No sir.

Jack introduced himself and after a few pleasantries, brought up the subject. "I've seen that wonderful church of yours, and I wondered if there might be a short space of time next Sunday for me to hold a service for our Canadian boys?"

The man didn't even have the grace to think the matter over. "Our congregation would not like that, Pastoor. We work to keep our church sanctified. Enemies of the Orange Free State would desecrate it. I mean no harm to you, Pastoor, but that's the way it is." He gave a slight bow, held out his hand to shake Jack's, and turned to re-enter his dwelling.

So that was it, then. Failed again. Would he never be a successful Padre? This downward path was so slippery, he seemed quite unable to return to the straight and narrow road he favoured.

In the end Jack made do with the building commandeered for a mess hall. Sunday mornings, the troops saw to their own breakfasts, apart from cups of coffee that the mess provided. He got up early to put up a makeshift altar.

He liked to prepare with some meditation and prayers as he was getting into his robes. But he'd had to leave them behind in Belmont. In the kitchen he still found a nook and composed himself, wondering about the service: who would come? Perhaps no one? Well, likely it would be smaller than usual. But he'd invited his Catholic patients, as promised, and even arranged for the daily orders to announce that all faiths and creeds would be welcome.

When the time came for the ceremonies, he found himself unduly nervous. A small but goodly number did turn up, and it passed uneventfully until his sermon. That's when his doubts and uncertainties made manifest. No longer a firm and often powerful orator, he let his self doubts betray themselves in minor hesitations and confused thinking. Anyone perceptive enough would declare him as inept. He cut the sermon short, which did no harm, certainly, and went on with the second half of the service, the Eucharist. As he himself took the bread and the wine, he earnestly asked for help. "Please, Lord, help me with my new suffering." But no help came in any blinding flash.

* * *

Sundays were usually days off, the afternoons given over to impromptu sports. Although one of the better athletes, he was not invited to take part. But they knew he loved playing. Was this disdain spreading? At every turn, his private anguish flourished.

Come on, stop wallowing in pity, he told himself, just go take in the sights. You're in a foreign country, so be a tourist.

Bloemfontein, although the capital of the Orange Free State, was not large by any standards. About a half a mile square, the town had a few broad streets lined with trees and a good assortment of public buildings. He tried taking an interest in the shop fronts, the style of homes, and then reached Market Square where only yesterday, a number of bullock carts had been tethered, unloading meagre produce. Now, being the Sabbath, it seemed empty, until one establishment across the square caught his notice. A few officers of the Imperials stood out in front, talking. No Canadians. He walked over.

Bless my soul, a hairdressing establishment! But much more, it sold ladies' perfumes and had an interesting display of Meerschum and briar pipes on sale inside. He read the sign: "J.J. Beranek, the Orange Free State Toilet Club. Baths, hot and cold, with showers. Razors of the best quality kept in stock, and strops" — surely one of the finer "Tobacconist, Hairdresser and Perfumers" he'd seen. And open on the Sabbath.

He exchanged perfunctory greetings with the officers, some of whom bore the scent of having just visited the establishment, and went in. The woman behind the desk took his name; if he came back in an hour and a half, the barber would look after him. So off he went, not stopping to talk with the officers, who viewed him condescendingly as a mere colonial. Even his clerical collar failed to elicit respect.

He passed a large building with a small watchtower and a curious striped pattern of alternating red brick and white stone — the post and telegraph office. And then saw the spire of a church that as he approached turned out to be the cathedral. He went in and found it empty, for the services had been held in the morning. Well, he thought, at last an open house of God.

He walked down the aisle between three massive arches on

each side, white stone at the bottom and brick above. The linked wooden chairs with woven seats would probably hold two hundred parishioners. Was it ever full? Entering the chancel, he noticed the absence of a pulpit, but liked the tall, upright candelabra and three high vertical windows, a tradition in this sort of church, about half the size of Holy Trinity Cathedral in Quebec but all one needed here. He went up to the altar rail and knelt.

He took a long time composing himself. Then, he did ask for help. "I really need it, Lord," prayed Jack. "I feel terrible." His mind turned over a number of items, slowly one by one. "When I search myself, I see that I'm really angry. I'm angry at the injustice of it all, angry also at the way my men are treated by their suppliers — and I guess I haven't yet come to terms with all this killing and maiming." He paused. "You know what? I'm even angry at You, for allowing all this to happen."

He bowed his head. There, now, I've said it. Angry at the Saviour. Horrifying thought. But true.

So what am I to do? It's up to You, Jack thought. And he let the silence fall.

In this modest, almost humble, cathedral, he waited. Waited for the Lord's voice to arrive — in a cloud, or in booming thunder, or as a soft whisper.

Nothing.

He remained a good while. The longer he knelt, the more pain he felt. Worthless? Almost. He had always sought to do the right thing. But now, there seemed no way out.

Only one other time had he felt like this: on the Canadian Labrador after his Lorna had left. What had he done then? Thrown himself into a frenzy of activity as a kind of absolution. But here, no frenzy of activity lay open as an option. Nothing, it seemed, could stop his slide into these forbidden murky depths of despair — a sin in itself.

He rose, bowed to the altar, and slouched out of the cathedral.

Once in the barber's chair, he struck up a conversation. His other haircuts had been on the Canadian Labrador with Uncle Tom Styles who cut hair in his kitchen, or Aristide Gagnon in Blue Point, who hardly ran an elegant barbershop, though it was warmed by a wood stove and made cosy by a spittoon.

"Well, I'm pleased to find you open — especially on the Sabbath. It means that I can even indulge myself."

"You and everyone else, it seems." The barber swept the cloth over Jack's head and fastened it round his neck. "I'm Jewish, so my Sabbath was yesterday. Mr. Beranek is a strict Protestant, but he allows me to do this because I can't work on his busy day, which in fact is Saturday. Just as well, too, we've never been so crowded, all these troops in town. After you came in, I had to put a stop to more customers. As it is I'll be working till late." He asked him how he liked his hair styled and would he like a shave?

"Oh yes please, a shave. I understand you have baths here?"

"The very finest. I'll go book one for you after this."

Jack reflected on this new-found delight: was it helping rid him of his despondency? In fact, no, this attention to personal cleanliness, although next to godliness, was only making him feel more dissatisfied. Here he was, attending to his body like any superficial narcissist. Another step on his descent?

But then again, it did have a calming effect: the smell of the soap as the barber lathered up his face; his pleasing chat about the features of his adopted town, asking Jack if he had seen this or that sight.

"It's nice to know that not everyone in the Capital is against us," Jack mumbled, "except for a few hostile stares from some who see us as occupiers."

"Most of us never asked for war, no doubt about that," said the barber, who'd introduced himself as Abraham. "Like Cape

Town, our population is divided. Even those who didn't go off to fight, like me, are distrusted. But you, Padre, what do you think about all this war business? Since you're here, you a Christian must approve of your troops coming here to slaughter us?"

Jack could see himself being drawn into another political argument, which was the last thing he needed now. Should he tell this barber about his inner turmoil? No sir, not right now. He'd have to face quite enough of it when he got back to the camp.

"You know, Abraham, I'd rather not discuss these aspects right now. It may end up as being a beginning for a great new partnership between the British and the Boers."

They changed the subject, and before too long, Chaplain Jack emerged with a stylish haircut, pampered and clean, and at once set off back into town. His pay from the last three months had arrived, and some of it jangled in his pockets. Never having had any sense of personal wealth, now he felt almost rich. Oh yes indeed, he was going straight to hell.

No question of going back to face the hostile stares of his comrades. No, wander about, he decided, and soon spotted what appeared to be an Olde English Tearoom. Why not have a cup of tea and with it, a little cake? Sample a simple pleasure — on his primrose path to damnation.

Into the modest, one storey building he went. It had been converted into a shop with a small assortment of rather unappetising baked goods. A young woman stood behind the counter in a dark floor-length skirt and blue blouse, sleeves fastened at the wrists with pretty white ribbons. She had done her blond hair up in a bun, and her slightly pudgy face radiated a kindness, through which seeped a kind of pain. But she was putting up a good front.

"May I have a cup of tea and a cake?" Jack asked.

"I'm sorry, Pastoor," she murmured, "I was just going to close. It's past tea time." She turned away to blow her nose, and leaned against her counter.

Jack paused, then offered, "I'm sorry if it's too much trouble. But I could eat it quickly. And since no one else is here... Why not join me? "

She remained head bowed, and then turned and gave him a solid look. "Why yes, why not? Why not make another pot of tea? Yes, Pastoor, let us share a cup. But first, I'll hang out a closed sign. You will be my last customer."

While she brewed up the tea, Jack chose a cake and sat down. He had noticed a wedding ring on her finger and also that she seemed unaccustomed to serving. Had her husband left to join in the defence of Pretoria, which Roberts intended to attack once his troops rested? Or had he been already wounded? Even captured? Or killed? He was away, in any case. Should he ask? No. Too forward.

She brought the teapot and cups over and sat down, first giving him another searching look. "So what religion might you be, Pastoor?"

"I'm Canadian. I mean..." he chuckled, "I'm Church of England. I'm rather muddled these days."

"Are you now? Well, so am I..." She forced a smile. "I suppose that's not hard to see."

Jack wanted to reach out and comfort her. Then a voice inside him shouted, so do it! He put his hand on hers and clasped it.

She clamped her eyes shut. Then she released her hand and lifted the tea to her delicate and full lips. A bloom had begun on her rounded cheeks, perhaps from emotion. She reached over and broke off a piece of his cake and popped it in her mouth. "I don't know why Hermanus sold this. I never liked it."

In spite of himself Jack smiled, and then started to laugh. He had no idea why it struck him as funny, but it did. Imagine selling cakes that you hated!

It struck her as funny, too. She smiled and began to giggle. In a deft way, she reached out and gave his hand a little squeeze.

They both sipped again, and sat there in silence.

"I feel better already," she said in a surprised tone.

"A laugh will always do that. Though I have no idea what was funny."

"Me neither."

Had they just fallen into an instant friendship?

Chapter Twenty-Five

They talked for about an hour at the table, discussing the rains, the onset of winter in a couple of months, and Jack's very different winters in northern Quebec, all inconsequential stuff. He learned how they dealt with the cold, and how they tried to deal with the heat. Her father was Dutch and had brought his family here to start a new life before she was born. But speaking of him, pain flickered over her features.

Jack told her something of his Old Homestead on the Gaspe coast, and tried to describe exactly where it was. Not a great success, for she knew little of Canada, thinking it populated by Wild West bandits and fur trappers. Well, that's how they were known, Jack supposed. To feed into that, he told her a little of the Canadian Labrador, and was gratified to see her blue eyes widen as she listened, rapt, at his stories of driving huskies and being snow-bound by blizzards, and nearly dying as he crossed ice floes on the shores of the mighty St. Lawrence River.

For a while, they seemed entranced with their respective environments and forgot their troubles. This was the first real Boer person that Jack had come close to, as indeed he was her first Canadian. Before they knew it, an hour or more had passed. She got up and looked out. "It's dusk already!"

"Yes." With sinking heart, Jack realized it was time to return. "I've got to be going."

She rose, and then paused, thinking. "I have an idea you've had no home cooking for a good long time?"

Jack choked. "A good long time? Not since last summer on the Gaspe. I've completely forgotten what a real meal tastes like."

"Well, if I'm not being too forward, I would say that you're about to taste one again." She stood looking at him, expectantly.

Goodness gracious, he thought, how lucky! "With your permission, I'd be only too happy to taste home cooking."

Jack followed as she went through the back of the shop and down a short passageway into her home. She unlocked the door and they went in together. She went across to the shelf and brought a lamp to the table to light it. "You know," Jack said, "we haven't even been introduced. What's your name?"

"Catherina Elisabeth. And yours?"

Catherina! Not possible! And Elizabeth? What did all this mean? "I'm John Macpherson Alford. You know, Catherina, Catherine is my grandmother's name." She looked up, startled. It seemed to have struck her with the same force.

"And what's more, my great-grandmother was called Elizabeth, Elizabeth Garret. My grandmother Catherine died in 1863, before I was born, of course. But I grew up with traces of her all over the house: the wool blankets she wove; some of my mother's clothes had been hers; the favourite crock we kept our molasses in; that churn that my father had given her when he was young and just back from Montreal, where he had worked one winter. He never talked about that, but my mother did often talk about her churn. In its day, it was a marvel. The first kind of churn that didn't require up and down pumping." He demonstrated.

She shook her head, surprised. "A real churn? We get our butter from the factory here. A butter factory. It's cheaper than from the store. We use a lot of butter in the tea room."

While Catherina busied herself getting the supper, he pondered all this. Surely the fact that she bore his grandmother and great-grandmother's names had a significance. But what? Don't think about it too much, he told himself, but still, a feeling grew that eluded his understanding.

"And you won't believe this, John, but my grandfather's name was the same as yours, Johannes: John in Dutch."

They both stood for a moment in silence looking at each other. Oh Lord, thought Jack, what is happening?

She whirled and went to find a saucepan in the cupboard, and proceeded to prepare the vegetables.

"Here, let me help." Jack rose to stand beside her.

"Have you ever peeled carrots?"

"Not exactly." Jack felt foolish. "But I could learn."

"Here John, set the table instead." She pointed to a drawer, and Jack took out the cutlery, and then looked through a couple of other drawers for napkins.

"All my friends call me Jack."

"Jack it is then. But no one calls me Cat."

"Of course not. Catherina has such a lovely lilt, I prefer it to Catherine."

"Just a minute, Jack. I had almost forgotten... "She bent and from a cupboard beneath the counter produced a bottle labelled *Mampoer*, a distilled fruit brandy. "I think, with what we've both been through..."

"Me too? Am I that obvious?" interrupted Jack. "I was sure I hid my problems rather well."

"No, Jack, you obviously haven't been anywhere near a woman for a good long while. We always know what our man is thinking."

What welcome words! During the evening, being with her

like this, even his depression might evaporate. And he hoped it would go some way towards relieving hers.

* * *

"My Lord, this is delicious!"

Jack savoured every mouthful. He didn't want to chew too fast, because then he'd have to swallow, and that would be one more mouthful gone. She had fashioned for him the traditional Boer dish, *potjiekos*.

"You didn't make this from scratch?"

"Oh no! Traditionally, it was cooked by *Voortrekkers* in a three-legged iron pot. You have to keep it going, adding meat and vegetables, which I just did, to the rice and water, and simmer it for hours. It's been going for days. Usually I don't feel like cooking when I'm alone."

And a good bottle of wine. They had already made a dent in the *mampoer*, which was so much stronger than Jack had anticipated. "This *mampoer*, what is it exactly?"

"Home-made. Hermanus makes it once a year, several bottles. You mustn't drink too much. Some call it *witblits*..."

"I hope it hasn't 'blitzed' my 'vits'!" One of Jack's many flaws was that he did enjoy a little drink from time to time. Or was it a flaw? Only if he drank to excess, he told himself. Well, before the dinner (the preparation had taken over an hour) he had certainly done that. And now, this delicious red wine: lovely, deep, rich taste. "You certainly make good wine here in Africa."

"In the Free State, you mean, dear Jack. Thank you! And *witblits* actually does mean white lightning, so we know to watch out." She lifted her wine, held by the lamplight so it glowed, and then took a mouthful. "My husband saved this. It was to be for our second wedding anniversary." And then in spite of herself she clenched her eyes shut. Poor Catherina. Poor Boer Catherina.

Jack caught the cue. Five years being a parish priest, he knew what to ask and when. He began a gentle searching. She had been a schoolteacher. She had wanted none of this marriage business, no truck with men, she confessed, even though, with those angelic features, blue eyes and fair hair, she must've been the mark for a good many young Boers. Much like his grandmother Catherine, Jack presumed.

He was glad they'd begun eating because, with all the *Mampoer* earlier, he felt a bit off balance. Goodness! It would never do for a clergyman to be without his wits. These warm spoonfuls of stew, with its chunks of turnips, other root vegetables and pork, such an amazing taste, it all made him feel better. "Astonishing dish, Catherina," he said. "You certainly know how to live well here."

"I'm glad you like it, Jack." He saw that she wanted to go on, but had stopped herself. He looked at her: soft, rounded features in this candlelight, with the lamp on the sideboard highlighting her blonde bun. What was happening? Everything so perfect. But at the same time, so dangerous.

Should he go ahead, venture onto this potentially risky ground? Or rather, try to help Catherina overcome her malaise. He sipped more of his wine. Yes, discover what exactly she was repressing. "You asked me how long it was since I had a home cooked meal. I told you, a long time. My mother prepared a lovely going away feast for me last time I was home. That was last summer. I miss my family so much." No no, don't grow maudlin, pull yourself out of it — it's Catherina you're supposed to be helping. "We had lots of relatives come. Old Poppa killed a porker. Not as tasty as this pot-what?"

"*Potjiekos.*"

"No, but it sure was good. How Old Poppa loves crackling!

Mama knows how to roast a pork, no doubt about that." All right, Jack, now time to probe. "So now I'm wondering, when was the last time you sat down to a family meal?" There he'd asked. Though he hadn't added, "with your husband." She looked at him, her blue eyes making a question. In his, he hoped she saw only warmth, and even yearning.

She dropped her eyes, took a rather large a gulp of wine, and answered, "Six weeks ago. We had a terrible fight. Hermanus was leaving and I did not want him to go. 'What's wrong?' I asked, 'with having the British running the state? We would still have our restaurant. People would still come. We would still have to pay taxes. You know, we both treat our Kaffirs better than most. That would not change. They'd still work for us. Just because the British give them freedom doesn't mean they're going to stop work. They'll still have to earn a living.'

"But Hermanus was angry, furious at the British, in fact. For my sake he had tried to stay home. But once the war was going strong, he decided to leave." She took another drink of wine. Jack remained silent. "And so, I prepared him this dish."

She glanced at Jack and then looked back at her plate, and took another mouthful. "He always loved it. He loved *potjiekos*. And so, although I was still angry at him, I prepared it for our last meal."

"Did you fight over dinner?" Jack asked.

She shook her head. "We just remained silent. It was awful. Because he knew I loved him as much as I could. He was rather abrupt, you know. I think he loved me in his own way, too. But we did have a good life together. I had settled in. And, as a matter of fact," her lip trembled, "he was all I had."

She took a breath. "You see, my brother died a while ago. My mother went when I was young. So I used to live with my vader and take care of him. But even before this war was declared, vader went off to learn how to fight. He trained with them, and then, they came and told me... They told me that he..." She stopped speaking, put her hands to her face.

Jack reached out and rubbed her shoulders gently. She took his hand and clung to it with a fierce grip. They remained silent like that, Jack saying nothing.

Then she pulled herself together, took another large gulp of wine, and cleared her throat. "So Father was killed right at the beginning. That was another reason I didn't want Hermanus to go. Not the perfect husband, no. But certainly, from what my women friends told me, better than most. I didn't want to lose him." She was managing to keep herself under control. "Please, shall we talk about this later? Let us have this dinner as though it's all very normal. Let's eat as if we knew each other all our lives. Let's have fun, drink, and forget the past."

"What a splendid idea!" Said Jack. "And there's so much I need to forget too. That's why," he cleared his throat and took a swig of wine, "that's why I would love to do just what you say. Forget..." And enjoy his dinner with this beautiful woman.

Chapter Twenty-Six

"Now what's this?" Jack looked down at another tasty dish.

Catherina had gotten up, taken their empty plates into the kitchen, and brought back dessert. "*Malva Pudding*. It's Dutch. I also... I also made it for the last..."

She helped them both, and Jack tasted it. "Marvellous!"

"I thought I had better make up for that awful cake I gave you at tea-time." She giggled.

He smiled, and went on eating. They reverted to discussing inconsequential things: their backgrounds, and what little she remembered from a trip to Holland that her father had arranged when she was quite young. Jack revealed more about his ministry, about Bishop Andrew Hunter Dunn, and what other things he had been doing in Northern Quebec. They kept off the subject of the war.

Finally, when the two candles on the table had burned down and they had eaten their fill, Catherina got up. "I'll make tea, Jack. You go sit on the sofa and put your feet up."

"Wonderful," breathed Jack, and got up. But he found his head spinning. He made his way gingerly to the sofa and sat rather suddenly. Were his wits in fact blitzed? Or was he falling in love? He didn't know which — only that it was delightful: being cared for in a cozy home, far from war, far from those "comrades" who misunderstood him, just as if he'd been lifted out of time into another glorious dimension. There was Catherina in her kitchen, making tea just the way his mother used to. Or indeed, Lorna. No no no, forget her. In any case, all delightful.

In came Catherina bearing two cups of tea. She sat beside him on the sofa. "Tell me what has been bothering you, Jack."

Jack winced. "It would take a lot of telling. Perhaps we should still just enjoy the evening."

"No, I want to know. What could a wonderful warm man like you have to regret?"

Should he tell her? His job, after all, was to help her into a kind of happiness. That's what clergymen did. They didn't pour out their souls. But then again, she did ask. And she had a right to know; she had cooked him a delicious meal and lifted him right out of himself.

So he did tell her the bare bones: how he had been ordered by his commanding officer to go back to minister to the wounded and those suffering from enteric fever. And how he had sat with them, some dying, day after day, until he could take it no more. And then, the most unkind cut of all, he told her, staring straight ahead, body frozen: those men who had returned from battle alive and safe now resented his absence and blamed him for being a coward.

"I can understand, Jack." She nodded. "Just so unfair."

Jack felt close to tears, like a little boy again. Was it the drink? "Yes," he said, "unfair..." He heaved another great sigh and took a sip of tea. "And then, of course, being a clergyman and having to watch the killing, and the cruelty, all of which goes so much against everything I..." He shook his head.

Well, at least he had spilled it out. And to someone who cared.

Both of them remained silent, and then he broached the other enormous question. "So what happened to Hermanus?"

"He left six weeks ago."

"But surely, he'll be back soon?"

She shook her head. "No, Jack, he won't ever be back. They told me he's missing, and I know very well what that means. I'll never see him again. I'll never be able to say I'm sorry for the mean things I did to him, I'll never be able to tell him how happy I was at the little things he did for me, little moments of tenderness that I know cost him the world. He was brought up to be strict, hard-working, God-fearing, and to put nothing ahead of striving for his family."

"And you never had children?"

"No. We were together just three years. I didn't want them yet. And you see, being a teacher before, I knew something about how we could still enjoy each other without bearing any of the fruit."

Jack reached out and touched her hand and she clutched his. "Such an awful thing," he said, "this war..."

"Yes," she answered. "But on that last night, why didn't I say to him all the things that I should have said? Why didn't I say, you've been a good husband, Hermanus? I could have. Why didn't I ask him to forgive my acts of meanness, my bursts of anger. Oh dear Jack, I'm so unhappy." She let tears fall.

Jack could not restrain himself: he put one arm around her and held her tight. She sobbed and sobbed. He comforted her with soothing words, stroking her, and as she calmed a little, she reached up and kissed him.

What a feeling! He turned his head, found her forehead, and kissed her. Then she lifted her mouth, found his, and suddenly their lips were pressing into each other's, two longing beings seeking respite from such a long, deep loneliness.

The last thing that night Jack remembered, after he woke in the morning, was lying on Catherina's bed while she helped him out of his uniform and then placed a pillow under his head and caressed his brow. Just the way his mother used to. Was that why he had reached up both his arms?

She leaned into them, and then closer and finally got into the bed next to him. He held her close.

Oh yes. Jack the clergyman then gave himself up to such a forbidden pleasure, such an extraordinary delight. Surely the primrose path direct to an eternal bonfire.

Now he opened his eyes and saw her standing over him, sunlight flooding through the curtains and over her flowered flannel dressing gown. She held a cup of tea.

"Here, dear Jack, I'll put this on your side table. But you must go back to sleep; you need it. If you don't drink the tea, no matter. But now, I must open the café for morning coffee. I'll be back at lunchtime, when I close. You just lie here and forget about everything. Thank you for helping me forget. Thank you, my darling Jack. Thank you." She put down the tea and turned and closed the door behind her.

Jack tried to sit up, but his head was spinning. Had he drunk too much? Oh yes, and that was a big enough mistake, and well, even a sin. As he lay there, he remembered his comrades back at camp. Now he was away without permission. He'd broken military rules. And by loving her with his whole body, he had broken an even worse biblical injunction.

Don't think about the future, Jack told himself, you badly need sleep, and as if to prove himself right, after a gulp or two of tea, he drifted off into another world once more.

* * *

Jack became vaguely aware of someone moving about the room. He woke up.

Catherina turned as she saw him open his eyes. "I'm back. Good, you slept. I'll bring us in some bread and cold *boerewors* (sausage) for lunch, and we can have a snack. Then I must go back to the tea-shop again for the afternoon. But no reason for you to move; you stay here, don't get up, just rest, and then I'll make us another special dinner again tonight."

An angel. But how could an angel appear when he had broken rules left, right and centre, sinned atrociously, and slowly but surely descended into an infernal abyss?

Later that afternoon, Jack treated himself to a lengthy bath. Soaking in the warm water, he avoided thoughts of Otter and the camp — tomorrow he'd deal with all that. Right now just savour this unexpected experience. How extraordinary to lie with the voluptuous and experienced Catherina! His previous adventures (as a youngster on the Gaspe or during his first year at university) had been in haymows or woods, buggies or sleighs, most awkward and unfulfilling.

What would it be like, he wondered, to stay in Bloemfontein? Other soldiers had decided to stay. Wouldn't he love to live here and work in the tea-shop beside this Catherina. Among the enemy? Well, that did seem such a foolish thought now — the enemy! Oh yes, these people his fellow Canadians had come over to shoot and kill. How easily he had been manipulated back then. What about that?

But were he to stay, what about his calling? Could he ever give up his cherished vocation? Perish the thought! He had seen the cathedral, so there must be a bishop. Would that prelate not accept Jack with open arms? Not if this wicked applicant had come with armed force to destroy the Free State. Well then, what about some other religion, the Dutch Reformed Church perhaps? Most churches were aching to get trained men. But he didn't even speak the language.

Just listen to me, he thought, as he lifted himself from his bath and began to dry himself. Crystal mountains in air — and all for the love of a beautiful woman. Well, was it love? Oh yes, what else? He had so little experience. He thought that's what he must be feeling: with all her gentleness, her kindness, and that wonderful time they'd had last night. The way she cared for him — wasn't all that love?

But look! When you were so attached to Lorna, he lectured himself, you made no move, well, no practical move, and she had left. So don't let this second opportunity slip past. Yes, but first, should he not find out how she felt? Hint, at least? Get her feelings? But wouldn't these become apparent if they spent more time together? Of course, but how could he do that? He'd be off soon, if not into the fight, then into the military lock-up. Could he put her through another loved one leaving?

Don't be silly, he told himself. Here you are, facing months, possibly years, in jail for being absent without leave. A deserter, surely. You could even be shot for that. And what about your bishop? Career ruined! Should he ask her to marry him under those conditions? No, better wait until he faced this new future squarely. Spinning with thoughts, he dressed and went in to her rooms to wait for her.

Once again they had a most wonderful dinner. Jack was careful not to drink too much beforehand, although they did consume another bottle of this time not very good wine. As they were eating, he felt transported into the wonderful world where love reigned. What a delicious healing, coming as it did two or three years after his time with Lorna. Had he been smitten since then? No sir. Of course in the north of Canada, some of his parishioners' daughters had taken a shine to him. He'd been invited to family dinners, not just as the parish priest, but because those pretty young farm girls — well, never as lovely as Catherina — had their eyes on him. Families saw a match with a young clergyman as being worthy, their daughters never left to starve. But truth is, he received such a pittance in return for his long weeks of work — well hardly work, but visiting the sick, tending to the thousand other details thrown at him in each parish, perhaps not quite as onerous as on the Canadian Labrador when he adjudicated disputes, questioned boundaries, settled scores — all that was done in northern Quebec by proper magistrates and courts of justice — but still, a very busy life, and not an unrewarding one.

Here, he would face the same duties. But for pity's sake, stop looking so far ahead! Had he not learned that? The future always contained frightening, often impossible, events. But look, he told himself, when that very future ended up being *today*, right here and now, had he not been ready? Able to face whatever? Of course.

He allowed himself again to stare at Catherina in the candle-light — so beautiful. His heart blossomed. Oh yes, if this were not love, he didn't know what love was.

When at last they had eaten their fill, she blew out the candles. What now?

Well, without discussion, they went into her bedroom and slipped once again onto her glorious feather bed, only too ready to give themselves up to delights so long denied.

While Catherina slept, Jack lay savouring the memory of each lovely portion of her body, letting his thoughts soar. What an idyll!

How wonderful it would be to lie forever beside her. To hear the call of their children as they awoke at dawn, getting them up from their sleepy beds and sending them off to school. And then, while she worked in the tea-shop, he'd write his sermons or visit local dignitaries. No hardships here like a Canadian winter, certainly. Whatever his new church might offer as sustenance, she would also need to work in the tea-shop. Hard to make a living out of this desert. But again, here he was, building more palaces in the air. After all, he had known her now, what, just twenty-four hours? Was he being a fool? Yes, but how nice. So be a fool.

But with all that, he knew the dreaded morrow would arrive.

Chapter Twenty-Seven

The next morning Jack and Catherina were awakened by a banging at the front door of her house, around the corner from the tea-shop. Catherine leaped up, threw on her dressing gown and left the room.

Jack sat up, wide awake. What... Had they been discovered? Had the Canadians come to get him? Or the Boers? Would they take him out and shoot him? What on earth should he do? All sorts of wild and hideous thoughts ran around his fraught mind. Anyway, get up quick and make ready. Shave and dress, oh yes, as fast as he could.

As he was putting on his socks and shoes, Catherina came back in, shut the door, leaned against it, and looked at him.

He looked up at her with a questioning look.

She did not speak for a long time.

He frowned. What had happened?

She still leant against the door, looking at him with... well, an enigmatic, quite strange look, betraying nothing.

Finally he spoke. "Who was that, Catherina?"

"A soldier."

What did that mean? "And ..."

She shook her head.

"Tell me, Catherina. What did the soldier want?"

She came and sat on the arm of the chair by the bed. Then she looked at him. "He told me that they have found Hermanus."

Jack sat up.

"He is a captive. He sent a message. They will release him, if he promises not to fight. He will be coming home soon."

"Hermanus! Alive? He's coming back?"

"Yes. He's coming back."

Jack nodded to himself. He got up and slowly finished dressing.

* * *

Although it meant arriving sooner at camp and his punishment, Jack could not stop striding purposefully back through the town. He had been given a hearty breakfast of eggs, small pork sausages, tomatoes and toast by Catherina, although they had both been curiously silent about the new turn of events. Perhaps they should meet again, once they'd had time to think? But it was clear to Jack as he walked along that Catherina would go back to her husband, she would accept Hermanus and return to her former life. Yes, the further he walked, the more convinced he became of that. And as for him, what could he offer her? Nothing, until he found out into what depths this degradation had flung him. His own life would likely be devastated, he knew that.

First of all, the punishment. Army discipline required a severe one. Although he had visited and ministered to prisoners in the lockup, he had little idea what sentence might fit his crime. Deserting was serious. Could they shoot him? Or lock him up for years? Or send him home in chains? He hoped not.

And worse, his bishop. And church. What would they say in Quebec when they heard their chaplain had let them down? Would his punishment be announced in the church bulletin? Or the Diocesan Gazette? Would they make him an example? Would he be, as they say, defrocked? Well, then he could go back to the Old Homestead. But it sounded as if Mac and Clare had things under control there, with Earle coming along fast. Three brothers, all of whom worked harder than he. No, no room at the farm.

What about some job teaching? Yes, but would he like that? What little time he'd spent teaching children on the Canadian Labrador he had not enjoyed one bit. He felt helpless when faced by youthful energies of children racing everywhere and cutting up such storms, the minute vigilance was relaxed. Dreadful. In church, he preached and they listened. That's how he liked it.

So what on earth could he do? For a second time he had lost a new-found love — together with any and all prestige he might have built up over the years. Already he was suffering disrespect from the troops, just for obeying orders. Oh yes, all shreds of dignity destroyed. Indeed, a lost soul.

He'd never felt more despondent, more destroyed. How could he ever climb back into the sunlight he had formerly enjoyed. Indeed, a real underworld journey! A journey with no foreseeable end.

Trudging through the chill morning before the sun had risen high enough to heat the town, he somehow hoped he would be brave enough to face his punishment. And after all, had he not had two glorious days? Perhaps these memories would nourish him in the coming weeks or months.

Did souls benefit from suffering? He could see no earthly good jumping out of it. Even his very purpose here had been undermined by meeting one supposed enemy and finding out that, if she were not to be a permanent love, at least her being was still powerful enough for him to say, stop this destruction of others, be they sweethearts, fathers or sons. No, this war, he realized, was just not right. He felt a bit better, now that he had admitted that to himself.

He knew only too well that his Lord had descended into the Underworld, a much worse one, and broken asunder the very bonds of death. But no breaking for this poor clergyman. Just a bedraggled soul, floundering in the depths of a mire he had himself created.

* * *

As he neared the camp, Jack pondered his first steps. Go at once to Col. Otter and confess everything? Probably not. Otter was not a clergyman. Otter, so far as he could see, had very little sympathy for, and even less understanding of, human nature. No, think further.

What then? Father O'Leary was alone and waiting for him. Oh no! He had abandoned his friend and fellow priest for the pleasures of the flesh. Oh, now he felt real remorse. If anyone were to talk about a sin, that was it. For he had completely forgotten him and thereby let down his church and his conscience. Abandoning a good friend for the sake of carnal pleasures. What a terrible person he had turned out to be. He felt mortified.

Well, he decided, his first job must be to attempt a redemption. He would arrive after the camp breakfast and go straight to the field hospital as if nothing had happened. Then he'd seek out Father O'Leary. He hoped the aged priest had not been taken from him by that blasted typhoid.

Father Peter O'Leary was lying on his cot upstairs in the old stone building that had been commandeered as a hospital, a feverish sweat glistening on his brow. He turned his head as Jack came forward. "Jack!" he murmured. "Good to see you. I missed you yesterday. You must've been off in other hospitals."

Jack sat without replying. Then brought himself to ask, "How are you making out, Peter?"

"Bearing up, bearing up. The Lord Almighty is at my right hand and I grip His own as best I can."

"I'm afraid, from what I've seen, you may have another week or two of this."

Jack saw O'Leary studying him. Oh dear. A clergyman too, he must also have that sixth sense. Jack looked away.

"It'll be a lot longer," O'Leary replied. "I'm older than the men you've seen. It gets me down worse."

Well, thought Jack, now is the time. He leaned in so that he could whisper.

O'Leary turned to study his face. "What is it, my son?" he asked. "You have something to tell me?"

"Father, I don't know the words..."

"You have sinned." O'Leary nodded. "I knew it."

"How does it work, this confession business of yours? I'd like to learn — for my own practice, of course. Someone asked me to take their confession, and it was just so much trivia. But I knew there were some phrases I should say. Not having been schooled in your branch of religion, I..."

O'Leary was watching him. "You begin, my son, with, 'Forgive me Father, for I have sinned.'"

"Forgive me, Father, for I have sinned."

"And then I wait, or I say, 'Go on, my son.'"

Well, the time had come. Try a real confession. No matter that O'Leary was strict and adhered to the tenants of his church. Jack deserved the worst. So he had to do this. He began haltingly. "Father, I have gone to the very ends of degradation. I am in such need of relief. But there's almost no way I can be forgiven, so grievous..."

O'Leary frowned. In reading his face, Jack could see that little priest could not believe what he was hearing. He waited.

"First of all, I have drunk to excess."

Jack saw a smile cross O'Leary's face — which quickly vanished. After all, this confession stuff was pretty serious, Jack imagined.

O'Leary nodded. "Go on my son. Tell me everything. And the truth."

"I have been absent without permission. I didn't come back to the camp on Sunday night, nor on Monday morning, nor even last night. I just feel awful."

"I'm afraid, Jack, I cannot absolve you of that because it's no sin. It's just breaking a military law. You'll have to see Colonel Otter about that."

Jack paused. "Oh. So that's not a sin? Even though I knew it was wrong?"

O'Leary smiled, as he might with a child. "In the course of daily life, how many times do we do things that we know are wrong, my son? They jump out unexpectedly. Lord Above, if a priest had to listen to all those inconsequential acts, we'd never get any work done."

"Well, I guess the next thing is..." Now how should he say this? Well, if there was any validity in this confession stuff, he'd better have a go. With an effort, he launched out. "I have lain with a woman, Father." He paused. "Not once, when I was inebriated, but twice, when I knew better. But so help me, I could not stop. And worse, Father," he gulped, "I even enjoyed it."

O'Leary seemed to be suppressing another smile. He nodded. "Go on my son."

"Well, that's it."

"That's it?"

Jack nodded.

"Was she married?"

"When we lay together, we thought her husband dead. But we found just this morning, he's still alive. And so I left."

O'Leary nodded again. "Just as a matter of fact, you did commit adultery, but neither of you knew anything about it then."

"Correct."

"All right." O'Leary sighed, the sigh of an old man who had dealt with this so often. "Now, Jack, this is the part where you bow your head, and ask in your very soul, to be forgiven. And then I make the sign of the cross as I say: *Ego te absolvo, in nomine Patris, Filii, et Spiritus Sancti.*"

Jack remained, head bowed, in silence.

After a good length of time, he opened his eyes and looked. Father O'Leary was grinning.

"What's so funny?"

"You haven't confessed to the one really bad sin you committed."

"And what was that, Father? I swear that's all I did."

"The sin of pride. You thought that your one silly little dalliance, well, let's not call it silly for you took it seriously — you magnified it into some great extraordinary fall into eternal damnation. That was your sin. Simply, my son, you fell a prey to physical desires. Not a thing unusual about that. You're absolved now, in any case."

Jack sighed. Was it really that easy? "Thank you, Father."

O'Leary reached out and took Jack's hand. "Jack, do you know how many of our young soldiers have gone to prostitutes? Do you know how many would just kill to have had your experience? Do you think they're all sinners in God's eyes? Not at all. It's normal. And you fellas in your heretic church are even allowed to get married. Of course, it is better to withhold carnal pleasures, make no mistake, until your marriage vows. But although Christ exhorted us to be as He is, Jack," he shook his head, "we are, after all, just very ordinary human beings. I hope that doesn't shock you."

Jack studied the old man. Wise, of course; had he not been a priest for what, thirty years? He sure knew whereof he spoke. So no more indulging in this sin of pride, as O'Leary had called it, thinking that he had just consigned himself to an everlasting bonfire. Chin up, get on with life, and forget about it.

"And now, Jack, comes the worst part, go see the colonel."

Jack nodded and started to rise.

"Wait!"

Jack sat down again.

"Don't make a full confession. That's reserved for the church. Just tell him... tell him you got drunk, and had a nasty hangover. That's all he needs to know. It's very much in keeping. Might even give the old walrus a new perspective... Who knows."

Jack at last smiled. "So you don't think he'll throw me in the lockup for six months?"

"Jack, you just got drunk. He'd have us all locked up, if that's how he saw it."

Then a really horrible thought struck Jack. "What about my bishop?"

"What he doesn't know won't hurt him, Jack. You Waspy fellows are all the same. Puritans all of you. You can't even commit one tiny transgression without blowing it out of all proportion. Now Jack, don't forget to come back and tell me what he said."

"I won't forget," promised Jack. And off he went to see Otter.

Chapter Twenty-Eight

All that day, avoiding the dreadful future, Jack went from sick-bed to sick-bed, writing letters for those too ill to do so, and even boxing the last mementos and precious items of those who had departed forever. This particular chore always upset him. He could never stop thinking of the faces of the loved ones when they would open their doors to receive the box. But then, it might be all they would have to remember of their son, their husband or brother. So he always did this frightful chore carefully, never throwing anything away, apart from handkerchiefs and suchlike, for who knew what might be considered important? And all the while, he waited for a summons from his commanding officer, Col. Otter.

The next morning, it came. Far better, he thought, to be summoned than to volunteer. This way, he'd be given a clear time with the colonel. Perhaps the old dog might even listen, before he imposed what Jack was sure would be a severe sentence, in spite of what O'Leary had told him. You can't let a clergyman get away with being drunk.

Adjutant Brown, with a smirk, showed Chaplain Jack into Col. Otter's rather spacious office. They had commandeered one of the larger houses in Bloemfontein and the colonel seemed well installed.

Chaplain Jack saluted.

"At ease, Chaplain. How are things going?" asked Otter. "Everything all right?"

Jack hesitated. Then he thought, yes, the old duffer is giving me a chance to confess, so I'd better take it. "I'm sorry, sir, but the strain of tending to our wounded, the pressure of seeing so many of my friends shot, dying, or taken by that dreadful fever, it's... well, it's been preying on me."

Otter lifted an eyebrow, cupped his hands, and leaned forward on his desk and waited.

"I'm afraid, sir, I became a prey to the unforgivable. I ... overindulged. I'm sorry."

"And that's why you weren't with us on Monday?"

"Yes sir." Jack thought being tight-lipped might serve him better than floundering around in a morass of excuses.

"So you've had one bloody great hangover?" asked Otter.

"I think you've put your finger on it, sir. A hangoverlike I've never had before."

"And being a priest, you weren't sure what was happening. You drank too much, had a blasted hangover and couldn't handle it?"

"That's it precisely, sir. I couldn't handle it. I'm sorry," he repeated.

"So you bloody well should be," exclaimed Otter. "Especially you, our one C of E Chaplain."

"Yes sir."

"Should I send you back to Cape Town for rehabilitation?"

Jack lifted his head, looked straight at Otter. "Sir, that would be a punishment too enormous for me to handle. You know what the men have been saying because I obeyed your order the last time."

Otter shook his head. "What have they've been saying?"

Of course, Jack thought to himself, he doesn't mingle. Then

he saw a gleam of recognition. "Ah ha!" went on Otter, "so that's the origin of a couple of snide remarks I've heard. I see."

"The men think I'm a coward, sir, because you sent me back to tend the wounded. I've been given a pretty hard time since coming back." Jack let that sentence hang.

Otter nodded. "I can see that. I myself even fell into the trap. I was praising O'Leary in front of you. I should have been more discreet, now that you tell me that."

Jack remained silent.

"Well, we'll have to put a stop right away to that nasty rumouring. I shall see to that in the morning. You have been following my orders in a first-rate fashion, and your behaviour has been exemplary. You wanted to be at the front, you wanted to be with the men, and I made you leave for a more important job." Otter nodded to himself. "I'd have to say, well done, Chaplain! And no, you won't be sent back to Cape Town. What do you think I should do?"

"Frankly sir, I don't know military rules. But I can tell you this. After what I've been through, it's even more unlikely that this sort of behaviour will be repeated while I am in your regiment."

Otter looked pleased, and paused, staring down at his desk. "You know, Chaplain, we're going to join Roberts on his march to Pretoria shortly. I think this time, you will do all of us some good if you stuck with us. Especially with Father O'Leary's indisposition. How is the old man getting on? I hear you've been tending to him rather well."

Jack allowed himself to relax. "Well, we are brothers of the cloth, no matter in what directions our denominations diverge, rather unhappily at times, I am forced to say. But he'll pull through, I'm sure of it."

Otter coughed. "Of course, of course."

Jack waited

Otter looked up. "Well, that will be all, Chaplain. I'll make sure to attend your service on Sunday. I do hear from the men that when you get a subject in your teeth, you shake the hell out of it. Just like a British bulldog. And... Good luck."

Jack saluted, turned, and left the room, suffused with relief and, it be must be admitted, no little degree of surprise.

* * *

Amazing the release Jack felt as he strode back through town, as if he were climbed up into the light from an enormous dark cavern. Now, there was nothing that he couldn't do. He would throw himself into caring for the sick as never before. And to whatever fighting lay ahead.

On his way to the campground, he passed an enclosure where a number of suffering soldiers had been quartered. Under huge tarpaulins stretched between wagons, they were hardly protected from any driving rain or winds. Nothing to lie on but blankets over rough ground. Should he stop? No, first, report to the good Father and see how he was faring. Then look into the matter of the men's quarters.

Heading from Otter's HQ to Father O'Leary, who had now been housed in one of the better buildings, Jack passed several more makeshift hospitals, an area he had not visited before. Many of these patients seemed sadly in need of even the most basic medical care. What could he do? He resolved to make enquiries this evening. He also wondered at his not having noticed this before — another example of how one's own worries so often took precedent over the suffering of others. He castigated himself for that, and swore to do better. Meanwhile, day after day, night after night, the ambulance wagons kept coming back with maimed, mangled, war-broken humanity.

On the other side of this small capital city, he reached the grey stone building, formerly a clubhouse. He climbed the broad outside stairs, entered the first floor, and paused to admire the notice board, which told of past club presidents on small silver plaques, and of riding competitions, and in a line down one side, pictures of their mounts. Amazing what war does to an entire culture, he thought. The panelled walls spoke to him of laughter and gracious banquets, pints of fine ale downed as rosettes were examined and mulled over. But they now held only a plethora of pain from suffering soldiers, on both sides.

Before he could climb the staircase to the second floor where O'Leary lay, he went to the men's room at the back of the building to relieve himself. Coming out, he passed a sunny ward with a sign: nurses only.

No orderlies? He looked in. Only three cots of the six in the decently appointed room were occupied. He frowned. Women patients!

As he stood uncertainly in the doorway, he heard a weak voice call his name.

He looked across. There in the corner — was that a familiar face? He walked closer.

The long, pale, drawn cheeks, dark circles under the eyes, the damp hair from the fever... Could it be? Two grey distant eyes tried to focus. "Jack?"

Was that the voice of Kelsie? Weak, almost hoarse, it carried the ring of the Hereafter. But still, the sound struck him with the force of a dum-dum bullet.

"I never thought I'd see you again..." she breathed.

Jack's stomach dropped and the walls of his heart pounded with surging emotions. "Kelsie! Kelsie..." was all he could say.

The two stared at each other, one so stiff, upright, trying to get a grip on his feelings, the other drenched in sweat, trying to focus, squirming slightly.

Jack shook himself, moved quickly to a corner, grabbed a stool, brought it over and sat down beside her. "You've been struck by the enteric?"

She nodded.

Jack reached over, and took her fevered hand in both of his. Pull yourself together, he told himself. Don't show your shock. Give her sympathy... understanding. Deal with your own emotions later. "You'll soon pull out, you'll be fine." He couldn't think of what else to say. "Father O'Leary, he's upstairs, it's been tough going for him too, oh yes, but in the end, you'll come through. You'll be fine." He tried to sound as confident as he could but a small voice within him kept saying, no, Jack, she won't be.

"No Jack," the weak voice whispered, as though repeating his thoughts, "I won't be."

They sat in silence for a moment, while Jack digested that and tried to decide on the best course of action.

"I see the signs. I've nursed enough patients." She closed her eyes. "I won't make it."

"Now Kelsie, you mustn't say that. Be confident, even when you don't feel it. That's how you'll get well."

"Tell me Jack, how have you been?" A tremor ran through her weakened tiny frame. She didn't want to hear empty words of encouragement, he could see that.

How had he been? Oh, just fine — off with another woman, forgetting Kelsie, doing all manner of dreadful things no priest should ever have dreamed of doing. What could he say? Better launch out, he thought, do your best. Take her mind off this predicament. "Well, Kelsie, I was sent back from the front to minister to the wounded at De Aar and at Orange River. The doctor, there, he sent me down to Cape Town to do some errands."

She brightened. "So you got my note?"

Jack nodded. "You can't imagine how it made me feel. So full of promise." Oh-oh, you shouldn't have said that. He squeezed the tiny fingers between his two large, but gentle, hands. "You didn't get mine, I suppose?"

She shook her head. "You wrote me?"

"Oh yes. And," he lied, "with just the same sentiment, even stronger, Kelsie. I told you how much I wanted to see you again." Well, only half a lie. But what else should he say?

She nodded slightly, and he could see her pain eased a little, and her body relaxed somewhat.

"Well, then I got some missions done, finding food and supplies for our boys. I came back to Orange River..." Should he go on? Why not? "I had to stay, because then, the trains came, full with wounded from Paardeberg. Unbelievable. You see, I missed that battle. I'd been ordered to leave." Don't apologise to her, she doesn't know, he thought. "I was ordered to go to Cape Town, as I said. So imagine! I missed the one battle we Canadians won and which, they all tell me, turned the tide of the war."

Kelsie nodded. "Our boys fought gloriously." She eased herself up a bit, and Jack arranged her pillows to help.

"Father O'Leary did a great job, tending the wounded, burying the dead. Fullerton was away, probably on errands for the battalion like me."

Kelsie nodded to herself. She smoothed her hair back in an effort to look better.

"I've more or less just come back. I gave a service on Sunday. You know, I've been with the colonel, who assures me that when the regiment leaves, he's going to send me out with the troops. No staying here."

"So you're going to go?"

Oh dear, he should not have said that. Now how could he answer her? Leave Kelsie like this? No, of course he couldn't. So how could he stay? By disobeying orders? No, but why not see the colonel again, ask to be let off? Then what would the men say! What on earth should he do now?

"You'll be much better by the time we go," he found himself saying, his instincts rescuing him at the last moment. "It won't be for a while anyway, I know that."

That seemed to reassure her.

"Now are you getting proper care?" He felt himself gathering strength for a possible onslaught against the administration.

"Oh yes, Jack." Her strength seemed to be improving, just by his presence, by his affection flowing into her hands and on through her body — yes, he felt he might almost be helping to heal her.

"We're treated better than most," she said. "There are three of us, all nurses. Caught them by surprise, us coming down sick. Put them in a real dither." She managed a weak smile. "Jack, it's scandalous how we take care of our boys. There are about a hundred of us, nurses from down under, New Zealand and Australia, from Britain, and yet military regulations forbid us to do our job. We can't bathe the men. We can't change them. We can't even make their beds; we're supposed to give advice, but what good is that — they don't have enough orderlies. Jack, there's not enough doctors around. No medicine, well hardly any, you see, the Boers blew up the railway bridge at Norval's Pont and supplies haven't been getting through. We're all run off our feet. I've been so worried — you know what a worrier I am — well, there's been plenty to worry about here, I can tell you."

"The other three Canadian nurses are here too?"

She nodded. "And doing so well. If I had been able to care a bit less, I might not have succumbed to this. But you see, I was so, so thirsty on the way. And I somehow felt that no disease could touch me. I'm a nurse. So I remember drinking some water from what seemed a clean bucket, and after a rainstorm, too. I think that's what did it..." She sunk back.

Jack nodded. After the burst of energy, she now seemed tired, and indeed in pain. Her hands went to her stomach and she doubled over.

Jack made as if to rise.

"Wait!" Bravely she tried to ignore her pain. Jack sank back, and waited as the spasm passed. She breathed, "Have you... Have you heard from your family in the Gaspe?"

"Oh yes, I got a letter. I'm going to write back. I'll tell them that I've found my really good friend, and she will come and visit. I'll have lots of time after this, and you will too, and you'll come to the Gaspe. If you don't," he wagged his finger at her, "then I'll take the train down to Halifax."

She sighed. "The only way I'm going to see the Gaspe now is through your words, Jack. You'll come back tomorrow and tell me more about it. I'll see it through your eyes, that's enough. It will have to be..." Her eyes grew moist.

Jack found himself at a loss for words. He did his best not to let the moisture creeping into his eyes flood into them, but her words made it so difficult, emotion taking over his entire being. Kelsie, his Kelsie...

"Jack, I really... would rather not die." Jack went to interrupt, but she motioned him. "I'm ready," she said, "but I really would rather not."

He shook his head, and then bowed it silently, gripping himself. Then he leaned forward. "Kelsie, I'll let you rest now, and

I'll come back tomorrow. You'll be better tomorrow, I'm quite sure. I don't want you to worry."

Kelsie nodded and closed her eyes. Jack almost felt she was glad he was leaving, so that she would not have to restrain her moaning, her writhing in pain as it attacked her insides.

Jack rose and went out of the room, a very different man from the one who had walked in.

Chapter Twenty-Nine

As he walked upstairs to see his next patient, the good Father O'Leary, he wondered if the Lord Above were good, what on earth had He been up to, letting Kelsie get so sick, and sanctioning this war? And what was Jack himself doing here, approving in appearance at least the whole dreadful affair. His mind was seething, and he had a good mind to go to the colonel and hand in his resignation, if that were possible.

But then, the thought struck him as he stepped on to the landing of the second floor: Father O'Leary, why not ask him? Might perk him up to have a knock-down tussle over the ethics of what the two of them were doing. Catholics were much better at seeing things in stark black and white. But was Peter too sick for this type of discussion? No, he decided, it might take his mind from the harsh fever wracking him.

Without further delay, he turned into the small, almost empty ward where the good Father lay in a corner. Jack went straight over to sit beside him, relieved to see that the only other officer there was asleep.

O'Leary opened his eyes as Jack came forward to fetch a stool. They widened as Jack sat down, with furrowed brow and teeth clenched.

Silence fell.

Jack, hunched over, looked at the palms of his hands, trying to decide how to bring up this juggernaut of a problem.

"Something bothering you, Jack?"

"You might say so, Father Peter."

"Them fellas, I talked to a couple of them, and they heard what Otter said. Now they're spreading the word that you were only doing your duty."

"Well, it's gone beyond that now." Jack about to launch into his whole problem, and then he remembered his first priority. "Can I get you some water? Or anything else?"

"No thanks. A new young orderly has decided to take special care. I have all I need. Except something to divert the mind, which," he managed a grin, "you're about to provide, I can tell."

"Not sure you'll like the diversion. But I've been wondering, honestly... Just what are we, you and me and Fullerton, doing here? What right have we got to be doing this? I mean, supporting all this fighting and killing?"

"What right?" O'Leary was firm. "We've got every right, Jack. This is a just war, and we're fighting it. Whatever made you think we should not?"

"Nothing much, I guess," Jack replied truculently. "Just that Our Lord happened to say, 'Turn the other cheek', He just happened to make plain that violence was wrong; He just happened to forgive those who crucified him; He just happened —"

"Jack! Jack, that's got nothin' to do with it!" O'Leary burst out. "Nothin' at all. He also said, If a wolf breaks into the sheepfold, you go right ahead and shoot it. He may not have used those words, exactly, but that's what he meant. Defend yourself! 'Onward Christian Soldiers,' ever heard of that hymn?"

"So once a hymn gives the okay, you run out and do it — to hell with what Our Lord says?" Jack's voice rose angrily, which even surprised himself. They were both slinging around the sarcasm like two veterans; what was coming over them?

"Jack me boy, calm down. If you have a problem, let's discuss it like two normal people."

"Just the point, Peter, we're not normal people. We're clergymen. We've taken our vows to follow the precepts laid down by Our Saviour. And you can be damn sure that in your branch of the church, just like in ours, any killing is plain wrong."

"Jack, you never read Saint Thomas Aquinas? There are two kinds of war: Just and Unjust. We're right now fighting a Just War — "

"How do we know that?"

"Jack, Saint Thomas laid down special criteria. You have to be sanctioned by your ruler, in other words, it's got to be started by Parliament, in our case. And only to right a wrong, or..."

"Yes?"

"I'm thinking, Jacko... Oh yes, to prevent further injustice. To stop aggression. And then, of course, there's Saint Augustine in the fourth century, and that pope who authorised the first Crusade, Urban II, they all had things to say."

"... in justification for killing others?"

"Jack! For going to war. To right a wrong, or to protect your members from harm. That first crusade started out within very strict limits. It was to protect pilgrims going to the Holy Land, and nothing more."

"Yes but look what happened."

"Man's nature, Jack, are we ever going to change that?"

He was about to go on when Jack interrupted, "And just how 'just' do you think this war here is?"

"We have right on our side. Don't forget Saint Thomas also said it's also got to be fought proper. Once you start a war, you can't do nothing immoral. No fighting with hatred. No attacking civilians. Being Christians, we just have to make sure our boys are following these sorts of rules. So you're in the clear Jack, we're all in the clear," O'Leary ended emphatically.

"Peter, at college when we got to Saint Thomas Aquinas, my mind slowed into the pace of an ox: it was all kind of boring; so maybe you're right. But does all that go along with what Our Lord said? I'm damned sure not."

"Jack, Thomas Aquinas was a saint. Those fellas back then, they studied more than you or me ever will. If they says it's okay, then okay it is! That's been drilled into us. That breakaway church of yours, you get no proper training, that's the damn trouble. No wonder we're the only religion."

It was Jack's turn to look at O'Leary askance. "Now Peter, don't let's start making this the C of E against Catholics. We're both here to do a job, and I came to get some advice, because I'm beginning to think this job we came to do is in no way justified. It's driving me crazy."

O'Leary was taken by a stomach pain and doubled over. Jack immediately felt remorseful. He reached out to touch the old man's shoulder.

O'Leary finally relaxed and lay back, panting somewhat. "Bloody fever, I wish it would go away."

"So do I. With all my heart. You'd think those darn bureaucrats or higher-ups would have seen we all had decent water. Specially before going on an attack. Shameful the way our boys have been treated."

"Aye, shameful it may be, but this is war, Jack. Who knows what their problems are, but you can be sure they got 'em. Supplying thousands, maybe hundreds of thousands, of troops down one little narra' gauge railway line, sabotaged half the time by the Boers. And oxen that don't travel more than a few miles a day. Not easy for the commanders neither. Us, we've just got to do or die. Let's beat the bastards and get ourselves back to Canada as quick as we can. You agree with me on that score, don't you."

Jack nodded. He wasn't sure that he did agree on the other points quite so emphatically. But he could see he wouldn't be getting a great deal of comfort, nor any of that good old-fashioned homespun wisdom that he had expected. All he was hearing was the doctrine of the Church, which made him even more fed up. He'd just have to make his own accommodation, he'd have to turn the matter over in his own mind and find his own conclusion.

With that, Jack walked out of the ward no more satisfied than when he had entered.

* * *

Jack kept ministering to his many patients and to Kelsie, who was getting worse by the day, and to Father O'Leary, who was taking a long time but seemed on his way to recovery. He'd made inquiries about how these dreadful conditions for the soldiers came about, and what could be done to mend that deficiency. Very little, he found out. So the days became especially long and arduous. Each morning's visit to Kelsie threw him into a black despair, which he tried not to reveal. And furthermore, he had to say goodbye to one after another of his soldier parishioners, and then pronounce their burial rites the next morning, those men whose hands he had held, whose bodies he had prayed over the night before. These duties at dawn, performed in Quebec and on the Labrador only every month or so, had now become a daily occurrence. He supervised the laying to rest of not only Canadians but those of other colonies and the Old Country, and indeed, even the enemy when their own pastoors were not available.

Field Marshal Roberts had decided that shortly, the regiment would march on to Pretoria, the capital of the Transvaal, a goodly distance of some three hundred miles. The regiment was gathering its strength: more supplies arrived from Cape Town, the food got gradually better, proper replacement uniforms were issued, but those who were sick remained sick. But still, this enforced inactivity prayed on the men, as it had earlier, but now they also witnessed, and could not be indifferent to, comrades down with enteric, or wounded, who were made to suffer in appalling conditions.

As he tended to the many diseased and wounded, Jack's sense of injustice and his natural antipathy to combat began to grow. The battles that had been so eagerly anticipated (and he counted himself among those who'd been deceived) were now seen to be a devastation to both body and spirit.

He had a duty to do, but on the other hand, what about his duty to his Lord and King — who commanded all followers to live in peace. Forget the Old Testament God who wreaked vengeance on all who crossed him, Jesus had changed that. And here am I, he thought, doing what I am expressly forbidden to do, be a party to organized murder.

What would the Bishop say? And Canon Scott's sermon expounding on the justice of their enterprise? But did those clergy back in Quebec really understand what conditions would be faced by young farm boys, by the incipient lawyers, clerks, and teachers here? Had they really looked ahead to the death and destruction this was bringing on our next young generation?

This wrestling with irreconcilable doubts was interrupted by an order to report to his commanding officer.

Chaplain Jack removed his helmet and was shown into the colonel's spacious office near the centre of town.

"At ease, Chaplain."

"You asked for me, Sir?"

"I did, Chaplain. The regiment will be moving out the day after tomorrow, at dawn." Otter waited for his reaction, which was minimal. "How is O'Leary doing?"

"It's a long slow haul, sir. But I do believe he will recover."

"We shall have to invalid him home, I think. Poor old soldier, he's done his best. He has given his very finest to the regiment, but I think now," Otter looked hard at Jack, "the burden will fall on you."

"On me, sir?"

"Yes. We have a couple of British chaplains looking after our sick here. I'm giving you the chance you have waited for. You will come with us to the front, where there'll be plenty of fighting, I can tell you." He smiled. "Enough to satisfy everyone."

Jack had some trouble finding his voice. "Thank you, Sir."

Now what should he do? This was a direct command. Should he face the colonel right away? Oh no, much too unprepared. Think about it overnight.

"You don't look pleased."

"Oh yes sir, very pleased. I'm just rather taken aback. This is, after all, just what I've come to do."

"Right-oh then. That will be all, Chaplain."

Jack, helmet under his arm, turned smartly and left the office.

* * *

That night Jack bedded down with the other two lieutenants, Robert Willis and Harry Burstall. They had grown friendly over time, now that Big George was gone and only three of them shared the tent. Willis was a wiry sort of fellow with short hair and a well-groomed moustache he took great care of every morning, shaving with a small hand mirror. Harry, six foot two, had a rather pudgy, almost baby face, which belied a fierce intelligence, great courage and an adherence to duty and rules that his troops found exemplary. He was certainly due for a promotion and everyone knew it, but he made no complaints. He led the men in fine fashion.

Most nights they would lie back as they were going to sleep and gossip about their homes, their families, and often complain of the conditions, all three of them topping each other with horrifying tales of neglect that they had heard about sloppy orderlies or stories of others on the wards who worked unbelievably hard and long into the night to make their patients better. During the day, no longer having endless drills, they were given lectures on tactics. The two officers saw to it that their privates were sharpening bayonets or practising their shooting and generally making themselves ready for the big push on Pretoria.

"I hear you were called in to the colonel's. Did he put you on the spot? More trouble?"

Harry and many others knew that Jack was not a favourite of the colonel's nor was he in turn esteemed by Jack. In fact, most of the regiment had grown to resent Otter, for they needed someone to blame for their lack of clothing, food, water, all the many shortages that this war had brought upon the regiment, although most these problems had by now been rectified.

"No," replied Jack. "He just told me we're off the day after tomorrow."

The other two sat up like bolts. "Did he now," said Willis. "You're sure?"

"That's what he said. I think he was a bit disappointed."

"Disappointed? By our going off to fight?"

"No, at the way I responded. You see, I'm having a bit of a battle with my conscience." Jack went on quickly, "But it will pass. Now, I went in to say good-bye to Peter O'Leary, who's being sent home tomorrow. He was sorry to leave you all, he told me to tell you that. But he's still weak, and surely not up to any more battling. I'm sad to see him go."

"Was he quite upset?"

"Not really. He can see that our main task is probably over. We've certainly given the Imperial Forces a hand up, and I doubt, apart from the next couple of weeks, we'll have much more to do."

Willis nodded. "Yes, but those next few weeks... I would have liked him there."

"Not up to it, I'm afraid. As Otter says, he's done far more than his duty." Jack was pleased to have diverted them from discussing his own doubts. Would they really understand his problem with the rightness of the struggle and the many lives so needlessly taken?

"Well, Jack, the problem of being a Christian, and then going out and killing your fellow man..." Harry asked with acuity. "I've often wondered how you clergymen do it. As for us soldiers, when the government orders us into action, we do what we're told. And we do our best to win for good Queen Victoria, and for the Canadian nation. That's what we're trained to do. But you, a clergyman taught to love your fellow man, no matter who he is — yes, I do see you might have a problem."

A problem that Jack knew he had to resolve on his own.

Chapter Thirty

And resolve it he did. But not before his disturbed sleep was cut short by a definite call — a loud one, his name, he felt sure. But who was calling? All around, the regiment tossed in their tents, but no really intrusive sound broke the night stillness. Could it have been Kelsie? Should he dress and go see to her? Or was he, as usual, dreaming heavily. Yes, that was it, his nights had become so difficult, recently, with all the mayhem of his days.

At the first hint of light, Jack arose, dressed as a captain with his chaplain's insignia, and walked out of the camp over a slight rise, down to a wooded area where burial plots of the various regiments had been laid out.

He was the first to arrive. He stood silently waiting among the piles of rocks and humps of freshly turned sand before their new wooden crosses and he reflected on that curious awakening in the night. He looked around at the haphazard array of death in this makeshift mortuary. How many young men from far-off lands had come to lie here in this bleak desert, cradled by foreign sand and shaded by trees never seen at home? He was interrupted in his thoughts by the Bugler who greeted Jack with a proper salute.

"Well, Private, I suppose this will be our last burial service for a time. Or are you staying behind when our boys leave?"

"I'm a staying, Sir. The colonel decided to send off a new fella what came with the Second Contingent." Canada had sent out another force in January, which had embarked from Halifax on the Laurentian along with two other steamers loaded with three batteries of field artillery, three squadrons of mounted rifles, and a squadron of specially selected scouts: 1,230 men in all and over a thousand horses, many of which died on the voyage. They had just joined Robert's army in Bloemfontein.

"I expect that the Chaplain from the new regiment will stay to take care of any burials," the private said.

Jack nodded. This high desert, before the sun rose, was definitely chilly. They stamped their feet, swinging their arms to keep warm. Far over the flat horizon, the wide sky was brightening as it blackened bushes and silhouetted humps of anthills and distant kopjes. From the wood nearby came a diminished dawn chorus; the large ungainly vultures had not yet begun their daily circling.

He squatted against a stump to ruminate on his coming decision, when he heard the rattle of an oxcart and grinding of its heavy wheels. At the approach of the "hearse" he arose and opened his prayer book. Then he frowned. The Kaffir driver and burial detail of two were accompanied by a fourth, a tall, slim figure. As they approached, he could see that it was indeed Sister Georgine Pope, the head Canadian nurse. What on earth did that mean?

The oxcart trundled forward with its Kaffir driver and stopped. The two soldiers on burial duty moved to the rear to remove their sombre burdens. Jack took his accustomed place by the grave, dug the previous night. The sun was just about to break over the horizon. Somehow, the burial cart always managed to get its timing right: military discipline, military orders, even in death.

The nurse detached herself from the others and came forward.

"Hello Sister," Jack said. "To what do we owe this unexpected visit?"

"Ah, 'tis a sorry occasion, Chaplain, one that should never

take place. I knew you hadn't heard." She paused, looked at the ground and then raised her big, dark eyes to meet Jack's stare, steeling herself for her next sentence. With sombre mien and strangled sob, she spoke. "Sister Kelsie... In the night..."

"But... I was with her yesterday morning." Jack's brain whirled. "She looked... I even thought she was looking better. I thought, in fact, there might be a chance now, that she would come through."

Sister Georgina shook her head. "Someone heard her cry out, and they summoned me. Of course, I called the doctor too. As I went into her ward, I saw her little form lurch up. She stared into the lamplight, and I heard her cry out, 'He's coming!'

"I looked for an orderly to get you, for it was probably you she wanted. But then I heard her gasp, 'The brightness'... Her eyes wide, so wide, Chaplain. I went forward to shield them, for I feared she might be hurting herself. 'The brightness', she cried out again, and then as she sank back, she breathed, 'How very, very bright...'" Jack bowed his head. "I didn't have to feel her pulse. I knew there was none."

Silence fell. The Bugler looked down, scuffing the ground with his foot.

Jack envisioned her lying on the cot, a wisp of the creature he had known, white face on white pillow, in the darkened lamplight.

"We tried to help. The doctor came, but it was no use." The Sister shook her head sadly.

Jack just could not get this enormity into his brain. Every faculty refused to accept it. His Kelsie. Gone? Not possible.

The burial orderlies laid the two men's bodies in the grave and went back to the cart. They lifted out their much lighter bundle. Jack looked sharply away, then turned his back. He bowed his head to say a prayer, held his eyes tightly shut and covered his face with his hands.

No, no time for tears! But how to stop his feelings winning out? Pull yourself together, he told himself: you do have a job to do. Mourn later.

Come along, he told himself more gently, just turn around, open your prayer book, and begin the service for your Kelsie. She would expect it. But this vision, and that sound of her cry, would stay with Jack through the long dreary months of duty that lay ahead.

He saw Sister Georgina looking at him with compassion; she too was holding back tears. The burial detail, having placed Kelsie's enwrapped body gently in a separate grave, stood back and snapped to attention, eyes averted. They obviously knew what had transpired, and although used to burials, they too seemed affected by this passing of an unusually brave young nurse.

Jack began the Burial Service.

When he began to speak, he was afraid his voice would waver. But no, he sounded firm and pronounced the words, which of course by now he knew by heart. As he read the words with half his brain, the other half was tormented by vivid memories.

So he mingled fragments of the rite with a renewed determination to end once and for all his participation in the carnage.

I am the resurrection and the life, saith the Lord: he that believeth in me, though he were dead, yet shall he live: and whoso-ever liveth and believeth in me shall never die. No, Kelsie, this is it. No more war for me! No more accompanying the troops, no more exhortations to victory. *For he must reign, till he hath put all enemies under his feet. The last enemy that shall be destroyed is death. For he hath put all things under his feet.* Yes, he conquered death, but you, Kelsie, can no longer see the sun rise over your Halifax hospital. No more will you help your little sister Orla with her homework. You will never walk back over the brow of the Hollow as we promised. I'm finished with war. I don't care what the outcome. *This corruptible must put on incorruption, and this mortal must put on immortality.* Yes, Kelsie, you shall put on His mantle... And so must I. I must turn away, no matter whether I'm shot for desertion, or clapped in the brig, I must go back to Canada with my blunt statement: war is wrong! *Come, ye blessed children of my Father, receive the kingdom prepared for you from the beginning of the world...*

* * *

Right after his painful breakfast and still trying to absorb Kelsie's passing, Jack set off for the colonel's office. Face him he would, no matter what the consequences. His mind was made up.

As he passed out of the camp with firm tread, a voice called loudly, "Chaplain! Chaplain Jack! Wait!"

Jack stopped and turned.

Eamon! Seeming healthy and recovered, he hurried up, arm still in a sling but otherwise in fine shape.

"Why Eamon, good to see you! I thought you had been invalided back to Canada. Or at least sent down to Cape Town."

"No sir, I'm going out with the regiment tomorrow morning. Into battle, yes, Chaplain. Very exciting. I made them pronounce me fit. Look." He took his arm out of his sling, lifted it, moved it in different positions. "I'm as good as the next fella — probably better, because I've seen fighting, I know the battle, I'm a veteran, Chaplain, you can see that now, eh?"

Jack took in his new companion. "Eamon, you're a hero. Coming back to fight again after being wounded once, well, we should all be proud of you. Yes sir." And that, Jack did believe.

He would salute bravery wherever it occurred. "I wish you well tomorrow, and onward into the fight, no question about it."

"Well, you're coming along, too. I heard that you saw the Colonel. He picked you out of all the other chaplains. You're the bye as we sez." Eamon broke into the sailor's song:

"I's the bye that builds the boat and I's the bye that sails 'er,
I'se the bye that catches the fish and brings 'em home to Lizer."

He seemed so pleased.

"I'm sorry, Eamon, but I've decided war is wrong. I spend my life burying poor lads who should be out pitching hay or teaching classes full of students. I'm determined to make a statement. I am not coming."

What next struck Jack was the enormous hurt on Eamon's face. "Jack... Chaplain Jack, you can't... You can't mean that. You won't let us all down? Would you? Let us fellas go off fighting without you near? You just can't." He finished weakly, despairingly.

"Just watch me." As soon as Jack said that, he regretted it. He saw the astonishment in Eamon's eyes. "But Chaplain, we're going into battle — some of us'll get wounded. We need someone like you. What if we... what if I get kilt? Who'll bury me? I don't want no stranger saying them rites over me body. You gotta come."

For the first time, Jack saw this tough young man, devastated, near tears. Eamon was begging him. Eamon was counting on him.

Chaplain Jack let the exchange sink in without speaking. And then, his mind swept over the many, many others who would feel just like Eamon. Was he, their chaplain, going to let them go off alone? To be struck by a Mauser, to be blasted by a dumdum, while he sat comfortably in a railway car heading south?

"Aah," said Eamon, "you was just kidding, wasn't yez." He relaxed somewhat.

Must have read my mind, thought Jack. "Yes, Eamon, of course I was kidding. Of course I'll come with you. Of course, I'd never let you down. Of course, I shall do my duty, as is right and proper. You can count on me. I shall be with you all when you march out of camp tomorrow morning."

And so, Chaplain Jack Alford went with his regiment into battle.

Chapter Thirty-One

Jack held services for the men on Good Friday and then on Easter Sunday, April 15th. On April 21st, he marched off with the whole regiment (which now numbered only 621 officers and men) eight miles to Springfield Farm to relieve the 19th Battalion. The men had left most of their possessions behind in Bloemfontein, not knowing that many were never to return. Roberts had assigned them to sweep the Boers from ridges and hills northeast of the city.

What now distinguished the marches was the right to sing, which had been withdrawn from the men up till now by foolish orders from Otter. The columns resounded with: "We are the Soldiers of the Queen, my Lads", "Home, Sweet Home" and other favourites, which made the steps lighter and the journey more fun.

Monday they attained Klip Kraal, and Tuesday skirmished and dislodged the enemy from the Waterworks. Tuesday evening, Jack had brought along his prayer book, of course, and as they prepared to bivouac for the night, he got it out. He saw that the sun was now dipping into the horizon, so he stood up and led a short service of Evensong. He felt gratified to notice that quite a few of the men took note and rose to stand with heads bowed, repeating the Lord's prayer. He invoked God's strength in their righteous crusade and called down his blessing on their noble enterprise. He could hardly believe the words that were coming out of his mouth, but then he was here to do a job, and a job he would do: the more courageous the men, the sooner this whole mess would be over. He also felt sure that knowing their Lord stood beside them meant that the regiment fought harder, attacked more courageously, and were thus emboldened to press on to a speedy victory.

After they had settled down, he closed his prayer book and made his way through the company.

A young private jumped up as he came by. "What're ya looking for, Padre?"

"I'm almost too embarrassed to say," Jack confided.

"The latrine is that way."

"No, it's the Bugler I want..."

The private peered into the gathering gloom and then pointed him out. Jack went over to crouch by the young man, who also had blonde hair like the one Jack had worked with at the Orange River Field Hospital. I wonder if they all have blonde hair, he thought to himself. "Bugler, I'm hesitant to ask, but the call for 'charge'... Would you mind just humming for me? You see, I've never been in an actual battle. That's the one thing they didn't teach me at university, nor when I was appointed Chaplain." He chuckled in spite of himself.

"Well, of course, Padre." The young soldier proceeded to give a good simulation.

Jack nodded. "Again, if you wouldn't mind." The Bugler blew through his lips, imitating a bugle sound two or three times until Jack was sure he had it.

"Thank you, Bugler." Jack began to rise.

"Wait!" the Bugler said. "Don't you think, sir, I should give you the call for 'retreat'? I know we hope it'll never be needed, but wouldn't it be funny if I blew it and you thought it was 'charge' and went racing off in the opposite direction toward the enemy?" He chuckled, and Jack joined him.

So the Bugler imitated for Jack the call for a retreat. After Jack had gotten that settled, the young man gave voice to a few other different ones that might come in handy.

Jack patted him on the shoulder. "You know, chaplains don't really get enough preparation for this sort of thing, I'm afraid. Most useful! Especially in battles, attacks, and so on." He was surprising himself by how much energy he was throwing into these endeavours, accompanying the troops and cheering them up.

He went back to his place near Harry Burstall and Robert Willis, rolled himself in his greatcoat, and fell asleep, contented.

* * *

The first time Jack heard the bugle's sharp demand to charge for real was the next day, in the battle of Yster Nek, or Israel's Poort. The Boers had been spotted on a line of kopjes. Now the Royal Canadians had to clear them from their easily defended positions before undertaking the major objective, Black Mountain. All morning, they had advanced warily, and now lay waiting in a shallow donga, or washed out gully, for the order to attack.

About three in the afternoon, an order came to proceed under heavy fire in open ranks at fifteen paces. With the Boers raining down a deadly and continuous fusillade, they stopped at a wire entanglement about seven hundred yards from their objective. Jack saw that to advance would be as great a folly as that ordered by the now dead Colonel at Paardeberg. Much more sensible to retreat, but then the Captains of the Companies, Harry Burstall included, leaped up and did a marvellous job of steadying the men. Colonel Otter himself came up to check the anxiety felt, not just by Jack, but everyone. He was unhappily spotted by the Boers, which occasioned a storm of bullets, one penetrating his neck within an inch of the jugular. But only at the end of the day did brave old Black Bill retire to a field hospital.

For over an hour Jack lay with the others, awaiting the clarion call to charge. They waited, and they waited. I think, Jack said to himself, this is worse than the coming rush into that hailstorm of lead! His heart kept pounding: thump thump thump, against his chest, making him lose his train of thought. When we charge, do I run zigzag? How long before I get hit? Will they mow us all down? Me included? And then what? But after a good deal more agonizing, Jack heard the bugle blare and they charged.

With the snapping of bullets all around them as the Mausers opened up, Jack felt his first twist of panic. And why not? "Into the valley of Death/Rode the six hundred." Lord Tennyson had that right, no doubt about it, thought Jack, as the Charge of the Light Brigade sprang into his mind. How apt, oh yes. He was looking straight into those two blank but frightening eyes of death itself.

He remembered to zigzag, his panic spurring him even faster. Don't you strike me, he breathed, don't you dare hit this healthy body, you killer bullets, you Mausers of death, go past, hit none of us, as on and on he ran and on and on he talked — willing himself through the desperate onslaught.

The faster he ran and the closer he got to those murderous muzzles, the less he spoke and the more fear grabbed at his innards and frazzled his brain. He was charging with the others right into Boer rifles pointing dead back at them. Count on his Saviour? No use. If a bullet were meant for him, take him it would, oh yes, no doubt about that! Too many fine young men, far finer than him for sure, had met their end.

He flashed on his Old Homestead, on Poppa and Momma, but that only frightened him more — the thought he might never see them again, stabbing him with such a sharp agony that he quickly put them out of his mind.

It's always the worst, he'd heard that, this first charge, it's always the worst. You'll get used to it. Yes, he shouted, I'll get used to facing death. My first battle, no blame — I'll get used to it. He realized he was yelling as he ran.

Uh-oh, Jack found he was a good bit ahead of all the others because he carried no rifle, no ammunition belts, little to weigh him down, and his rugby training gave power to his legs, agility to his feet, dodging the stones and bushes. He had almost welcomed the good sprint. But no, it would not do, look, he could even see the Boer farmers as they popped up, took aim, fired, and dropped out of sight. His own troops behind him banged away at them, one after another. So he slowed down. And just as he did, he saw the other front runners drop. Hit? No, the rapid firing had become too intense. They knew to drop to the ground and to fire back as lesser targets. Jack followed suit.

Then he saw them crawl forward on their bellies and he did, too. But without the adrenalin of a breathless sprint, the situation struck him with even more force. Any one of these bullets whizzing past, spurting sand when they bit into the ground, or twanging off rocks — any one of them could end his life, right here and now.

Stop! Don't think of dying, think of winning, concentrate on crawling, look where you're going, creep up fast behind an anthill or any boulder.

All at once, he heard a chilling scream to his left. The others kept moving forward on their bellies, as if nothing had happened. Of course, someone got hit, but what could he do?

Jack frowned. What should he do?

He turned left, crawled as fast as he could, reached the soldier who was crying out, writhing. What now? Bring him back to a doctor, of course. Fiset would not be far behind, he knew that. He grabbed hold of an arm, began to pull, but that only caused an anguished yell.

He stopped. Then he crawled closer. He rolled over, lay on his back, pulled the lad as gently as he could onto his chest, turned toward the rear, and with his feet propelled the two of them over the rough desert, through thorn-bushes and around rocks. It tore his uniform, scraped his back, hurt his neck, but he kept going. Suddenly, he found himself going downhill and they dipped into a slight donga, which meant they would both be safe for the moment.

Panting heavily, he let the soldier roll off onto his side. The private had lost consciousness, but was still breathing.

Now, what do I do? thought Jack. He's safe here for the moment. They need me up ahead. More will be hit, some may be killed, I must get up there. Then, he decided, first go back, find a stretcher-bearer. He'll know what to do. That's their job. They'd come get the poor wounded lad.

He rose onto all fours and turned for one last look, and to orient this position. Something about the lad's body stopped him. He crawled closer, put his head to the man's chest.

No breath. No heartbeat. No life. He knelt over the body and said a prayer for the ascent of his soul. This young soldier, most likely the darling of someone far away, had died in the sand without even the touch of a loving hand. He now lay, gazing blankly upwards, never to see the Southern Cross, which would soon emerge to christen the night. Would he sleep as well as under the snows of Canada? A sigh escaped Jack. Then, dropping flat, he made off on his belly after the rest of the men who were now rapidly approaching the enemy Boers.

The charge, and the overwhelming Imperial force backing them up, meant that the Boers finally called the retreat, and Jack could see them taking off. Later that evening, General Smith-Dorrien came to congratulate the Canadians.

But the battle for Thaba 'Nchu, the Black Mountain, lay ahead.

Chapter Thirty-Two

The next morning, the acting CO, Major Buchan ("Good Old Larry") marched the exhausted regiment now called The Fighting Brigade, six miles to the base of Black Mountain, two thousand feet high, the most important kopje on which the Boers had entrenched. From Bloemfontein the RCR had fought doggedly forward, overtaking the Boers, clearing them off vantage points, erasing their presence to permit the vastly superior force under Roberts to march onwards towards Pretoria.

For another three days the company skirmished, attempting an assault but failing, and even attacking and gaining Eden Mountain, but having to withdraw. On Sunday Jack was not required to fulfill his service commitments. But when he heard from the little village of Theba 'Nchu below, its church bells calling the villagers to worship, how he longed for his own St. Paul's Church in Shigawake and its little bell tolling an invitation to worship across a snowy countryside.

The day before, the Canadians had fought their way across open country bombarded by Boer guns at Thaba Mountain and Hout Nek. The Boer Gunners directed their artillery on the Canadians as they advanced, sending shell after shell with unexpected accuracy into the advancing line. Men were stunned, knocked down, one even tossed in the air, but only one killed. A real baptism of fire.

That night, with only two biscuits and tea for two days, Jack and his companions bivouacked for the night, cold, tired, and hungry. They had no blankets and the night was piercingly cold; they had to maintain absolute silence for fear of attracting the enemy's attention, and avoid lighting fires for the same reason. Jack munched his hard tack, and huddled, shivering with cold, waiting for the morrow and more fighting.

Now at dawn, gathered part way up the hill, the men, Jack among them, crouched among boulders. First thing to be done was reconnoitre the large summit, and a private volunteered to do so. Later in the morning he came back with a leg wound for his pains to explain that there was indeed a prominence that offered an excellent vantage point over the rest of the summit: that was now to be their target. Meanwhile, naval guns appeared on the scene and began to lob shell after shell on the Boer trenches above.

Looking up the mountain, Jack could see that its steep sides were clear of large obstructions, but strewn with bushes and boulders. He knew what was coming next. He'd heard that call to charge not once, but now, three times. He knew it well. And he also knew that awful feeling in his guts while waiting for it to resound loudly in the desert air. This time, he expected a real slaughter. Climbing that clear slope of the kopje ahead with the Boers shooting down, so very few would reach the top.

But before the clarion call of charge, Jack heard a very different one. He looked around. Oh! Fix bayonets! Heavens, slaughter for sure. Well, all he could "fix" was his cross. A small one hung round his neck, but fortunately he had brought a second one in his pocket; he now gripped it in one hand as his bayonet, as well as his shield.

With bayonets unsheathed and fixed on the end of their rifles, they waited. B company was in the van, led by his friend Harry

Burstall. But Jack was afraid that this Captain would not see the light of tomorrow's sunrise. In fact, Jack realized, this chaplain too might not be alive to greet the next dawn with his usual morning prayers. This was to be, he just knew it, his last fight.

Any regrets? No. He had fought alongside these men now for several days; he had become inured to the difficulties of wartime, of the marching, the hunger and thirst that goes with being ahead of supply lines, being in the forefront of what amounted to an invasion. He had made his decision consciously, and now he must carry it out with all the vigour he could maintain. Too bad, in a way, to meet his end here in a foreign land, but he'd be joining a multitude of others who had made the same decision and now lay resting on foreign soil.

The Canadians were not of course alone, they were backed by a huge Imperial army travelling across the desert with them. One contingent on the right had kept moving ahead, while far in the distance on the left, another battalion was marching, expecting to eventually surround this kopje and cut off any escape. But first, Black Mountain had to be cleared. And it was up to B company to do it.

Jack wondered why they had been ordered to attack in full daylight. Surely the cover of darkness would make it easier? But it was not to be. The men knew it, and he knew it. The crest of the hill had to be won, and the Canadians were there to win it.

He looked about at his friends, all with the same queasy fear, he felt sure, as they gathered for this final onslaught, perhaps the last battle any of them would ever have to wage. Indeed, in Jack's mind, this was a do or die endeavour.

Then Harry caught his eye, winked, and gave his Bugler the order. No more ruminations hampered Jack's will to live, as he heard blasting from the brass-throated bugle: Charge!

The men rose and scrambled with their bayonets unsheathed

up the clear slope of the kopje towards the left hand bulge, which gave a view over the rest. Oddly, no veritable storm of lead greeted them — instead, sporadic and seemingly accurate shooting picked off one or other. But still the soldiers advanced, zigzagging, moving as fast as they could. Tough going, Jack thought, as he gritted his teeth and dug his toes into the loose sand. He'd made other charges, sure, but was he not still afraid? Oh yes, for this was to be his last, he just knew it. But he'd learned how to divert his mind, to press on regardless, although beside him one after another of his companions was struck down. When would his turn come? At any minute. But upwards he climbed.

Beside him he heard Harry yelling: "Let's go, lads! The quicker we get there, the fewer we lose! Give 'em hell!"

Damn right, thought Jack, let's just get there. And with that, he took off even faster, weaving back and forth, running, scrambling, panting and tripping.

If I'm finished, it'll be doing my best, he growled, yes sir, nothing but a well-aimed Mauser is going to stop me, as he fell again.

He rose and dashed even harder, tripped again while a bullet spun past and twanged off a rock behind. Lucky trip — saved my life. How many more times will I be so lucky?

Well, the faster we get there, the fewer bullets we'll take. Jack was now a good bit ahead of the other soldiers, who carried extra rounds of ammunition, heavy, oh yes, and rifles, and packs. They were panting, working at climbing. But Jack just had his cross, which he gripped in one hand as he tore on up. Random thoughts drove through his brain, but in the main it was: Get there! Get to the top, go through the bullets, past the blood, just get to the top!

Not much further now! He'd made it this far. Oh yes. But

then, just ten yards dead ahead, a Boer farmer, black hat, rose from behind a stone-piled balustrade, lifted his rifle, pointed it directly at Jack. An open target!

Jack froze. About to meet his Maker — at last. But in that split second, that fraction of an eye-blink, did any great image of Paradise open? No, though time itself stretched into eternity. As you finally face your death, does your life flash before your eyes? Oh yes: for Jack now, time expanded.

Jack saw Lorna, saw his parents, Kelsie, her canvas-wrapped body lifted from the cart. He saw Big George expire, he now saw himself looking into the hollow barrel of a rifle pointed directly at his chest. What immense blink of an eyelid, huge chink of shattered instant, did these images fill?

The finger tightened, for they were that close. Jack shut his eyes, thrust out his cross in firm fingers, arm straight ahead — as if it would help. Drop to your knees! Die in prayer!

BANG! the barrel flared.

Jack dropped.

The helmet leaped from his head.

But Jack was alive.

The Boer turned tail and took off. Jack leaped up. He bent to grab his helmet with its new bullet-hole, thrust it on his head and tore up onto the balustrade, leaned for a moment against it, panting and retching. Then against the blood-red setting sun, he saw black forms fleeing, twenty or thirty, racing off. The Boers in retreat!

He turned. His companions struggled painfully upwards, cautious, moving as best they could.

"No no, come on!" he yelled, and waved. "They're in retreat! We're safe. We've won. We've won!" He waved and waved.

The privates of B company rose without further thought and scambled up to join their chaplain on the top of the kopje.

Objective achieved — the enemy had cleared off.

Harry walked past Jack, clapping him on the back. "Good work, Padre!" The men gathered, orders were given for mounted scouts to chase the Boers regrouping beyond the hill for a dash into the desert.

Jack looked up and saw the sun dipping towards the horizon. His companions had gathered on the flat surface, collapsed on the ground, panting, leaning on boulders, exhausted. With a smile, still panting, he pulled out his prayer book. In a loud voice, he began to read the service of Evensong.

One after another, the men rose. They cheered as Chaplain Jack praised the Good Lord on High for having given them the victory. Then they joined him in the Lord's Prayer.

But Jack could not take his eyes off the men as they looked to him for the prayers. In the eyes of each and every man, Jack saw admiration blossoming, and, yes, a love returning in full force. Had he finally vindicated himself?

As he read the closing prayer, Chaplain Jack Alford decided that he was indeed a happy man.

Afterword

The Reverend John M. Almond, upon whom this story is based, continued to serve in the Royal Canadian Regiment while they fought more battles over the next few days, culminating in the battle of Zand River. On the fifth of June after more skirmishing, he marched with the regiment (38% of their original strength) into Pretoria, the capital of the Transvaal, which had surrendered to Field Marshall Roberts.

The remainder of their tour in South Africa became mainly guard duty, protecting railway lines and troop establishments through these winter months, June to October. The next phase of the war, which began after they left, lasted two long years — years when many of the criteria set out by Saint Thomas for a "Just War" were overlooked. It was brought to a close by the signing of the Treaty of Vereeniging in May 1902, ending the Transvaal and the Orange Free State as Boer republics. However, the British in 1907 granted the Boers £3 million for restocking and repairing farm lands and promised eventual self-government.

Their one year of duty over, on the seventh of November the regiment sailed on the *Hawarden Castle* to Liverpool. Although aching to get home, they spent ten days being, quite literally, royally entertained. At Windsor Castle, the good Queen Victoria (shortly before her death in January 1901) greeted and honoured them in special ceremonies of thanks.

On the tenth of December, they boarded the *Lake Champlain*, crossed the Atlantic, and arrived back in Canada two days before Christmas 1900.

Acknowledgements

This book required a good deal of research. As with *The Pilgrim*, I patterned my hero, Rev. John Alford, after my uncle, Col. the Ven. John Macpherson Almond, M.A., D.C.L., C.B.E., C.M.G., V.D. (1871-1939), the eldest brother of my father, Eric. First, I must acknowledge the help of my cousin, Ted Wright, who discussed many aspects of this novel over breakfasts as the sun rose around five in the mornings, or as we weeded our fava beans and cabbage in late afternoons. When not building crab traps, splitting the winter's wood or hanging nets, Ted spent days trolling the Internet for many of the facts I needed. When something eluded him, I relied upon my young graduate friend now at Google, the dazzling Ksenia Shubina.

I visited the Imperial War Museum in London and our new National War Museum in Ottawa, where I'd like to thank Jane Naisbitt and her helpful staff for guiding me through the books and letters in their excellent Boer War exhibit. The archivist at Bishop's University, Anna Grant, found aspects of Uncle Jack's early life in *The Mitre*, including the actual text of Canon Scott's sermon, and in the *Diocesan Gazette*, with its astonishing account of how John Almond got to serve in the Royal Canadian Regiment, and so be awarded the Queen's Medal with three clasps. I acknowledge also the helpful guidance of the Archbishop of Quebec, the Most Rev. Bruce Stavert, his archivist, James Sweeney, and his brilliant historian, Dr. Mary Ellen Reisner, who also helped with my opening chapters. Moira McCaffrey of the McCord Museum in Montreal took time to guide me through its collection of useful rare photographs.

Rather than make these acknowledgments longer than the book itself, I shall just mention below some of the more important. First, the most vivid moments in the book would not have seen the light of day had I not chosen to adapt some of the stunning material in letters written by our soldiers in South Africa. Our army at that time was unusually literate, and indeed, not censored in their writings, as in later wars. Imagine how I felt when I held with gloved hands the actual pages written in the Karoo desert to loved ones in Canada and thence, by their good graces, sent on to Ottawa to be preserved in our fine national institution, Library and Archives Canada (LAC), which the Conservative Government seems intent on destroying.

To make this book as lively as possible, I borrowed liberally from these letters and books. I did this in all conscience because I believe the soldiers themselves, authors of such devastating descriptions, would have been pleased to have their writings made more widely available. I mention especially Russell Hubly (*Everyday Life of the RCR*, [J&A McMillan, 1901] available in the McGill University Library), whose marvellous personal account of Paardeberg I translated into the last words of my fictional George Bursey, his account of drinking the Modder River water into the dialogue of Eamon McAndrews, and also his account of the aftermath into the mouth of correspondent Brown on the station platform. Several long pages of beautiful remembrances written from the trenches by another soldier, I translated into the vernacular of Corporal Ferguson on the platform. Just wonderful writers, those soldiers; no one could ever hope to create anything to compare with their descriptions. At LAC I also copied the daily diaries of Colonel Otter, carefully preserved on microfilm, so useful on the whereabouts and other details of our Royal Canadians. Otter's biographer and grandson, the McGill historian Desmond Morton, provided in *The General* any further background I needed. Finally, I want to acknowledge the contribution of Corel's Canadian WordPerfect, the superb program by which I entered the text of all eight books.

The events of Black Week are chronicled in a clear fashion by Rayne Kruger in *Goodbye Dolly Gray* (Cassell 1959), from which I fashioned my truncated description, and wish also to thank Stephen A. Pagaard for his recent scholarly treatise *Disease and the British Army* (Military Affairs, Vol. 50, No. 2). The lectures of Lieut.-Col. G. Sterling Ryerson, Canadian Commissioner for the Red Cross (published in Toronto, 1900) gave me useful descriptions of wounds, fevers, cures, and hospitals in this, Canada's first foreign war. I also want to thank Duff Crerar for his excellent *Padres in No Man's Land* where I found the tip about my uncle's indiscretions (Otter to Molly Otter 26 June, 1900) that led to the final section of this book. He has been most helpful with advice and reading the manuscript.

My South African friend, Bernard Unterhalter, helped with the habits of the Boers of the time, and lent me Van Riebeeck Society's *Reminiscences of A.E. Hilder*, (a Canadian) as well as *The War Diary of Burgher Jack Lane*, (a Boer Farmer) He also read drafts, and advised me on the era.

And for a proper perspective and narrative of what happened, no historian is better than my friend Carman Miller, Canada's leading Boer War expert and a distinguished professor at McGill. I thank him for allowing me to use some of his actual phrases verbatim from *Painting the Map Red* and *Canada's Little War*, and also for reading and correcting a draft.

With the help of Abe Books, forever my stand-by, I was able to snaffle many of the accounts written in 1900 and out of print for over a century. Dear Stanley Brown in *With the Royal Canadians*

(Publishers' Syndicate, 1900) gave such a graphic detailing of our first contingent from its departure from Quebec City right through and past Paardeberg, including the attack on Lubbe's Farm. Brown was wounded in the Zand River engagement and invalided home. E.W.B. Morrison, an Ottawa war correspondent and Gunner Officer with the Second Contingent, collected his own equally brilliant columns into *With the Guns in South Africa* (Hamilton, 1901). T.G. Marquis's *Canada's Sons on Kopje and Veldt* (Toronto, 1900) was my other favourite stand-by. A lively, illustrated British book, *Private Tucker's Boer War Diary*, though mainly British, provided background. Winston Churchill's account of his experiences as a correspondent in that war (which he covered for the Morning Post, for a princely monthly £250) also gave me revealing insights.

I was surprised, after writing the book, to discover that Dr. Fiset, later Sir Marie-Joseph-Eugène Fiset, KCMG, three years after the war became a colonel and Director-General of the Army Medical Service. In December 1939, he was appointed the first lieutenant-governor of Quebec. Mr. Morrison was also a soldier and won the DSO for bravery at Leilifontein. Harry Burstall retired in 1923, as Lt.-Gen Sir H.E. Burstall, KCB, KCMG after 35 years in uniform. Among the Canadians, only Arthur Currie was more highly decorated than Burstall in the Great War. This was all pointed out by splendid Major Marc George, my main advisor on Book Six, and head of the Canadian Artillery Museum in Shilo, Manitoba, who read and made some final, but crucial, corrections. He was also a great help with many of the army terms and information, and corrected much else. He has been a tower of strength for my war books in the Saga.

The actual daily weather and the conditions faced by the Royal Canadians herein are all accurate. But this is after all, historical fiction, and let me be clear that I have imagined Jack's actual story, as well as some of the characters he interacts with: correspondent Kandinsky, Adjutant Brown, Captain Forbes, Privates Eamon McAndrews and George Mckinnie, Sister Kelsie Maclean and, of course, the divine Catherina. Although no Canadian nurse died, mortality among the other nurses was significant. I have also chosen, as I mentioned, to use the language then invoked, such as Kaffir (now a slur), kharki for khaki, and the practise in wide use in 1900 of telling stories through the eyes of another narrator, as I did with Paardeberg. One might note that tracing Jack's actual movements allowed me to look into other aspects impossible had he simple stayed with the regiment.

Of course, the Internet (once one knows how to mine its depths, as Cousin Ted does) is full of letters, essays, newspaper columns, and indeed whole books, that may be consulted. As they are publicly accessible, I shall not list them here, save to acknowledge the help of that great resource. And as is my wont, instead of a line from a poem, I have buried another secret herein: a blatant anachronism, find it who can.

Finally, I must acknowledge my many readers, who have through so many pages detected errors, infelicities of style, awkward sentences, and all manner of little ineptitudes and anachronisms that creep into my writing: Peter Duffell, that wise and wonderful film director; Diana Colman Webster, the J.K.Rowling of textbooks; Nicolas Etheridge, a talented diplomat: all got out their blacksnake whips to force me back at it just when I was sure I had finished. I'd also like to include: Philosopher Lou Marinoff, canal-boater Dr. Rex King, my step-son Chris Elkins with his scapel-like eye for detail, a dear friend and linguist Prof. Danielle Cyr, the Rev. Susan Klein who has read and advised on all my books, and the brilliant ex-ambassador, Jeremy Kinsman.

And the novelist and friend, David Stansfield, edited and did his utmost to perfect this book after I thought it well finished.

All books in The Alford Saga are dedicated to Joan Almond, and I want to make clear that none would have been written without her support and encouragement.

Appendix

Except from the Quebec Diocesan Gazette, Jan 1901

The Bishop employed John Almond as a traveling missionary to visit Quebec districts with headquarters in Quebec City. When he was doing this, it appeared as if the First Canadian Contingent, made up as it was of the English churchmen, seemed as if it would be sent forth without an Anglican chaplain.

In the nick of time and without any suggestion from others, Mr. Almond volunteered to go if the matter could be arranged. At once therefore, very earnest representations were made to the Federal Government, and at the same time the very solemn service held at our cathedral gave a tremendous impetus to the project. On the very day of sailing, the Bishop, the Dean, and the city clergy, introduced by Sir Henri Joly de Lotbinière, went as a deputation to Sir Wilfrid Laurier, and it was by the kindness of the Premier, ably seconded by General Hutton, that the matter was carried to a successful issue.

THE DESERTER

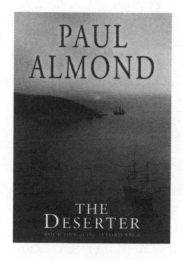

Imagine you're in a swaying hammock on a British man-o'war around 1800, riding out a harsh spring storm in a deserted estuary of the Gulf of St. Lawrence. Behind those high red cliffs lie a hundred miles of uncharted wilderness, populated only by indigenous peoples. If you jump ship and are caught, you will be branded a deserter — subject to death by one thousand lashes. What can you bring to help you survive? Within minutes, the ice-strewn waters could freeze your body and claim your soul. If this were your one chance for a life in the New World, would you jump?

Thomas Manning did, and his leap into uncertainty begins the epic tale of a pioneer family, one of the many who built our great nation. Through his and his descendants' eyes, we watch one small community's impact on the great events which swirl about them and bring conflicts they must face in their struggles to create homes and families.

Absorbing, touching and full of adventure, THE DESERTER is Book One of the Alford Saga, a series chronicling two hundred years of Canadian history, as seen through the eyes of a settler's family.

ISBN 978-1-55278-977-3
mm paperback $10.99 CAD

THE SURVIVOR

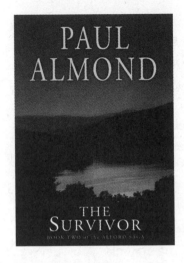

Thomas Manning, branded a deserter from the British Navy, is forced to change his name to James Alford to avoid the death penalty. Determined to forge a new life on the Gaspé Peninsula, he struggles to survive the harsh landscape and win the hand of Catherine Garrett.

After working in harsh sub-zero woods, he saves the life of an orphan working in a sawmill, and so gains crucial lumber to build a homestead out of intractable wilderness. But first he must battle murderous brigands to rescue a starving bull calf he hopes will be the first of the oxen he so desperately needs to clear his land. Finally, heroically surviving Canada's worst famine, he faces down implacable bureaucracies to keep the farm he has been fighting to bring under cultivation.

A captivating and fast-paced adventure, THE SURVIVOR is Book Two of the Alford Saga, a series chronicling two hundred years of Canadian history, as seen through the eyes of one settler's family.

ISBN 978-1-55278-967-4
C Paperback $19.95 CAD

The Pioneer

The riveting Alford Saga continues with James Alford, the Deserter, battling old age and ferocious winters, but even more crippling, the departure of his son and only heir, young Jim, who sets out on snowshoes for Montreal, seven hundred miles away from their home in Shigawake.

Arriving at last in Montreal, Jim is driven by starvation into a back-breaking job constructing the Victoria Bridge. He finds lodgings with an Irish widow in Griffintown, and falls in love. But after a stinging deception, he rejects the bitter realities of urban life and returns to the Old Homestead and its community of pioneers. His ageing father recruits him to rally recalcitrant neighbours to found a school for their children and a church for their worship in Shigawake.

Enthralling and adventurous, THE PIONEER is Book Three in the Alford Saga, a series chronicling two hundred years of Canadian history, as seen through the eyes of a settler's family.

ISBN 978-1-77087-123-6
C Paperback $19.95 CAD

The Pilgrim

THE PILGRIM, the fourth book in Paul Almond's thrilling Alford Saga, opens in 1896. After graduating from Bishop's University, young rector Jack Alford is sent to his first parish — the implacable granite shores of the Canadian Labrador on the vast St. Lawrence River. Hazards imperil his life as he travels this harsh 450-mile coastline in summer and winter, by boat and dogsled, to visit communities in his far-flung parish.

Jack's zeal for the welfare of Labrador's hardy parishioners diverts him from his blossoming romance. Through summer storms that menace his tiny mission boat and fierce blizzards that almost annihilate his dog team, Jack brings succor to stranded families, care and leadership to villages perched on the windy granite, and inspired teaching in hill-top churches that stand as beacons of hope among the seal-fishers and rugged pioneers of Labrador.

ISBN 978-1-77087-163-2
C Paperback $19.95 CAD